Failure is n...
failure is not an option.

Wally's legs, which generally loped along with ease and spring, now seemed weighted with lead. There was an agony of fatigue throughout his body that was something more than muscular, something baser than chemical. It was the warning from the physical world that he was attempting something that broke a fundamental law. A perverse action that should not be easily committed.

His body pleaded that every step be his last. His mind forced his legs to pump faster, every step *faster*. There was no time to maintain, no place to backslide, no alternative but to run *faster*.

Failure is not possible, failure is not an option.

It was sheer willpower against the laws of physics. Speed power in defiance of the universal constant.

The atoms in Wally's boot treads had long ago ceased to bounce off the atoms of the road over which he virtually flew. Now his mind began to divorce itself from any remaining attachment to the physical universe. The definitions that were the road, the fields, the sky, and stars all faded until all that was left was the radiance.

The domain of light.

Failure is not possible, failure is not an option.

The radiance grew in intensity, then exploded into shafts and cataracts racing out to meet him, as he threw himself forward into one last surge, the last he had to give.

So beautiful.

He was lifted up.

Also available from Pocket Books

Justice League of America

Batman: The Stone King
by Alan Grant

Wonder Woman: Mythos
by Carol Lay

JUSTICE LEAGUE of AMERICA™
THE FLASH®

STOP MOTION

MARK SCHULTZ

POCKET BOOKS
NEW YORK   LONDON   TORONTO   SYDNEY

The sale of this book without its cover is unauthorized. If you purchased this book without a cover, you should be aware that it was reported to the publisher as "unsold and destroyed." Neither the author nor the publisher has received payment for the sale of this "stripped book."

This book is a work of fiction. Names, characters, places and incidents are products of the author's imagination or are used fictiously. Any resemblance to actual events or locales or persons, living or dead, is entirely coincidental.

An *Original* Publication of POCKET BOOKS

A Pocket Star Book published by
POCKET BOOKS, a division of Simon & Schuster Inc.
1230 Avenue of the Americas, New York, NY 10020

Copyright © 2004 by DC Comics. All Rights Reserved.
Justice League of America, The Flash, and all related titles, characters, and elements are trademarks of DC Comica.

Cover design by Georg Brewer
Cover art by Alex Ross

All rights reserved, including the right to reproduce this book or portions thereof in any form whatsoever. For information address Pocket Books, 1230 Avenue of the Americas, New York, NY 10020

ISBN: 0-7434-1713-5

First Pocket Books printing March 2004

10 9 8 7 6 5 4 3 2 1

POCKET STAR BOOKS and colophon are registered trademarks of Simon & Schuster Inc.

www.dccomics.com

Manufactured in the United States of America

For information regarding special discounts for bulk purchases, please contact Simon & Schuster Special Sales at 1-800-456-6798 or business@simonandschuster.com

For Denise

Acknowledgments

Acknowledgments are a dicey business—some deserving soul usually gets left unacknowledged. Up front, my apologies to any or all I may be unintentionally slighting.

Thanks to Michael J. Ryan, my science advisor, although no blame should be transferred to him for all the "scientific" liberties taken. To Vincent Rush III, who helped give bloody life to my crime scene procedure. To Geoff Johns, for feedback on the Flash characters he's developed. To Joey Cavalieri, for Flash background and for suggesting the idea of an artificial speedster in the first place. Good suggestion, that. To Denny O'Neil, for generously lending his experience.

Of course, to my editor, Charlie Kochman, who gave me the chance, and who skillfully and patiently piloted me through unknown waters.

And a big tip of the hat to all past Flash writers, artists, and editors, with whose wonderful characters and concepts I've been privileged to play.

JUSTICE LEAGUE of AMERICA
THE FLASH

STOP MOTION

well separated from him and one another by him.

CHAPTER 1

Mystery in Space

The scarlet-clad form of the Flash rocketed straight up through the atmosphere alone and without benefit of mechanical aid. Had anyone else been there to follow his trajectory, that person would have naturally assumed the Flash could fly. That person would have been wrong.

The Flash was a super hero, and one who did not possess the power of flight. He was, however, the Fastest Man Alive, a skilled superspeedster, and that gave him compensatory options. His pistoning legs pumped so fast that they compressed the molecules in the air beneath him into a precise, controlled column that allowed him to climb through the troposphere like a runner sprinting up a staircase.

If this didn't give him the maneuverability of a true flier, it was the next best thing.

The true fliers were up there in the night sky as well, separated from him and one another by hun-

dreds of miles, but closely coordinated by alien telepathic link and hard-won experience. They, too, were
heroes—Superman, Wonder Woman, Green Lantern,
and the Martian Manhunter—and, along with the
Flash, members of the Justice League of America, all
sworn guardians of the Earth and its people.

As such, they now found themselves rushing into
the skies high above Eurasia, radiating out from a
common point to which they had teleported from the
Watchtower, their headquarters on the Moon. Only
minutes earlier the League had been sent scrambling
by the astounding reports: From a point of apparent
nothingness midway between Earth and her satellite,
a barrage of otherworldly radar blips of incredible dimension had sprung into existence, many careering
on courses that would smash them full into Earth.

That had been no more than two minutes ago.
Within ninety seconds the League had assembled a
mission team. Now, they climbed skyward to meet
the unknown invaders.

The Flash squinted up into the black and saw the
mysterious intruders for the first time, racing straight
down at him. They were igniting into fireballs as they
hit the upper atmosphere, appearing, from his perspective, to be coming straight out of the constellation
of Cassiopeia.

He reckoned their rate of speed, as they left the
cold void of interplanetary space, to be almost exactly
fifty-two miles per second. That was fine. He could
keep pace with them with only minor exertion—noth-

ing unduly stressing. Their individual masses he could only guess; maybe up to millions of tons. The truth was, the Flash was much better at gauging speed than he was at estimating mass. Speed he knew intimately, mass was only cold physics.

To himself, he labeled the invading bodies, with purposeful ambiguity, as *phenomena*, a term that left plenty of room for interpretation. What from a great distance had seemed most likely a storm of simple, if colossal, meteors, had lost perspective and definition the closer he approached. Oddly enough, the closer he drew to them, the more difficult they became to *look* at.

Very odd.

Besides, simple meteors did not appear out of nowhere halfway between Earth and the Moon, catching every astronomical observer with his pants down.

Experience had taught him that it was safest to refer to such an exceptional unknown in the broadest of terms. Categorization would come only when knowledge and certitude were gained.

There were a series of silent explosions of flaring light that suddenly extinguished a number of the still distant fireballs. The Flash recognized the hands of his teammates in this—they were high above, efficiently destroying the potentially lethal invaders. Whatever they were, the fireballs could be met and stopped with physical force.

But they were coming in fast, and not every fireball could be met by the first line of defense. The Flash saw one shoot through, burning past the net of explosions that winked like fireflies. He altered his direction slightly, and put himself on a course to intercept. As he raced toward his particular assignment, he fought hard to concentrate on its strangely elusive nature. The radiant body began to take on a confused sort of form, although it was by no means *defined* in his gaze. Focusing on it made his head hurt, he suddenly realized. It made his eyes strain, made the surrounding universe turn a little milky, and that had nothing to do with the effects of the 200-plus Mach speed he maintained; he was very comfortable with the bizarre but familiar compression distortions that were part and parcel of ultrahigh-velocity states. No, there was something extremely unsettling and *painful* about the nature of the object itself. He absorbed a rapid-fire succession of fevered, nonsensical impressions: a mad spaghetti tangle of writhing extrusions, blocks, and prisms turned inside out and rebuilt backward, colors that should not exist, and an eye-crossing lack of any recognizable substance or structure. Each impression ended as his attention repeatedly slid off the slippery, pulsing fabric of the fireball. It was all profoundly *disturbing*. He had seen plenty of alien worlds, and this was unlike any of that.

What, he thought, *what . . .*

With a self-conscious curse, he shook off the unsettling queasiness the fireball's appearance had cast over his mind and focused again on the task at hand. This was not a time for analysis, it was a time for action. Increasing the speed of the pumping motion of his legs by half again, he prepared for his assault on the invader. His scarlet-clad form tensed; he knew it would be a near thing, this tactic he was about to employ. It was a desperation move, perhaps suicidal, but he felt there was little choice. Not one to normally take unconsidered risks, the stunning appearance of the phenomena, exploding out from some undefined point in the middle of empty space, had left no time for strategy.

The truth was, the Justice League had simply reacted, had scrambled, was relying on experience and teamwork and personal initiative to deflect those fireballs that screamed on collision courses with Earth. They were coming in at an oblique angle, over the skies of eastern Europe and western Asia, and that was a lot of sky to cover, with a lot of lives at stake below. Given the size of the fireballs, it was quite possible *all* life was at risk. The Flash knew he had no choice but to pull out all the stops to counter this, his chosen target. *His* responsibility.

The unsettling object was far more massive than anything he could hope to outright destroy, despite the incredible energy generated by his superspeed. His hastily constructed plan was to graze the hurtling body, to deflect its shallow angle of descent just slightly enough to cause it to skip off the skin of the upper atmosphere, past the Earth, and back into the void. He would have to rely on the pillow of lower atmosphere air that remained concentrated like a prow before him, caught up in the rapidity of his ascent, for any chance of survival. A slim enough thing, but it might be enough of a cushion to save him from vaporizing on impact.

From his perspective, the Flash's exertions equaled those of an average athlete slowly gearing from a healthy jog into a brisk run. He instinctively monitored his body functions; his heart rate remained at an acceptable stress level, and the lungfuls of oxygen he had gulped before leaving the troposphere below was still sufficient for the job. In his accelerated mode, as he arced high into the thin twilight of the upper stratosphere, the fireball appeared to approximate his rate. Had any mortal eyes been there to look, they would have seen nothing. What has taken this long to describe transpired in a fraction of a fraction of a second, and normal human perspective cannot register those quantums of time.

So this was it. *This,* he told himself, *is what I do.* He was a hero and all he knew was to act the hero, and damn the consequences. Buffered by the bubble of air, he set his course for what he hoped would be a glancing blow.

Now he began pistoning his legs furiously, driving himself upward to Mach 300. Although the atmospheric gasses of this altitude had grown incredibly thin, the momentum he had built up in the lower atmosphere, his legs working against the mass of the air itself, continued to rocket him spaceward.

This was it. The fireball loomed close.

Suddenly, a streak of eternally extended blue and red slashed past him, angling in from the right and above. *Something moving even faster than me?* Catching the invading fireball about thirty degrees off its trajectory, there was an impact explosion that sent tons of fragmented material burning off into space. As his mind caught up with the event, the Flash watched with a combination of relief and irritation as the streak settled into reasonably human proportions and set about methodically trip hammering the remainder of the mind-twisting oddity into oblivion. The figure's massive fists smashed down four times onto the million-ton mass, in Mach speed to beat the invader's own rate of travel, and then all that remained was debris small enough to be easily consumed by the atmosphere.

The task complete, the blue-and-red figure hovered around to lock eyes, and spoke through the mind link provided by the Martian Manhunter to all League members.

No one doubts your courage, Flash, but the situation calls for brute force, and that's our domain.

There's no need yet for you to risk life and limb. Just pinpoint any fireballs we may not catch and give a shout. We'll take care of them from there . . .

Superman smiled benignly, and ducked his head in a gesture of comradeship, but the exclusionary "our" and "we" rankled. The Flash knew he was referring to the team's big guns—the heavy hitters who could stand toe to toe with a phenomenon of this scale without fear of obliteration.

He knew he was not part of that "we." The Justice League of America may have represented a confederation of Earth's superhuman elite, but even within that lofty station there were subtle differentiations in status.

The Flash stood on the crest of the Caucasus mountain ridge and pushed back his cowl, glad to be free of the clinging material. Unmasked, he no longer cut quite the same figure. The regal super hero became Wally West, a handsome if somewhat average young man with distant, sad eyes.

It was cold up here, under the summit of Mt. Khalatsa. It was colder high above in the upper atmosphere, of course, but up there his supersonic motion had kept the surrounding molecules agitated and radiating heat. Now, no longer isolated by the results of his superspeed, he was able to absorb the severe alpine environment. His sandy hair was whipped by a stiff wind; it smelled like a spring snow might be coming. His skin tingled.

Wonder Woman stood nearby. Glancing at him, she caught his impatient fidgeting.

"Relax, Wally. We did good. The job's done. You can come down off that runner's high of yours."

She was ribbing him in her own proper, old world way. He knew she knew it wasn't that easy for him—that shift from ultraspeed consciousness to normal time. No matter how much raw speed Wally could generate, it wouldn't do any good if his mind couldn't keep up with the movement. Like all effective superspeedster minds, his automatically jumped into an accelerated mode whenever he turned on the juice. He thought as well as moved in ultraspeed mode, no problem. The problem, however, was in the coming down, the deceleration to normal time. Wally always found himself having to fight his mind back down; it didn't want to stop racing. It lingered like a clutch stuck open, and led him into fits of restlessness, constantly waiting for the rest of the world to catch up with him.

Wally knew Wonder Woman understood because she was so completely empathic. She noticed things that the others on the team, as perceptive as they were, would never catch.

She was also one of the big guns, one of the heavy hitters.

"I could have done more. You'd think that someone who can move as fast as I can would be of more use."

After Superman had disposed of his fireball, Wally—the Flash—had resigned himself to his reconnaissance assignment and dropped into a dragnet pattern, criss-crossing the skies above Asia, taking note of any other invading bodies that slipped past the rest of the mission team stationed high above. The three fireballs that did make it to his level were quickly dispatched by team members he alerted telepathically—the Green Lantern had proved especially effective at casting his powers over the enormous distances necessary to reach these intruders. Wally knew full well that the Flash's speed and observational skills served an important purpose within the balance that was the Justice League, but he couldn't help but feel he had been relegated to second-string status. And it rankled him.

Diana, the Amazon Princess of Themyscira, known to the world as Wonder Woman, spoke softly again. "No, Barry would be proud. You wear the mantle of the Flash well."

She made reference to Barry Allen, the Flash who had preceded Wally, the hero who had mentored Wally and changed his life. To save the universe, Barry had run himself to death.

Wally fired back, the lingering effects of his accelerated state lending his words an edge he regretted. "Barry Allen—the Speed Force bless and keep him— has been gone for almost four years. You'd think I'd be of more use by now."

Diana, too much the diplomat to press an issue she knew Wally was not ready to address, did not reply. She returned to scanning the starry sky, with the casual alertness of a satiated hawk. For a brief second, Wally took the liberty of eyeballing her form. She represented perhaps the ultimate contradiction to male preconceptions of femininity. Her every curve dripped sexual allure, while her every sinew bespoke a warrior's regimen. *The true Greek ideal, I suppose*, thought Wally. Her ivory face and foaming black hair were literally breathtaking, those of a goddess created for pleasure, but her eyes shined with wisdom and restraint and, when angered, a killer's ruthlessness. She was the one true and primal warrior on the team, forged to the arts of war by the ancient Amazon culture; the pragmatist, the strategist, the field tactician. She was also the most perceptive, the most giving, and at times the most annoyingly distant. Wally, like everyone who spent time with Diana, was endlessly falling in and out of love with her.

Now, she was idly wiping her hands across the loops of the glowing gold lasso she kept fastened to the right hip of her sleek, armored field dress, resplendent in its stars and intricately worked gold. Wally watched as the stuff on her knuckles, the shimmering remains of the intruding fireballs she'd personally dispatched, disappeared, as if washed away by the lasso. As if by magic. Not as *if*, he reminded himself; the lasso *was* magic. Wally still had a hard time wrapping his mind around that concept and its mythological context. He remembered the stories he'd heard, that Diana was born directly from clay, a creature of myth. Although he tried, he couldn't fully comprehend that.

His mind was slowing, but he remained impatient. Where were the others?

Hearing a slight rustling from above, they both looked up to see the Martian Manhunter and Green Lantern hovering down out of the darkness together. The two emerald teammates alighted on the ridge, with the Lantern in midcomplaint.

"Okay, so who picked a mountain peak for our rendezvous? Jeez, as if the upper atmosphere wasn't cold enough—at least I was generating heat up there."

The Manhunter's usually impassive face was frozen in a slight, indulgent smile. Wally understood—he knew the young and undisciplined Lantern couldn't be *that* uncomfortable in his protective uniform.

Wally noticed that the Martian was bouncing something up and down in his hand. Something Wally could not clearly see, but which seemed to be engaging the Manhunter's intense interest.

Before he could ask the Martian about the thing, Diana brought them back to the first order of business. "I'm assuming all the invading phenomena in your quadrants were taken out?"

Green Lantern, even more inexperienced than Wally, looked a little sheepish as Diana's words snapped him out of his pique. The Manhunter, looking up from the cryptic object he continued flipping, jumped to debriefing mode without missing a beat.

"All but six bodies of noncatastrophic mass were destroyed in the ionosphere, all fragments disintegrating no lower than the stratosphere. I tracked the six smaller bodies that did hit Earth, and found the damage to be minimal. Loss of life restricted to invertebrates and vegetation, no property damage, no known witnesses. Disintegration was complete upon impact."

The Lantern reported similar results, and Diana appeared to relax somewhat.

Wally's mind was almost completely back to normal time now, and his indignation at having to play a supportive role to the main action was at least temporarily receding. He took a minute to appreciate his surroundings, which few men would ever experience. Wally believed with absolute clarity that he was a man who would have amounted to nothing if not for a string of coincidences and guiding spirits and dumb luck, a nobody who had no reason to expect to become part of Earth's most exclusive company of public servants. And yet, here he was in their midst, braced against the wind on the spine of the world. He could appreciate the absurdity, while at the same time marvel at the majesty of it all.

The pale ghosts of the surrounding peaks surrendered gusts of icy ash as the winds wailed through their bones. The stars glittered so bright it seemed he should be able to reach out and sift them through his fingers. *How many*, Wally wondered to himself, *how many have ever experienced anything like this?*

Not many, he knew. Not many were chosen to stand alongside giants. And he feared that maybe it was a mistake that he was here. That he might be revealed as a poseur and returned to the ranks of the mortal, the mundane.

Wally knew he could never do enough. For all his speed, he could never do as much in his entire career as someone like Diana accomplished in one week.

He shook his head; gave himself a mental kick. He had no patience for introspection. *Keep it in the moment*, he told himself.

The Green Lantern wandered over to him as Wally casually noted the Manhunter motioning for Diana to come see the object he endlessly tossed in and out of his hand. He would have liked to have joined his two seniors, but the Lantern obviously wanted to talk. As always when in the midst of the gathered team, the Lantern seemed a bit ill at ease.

"Did you get a good look at those things, Wally? I

mean—*could* you get a good look at them? Was it just me or—Christ. I . . . I've never seen anything close to that screwed up. Made me feel sick."

"Well, I was kind of hoping that with your off-Earth ties that you'd have a handle on them," Wally countered. "Me, I haven't a clue. Extradimensional, maybe."

Wally liked Kyle Rayner, the Green Lantern. He felt closer to him than anyone else in the Justice League. Their personal stories were somewhat similar. As Wally had inherited the mantle of the Flash from Barry Allen, so had Kyle been passed an overwhelming responsibility from another Green Lantern before him. Both of them knew they had an awful lot to live up to. Both of them feared they wouldn't make the grade. Although Wally had a couple years on him, they were closely matched as the youngest, most inexperienced members of the team.

However, they differed in two ways. Where Wally held his fears and doubts inside, Kyle had no problem keeping his teammates in touch with his insecurities. Sometimes, it seemed to Wally, to the point of whining—but, hey, he was just a kid. One who had been thrown into the brutal and numbing world of superhumans and villains without really asking for it. One who wasn't as sure as Wally that he wanted to spend the rest of his productive years tempting fate on the razor's edge of the high frontier.

And, unlike the Flash, the Green Lantern was one of the heavy hitters, his potential power maximum perhaps the greatest of any member of the team.

Whereas Wally's Speed Force was never likely to accidentally injure anyone other than himself, if Kyle made even a slight miscalculation in the utilization of his power, the effects on the environment and populace could be catastrophic. Maybe even another Coast City. Wally felt a familiar taste of horror rise in his gorge at the thought of the holocaust of Coast City, where a previous Green Lantern had gone mad and sought to remake the universe.

What must Kyle go through, knowing he held that kind of power in trust?

Wally glanced down at the alien emerald ring that Kyle always wore on the middle finger of his right hand. It was the source of his power. Its simple lantern design threw a soft glow over the green and black of his armored battlesuit, eagerly waiting for the moment Kyle would feed it the next mental image that it could form, with incredible speed, from pure energy into a workable tool—or weapon. *Sinister*, Wally shuddered. *Anything he wants, the ring can give him. How does he deal with it? How does he stay uncorrupted by such power? How does he stay such a kid?*

Kyle continued their exchange. "Extradimensional, at the very least. I'm thinking antimatter; they started blowing apart at first contact. Lots of free energy. I don't know jack about physics and such, but those flaming wild cards didn't look to be following the rules of any science I've ever seen."

Wally didn't feel he knew jack about science, either. "I don't know. But they *can* be destroyed, and I guess that's what's most important."

"Yeah, but don't you have the weirdest feeling that all this could be the work of some sort of cosmic sniper out there, somehow hidden from all our scanners, just waiting till our backs are turned? Meteors, weird-assed or otherwise, don't just pop up out of nowhere. I don't mind telling you, I think I was lucky up there . . ."

He's getting dangerously close to whining, thought Wally. The speedster really did want a chance to see what it was that the Manhunter was showing Diana.

" . . . I don't think I could have focused and kept up with all of them falling through my quadrant if I wasn't set up by Diana and the Manhunter and Superma—"

Suddenly, there was a stirring, a parting in the vortex of snowflakes above and, as if invoked by the speaking of his name, the last of the field team descended, all effortless flight skill and dark blue and red silhouetted against the stars.

"Superman, if you weren't so consistently humble, I'd accuse you of the purposely dramatic late entrance." Wonder Woman's greeting, while pointed, was noticeably relaxed compared to the terse inquiries with which she'd met the other arrivals.

The truth was, the Last Son of Krypton couldn't help but make a dramatic entrance. Even had he telegraphed his approach from miles away, and come down whistling "Dixie" in his birthday suit, Superman had a quality of presence that eclipsed his teammates. He commanded respect and awe even among his fellow super heroes, and Wally felt betrayed by the thrill the man's arrival brought; it reminded him of just how far he felt separated from a truly great man with truly great achievements. It was as if Wally devolved into a child again, a kid experiencing his first encounter with a hint of a vast and majestic universe lurking just beyond his field of vision, experiencing his first encounter with the highest aspirations and greatest possibilities held in the human form. Wally didn't know if the others felt anywhere near this much reverence for this first among equals, but he expected they did.

None of this changed the fact that Wally still felt a twinge of resentment aimed at Superman's actions up there in the sky. The icon had taken away his kill, and that did not sit well.

"You don't think I'm capable of engineering a dramatic entrance, Diana?" Superman's voice rolled like soft thunder, with all of the authority and none of the menace. "You know I like attention as much as the next guy."

He was making a crack at his own expense, as well as the others'. It was no secret that they all had healthy egos, all enjoyed their times in the spotlight, and although the man did a better job than most of keeping his ego in check, he had no problem pointing out the truth.

More important, he was in an obviously good humor, and Wally knew that signaled the immediate danger was officially over.

The Manhunter suddenly flipped his mysterious object high into the cold air. Superman's attention immediately went to the object, and then to the Martian, who nodded his head. Superman's eyebrows went up—he understood whatever it was that the Manhunter wanted to communicate. Then Diana and Superman exchanged knowing looks. Wally sighed to himself. The old guard, with years of experience between them, could communicate in subtleties far beyond youngsters like himself.

It had become painfully clear to Wally that neither the Manhunter, Diana, nor Superman wished to share the mysterious object with Kyle and him at this time. This was typical—the junior partners would have to slog through a mission debriefing before new information was introduced.

The five League members moved in closer together and Superman began the postoperation comparisons.

"I've been around the block a few times, but I'll admit I've never seen anything like *that*. Diana? Anything you recognize from the world of myth?"

"No—and they didn't require sorcery to dispatch." The Amazon echoed Wally's thoughts. "They were strictly from the realm of science. But not any science I've seen."

"J'onn, how about you? Something Martian science might have been familiar with?"

The Manhunter shrugged. He continued flipping the piece of *something* into the air. "Neither ancient Martian science, nor I, ever encountered anything like that. Apparently, there *is* something new under the sun."

The three veterans, finally satisfied that their extensive experience could offer no insights, turned to Wally and Kyle, and Superman spoke.

"Kyle, you've spent some time out there . . ."

But Kyle could offer nothing.

"Wally, your senses function better at ultrahigh speeds than any of ours. Could you get a good look?

Wally wanted to say he would have had a chance for a very close look if Superman hadn't intervened but, his accelerated high now worn off, he chose to let his frustration ride.

"They made my head hurt. Trying to look at them, I mean. It was like," Wally struggled for the words, "like my line of vision kept *sliding* off them. And the one I got close to—it only got worse. It was like the more I tried to focus on the fireball, the more my eyes didn't want to see it. I got impressions. It made me sick to keep trying to focus on it, but I did keep fighting and I sort of saw some, some—stuff, but none of it made much sense . . ."

Wally's words trailed off; he felt his attempts to communicate the event were leading nowhere. He was surprised that the others continued to listen as closely as they were.

"Go on. Tell us more," Diana urged. Superman nodded.

"Well, you know that objects are always somewhat distorted anyway when you're traveling that fast, so take what I say with a grain of salt. I guess the only way I can describe it is to say that I could get no sense of—*geometry*. It didn't sit in space the way something should, it didn't have a structure based on points and lines and planes and solids—it was inside out and outside in and all foggy and prickly and it made me nauseous and was completely lacking in, in . . ."

Words failed him and Wally spread his hands in a show of exasperation.

No one could offer a clearer insight into the event. Superman and Wonder Woman looked concerned, as if some fear had been confirmed.

The Manhunter continued to play catch. "Based on Wally's description, I could theorize that the phenomena came from *outside* what we informally refer to as the universe."

Superman and Wonder Woman shot the Martian sharp looks, and Wally realized the green alien had given voice to their fears.

"Maybe, but it'll stay a very tenuous theory without a lot more evidence," Superman flatly interjected.

The Manhunter eyed the object he juggled. "Absolutely. Some very solid evidence."

Of all the members of the League, Wally felt the least connection to the Martian Manhunter. Not because the hulking green figure with the beetling brow was not human. Technically, Superman, too, was not of the Earth; but the Kryptonian had absorbed Earth customs and mannerisms so completely that, beyond his superior physique and metapowers, you would never guess he was anything other than a normal earthling. The Man of Steel was the ultimate assimilated immigrant, raised on Earth, more at home here than he ever could be on the world of his birth. The Manhunter on the other hand was outré, plain and simple. He tried hard to make like a human; it was almost painfully obvious that he wanted his teammates and acquaintances to feel comfortable with him. But his honest attempts at earthly mannerisms, gestures, and habits were always a little *off*—they always left Wally feeling vaguely uncomfortable. The Manhunter was, to his very core and despite his best efforts, a thing apart, distant and different.

That wouldn't have bothered Wally half as much as it did if it wasn't for the fact that the Martian was both a shape-shifter with the creepy ability to mold the molecular structure of his frame into any conceivable shape commensurate with his mass—including a perfect mimicry of Homo sapiens sapiens—as well as an accomplished, extremely powerful telepath. That his telepathic abilities allowed for the convenience of mind-to-mind communications between all League members, and his strict moral code forbade his ever scanning his comrade's thoughts without permission, did little to relieve Wally of the anxiety of having his inner self exposed. Who could ever really trust a telepath? A shape-shifting telepath, to boot?

Well, Superman, Wonder Woman, and the rest of the old guard had worked with the Manhunter for years and had no trouble trusting him, oddball attempts to mimic humanity and all. They referred to him as the heart of the League. The truth, Wally admitted, was that the poor guy was the sole survivor of an alien race, the last scion of a dead planet, and how lonely must that be? Could he be blamed for working so hard to fit in somewhere? At least he was trying.

The five members of the field team continued to
mull over the unspecified nature of the menace they
had encountered, there at the crest of the Caucasus
Mountains. Superman and Wonder Woman's atti-
tudes, apparently affected by Wally's report, hinted at
a vague uneasiness, although they offered no reasons
why. The Flash and the Green Lantern felt their seniors' concern and fell under its shadow.

Suddenly, without warning, the Manhunter announced, "O'Brian is transmitting."

The communications facilitator for all the League's
needs, the Martian flipped the telepathic switch in his
brain that opened the team frequency, allowing all to
listen in on the mind-to-mind call.

*Oh, yeah, this is O'Brian himself transmitting from the
home of the hits on Luna Central: the mighty, still-standing
Watchtower. Does anyone down there remember me? Or
even care?*

It was Plastic Man, the hero of a thousand rubbery
shapes and a million impolite affronts, calling from
the League's base on the Moon, the telepathic approx-
imation of his oily, lounge lizard voice licking at
Wally's brain unpleasantly.

The man was bona fide, a time-tested hero, but,
man, oh man, he worked as hard to be annoying as
the Manhunter did to be accepted. O'Brian was a
good deal more successful, too.

*We're just trying to figure out what exactly we encoun-
tered, O'Brian,* Superman deftly maneuvered his
thoughts through the telepathic field. *Sorry, we got a
little involved. What's your status?*

Not that any of you glory hounds really cares, but us unassuming sorts on the home front have done quite well today, thank you very much. Watchtower wave and particle defenses have deflected or pulverized all seventeen chunks of mayhem on collision courses with Luna. No, repeat no, eagles have landed. The home team is batting one thousand!

The knucklehead thought himself an absolute card, but he did always manage to communicate the necessary information. Wally knew he couldn't have been happy to have been left behind on homeguard detail; Plastic Man, too, was no big gun. In this instance, Wally could sympathize with the guy.

Good deal, Plas. What did they scan as? Kyle's tentative offering blared harshly and with no rhythm; it took years of practice before one could smoothly navigate and nuance the Manhunter's telepathic field.

O'Brian, more experienced, clearly communicated embarrassment. *Um . . . yeah, about the scanners. Well . . . Jeez, you know how I've got this reputation as the team screwup? It seems I've justified it this time. I must have done something to louse up the scanners' master setting because, damn it all, they registered absolutely nothing. Not one of them. Nada. Sor—*

Superman overrode his signal. *Don't think it's your fault this time. We're having the same problem with our own senses.*

After Plastic Man had finished his many and profane expressions of relief, Wonder Woman asked Wally, much to his chagrin, to describe his perceptions of the intruding fireballs to the homeguard. Wally had hoped it wouldn't come to that; he hated to speak

telepathically any more than was absolutely necessary. It made him feel exposed, like maybe he might
accidentally reveal too much of himself. He was more
adept at the skill than Kyle, but not by much.

Still, the fact was that this was what was required
of any League member, and the request made tactical
sense—he was the only one who had come away with
any kind of description, so he did his best and bleated
out a summation for O'Brian to digest.

When that was done, and O'Brian had had his opportunity to cast aspersions on Wally's lack of de-
scriptive ability, they wrapped the session up and the
Manhunter broke off linkage. Wally shook his head to
clear the lingering psychic cobwebs—navigating the
telepathic airwaves still took a lot of concentration on
his part, and left him feeling divorced from the physical world. He blinked his eyes and looked around to
see the Manhunter, Superman, and Wonder Woman—
all far more adept than he and Kyle at compartmen-
talizing these telepathic group sessions—engaged in
examining the Martian's object. Or, it more accurately
seemed, *trying* to examine the object. Now Superman
was the one flipping it in and out of his hand.

Wally felt the heat of resentment again building inside him—*Really, how long are they going to keep Kyle
and me in the dark?*—when Diana abruptly turned
toward the junior members.

"Are you two fully returned from the link? Yes?
Then come here and look at this." She indicated the
object in Superman's possession.

Wally and Kyle walked tow... ....
did not get any easier to see.

"What—is—? I can't focus on it . . .
squinted hard. "It's like the . . ."

"It's like the fireballs," the Manhunter ... ...d
Kyle's thought. "In fact, that's exactly what it is—a
fragment from one of our extraterrestrial intruders."

The fragment *was* just as difficult to see—to
perceive—as Wally's fireball had been.

"So how did you manage to capture it?" Wally
asked, fascinated, his resentment forgotten.

"Totally by accident," the Manhunter admitted.
"At one point I found myself confronted by three fireballs hurtling simultaneously through my quadrant. I
spread myself thin in my tentacled configuration, and
was able to disperse enough muscular energy to each
extended pseudopod to deflect all three. But the effort
was numbing, and somehow this fragment got caught
up in a tangle of exhausted tentacles. At first I didn't
understand what I had; it felt like there was a diesel
engine tearing into my brain and either it, or I, were
going to explode. But then I put two and two together—and even though it seems obvious now that I
could have come in contact with debris, it didn't come
to me easily then—and I realized that if I held the debris lightly, kept it moving with minimal contact, I
could keep control of it."

Wally, for all his difficulties with the Manhunter's
"alienness," felt nothing at this time but admiration
for the being's extraordinary skills and presence of

...d. Who else but the Martian could have made this capture?

Kyle, also impressed, reacted more openly. "That was so—*coordinated*. I *never* could have pulled that off."

As Superman flipped the fragment—that was how Wally now mentally referred to the indistinct object— his Kryptonian eyes precisely followed its trajectory as if guided by optical gyroscopes. By the faint reddish glow they were emitting in that dark setting, Wally surmised he was using his microscopic vision, or who knew what other observational power he carried in his repertoire, in an attempt to understand the thing.

Suddenly, the Man of Steel diverted his eyes, squeezed them shut, and drew an unsteady hand over his brow. "Great Rao! My head feels like it's going to split open! Now I know what you meant, Wally. My focus seems to keep *sliding* off the crazy thing. It hurts to keep at it! It's *there* . . . I know it's *there* . . . but for the life of me, I can't focus on what it *is*!"

Wally didn't want to do it, he felt a hollow in the pit of his stomach, but he stepped forward and held out his hand. "Let me try. It seems I got a better look at the fireballs than anyone else."

Superman, still visibly uncomfortable, lightly lobbed the fragment to the Flash. Wally caught the object gently with both hands and closed his fingers around it. Immediately, he understood what the Manhunter and Superman had already discovered. The thing pulsed with an energy and vibrated on a frequency that was all out of step with anything familiar or natural. It just felt all wrong and crazy and mindrending, and he was getting sick again and everything was going milky and prickly, and all that he could do was toss it in the air like a hot potato and commence to juggling. That action, at the very least, made his relationship to it tolerable.

But only barely tolerable. The minimal contact was still enough to keep him feeling miserable and oddly disoriented. He swallowed hard, steeled himself for what he knew would be most unpleasant, and forced his concentration on the fragment. Wally seriously doubted any success this time; he was no longer experiencing accelerated consciousness. He was driven more by a burning desire to contribute, to again prove his worth to the team.

The strange thing was, he *did* get a glimpse into the object. At first it was the same: frustration and eye strain, brain pain and utter disorientation. One second his perceptions were sliding around and off of it, like feet trying to gain balance on top of a ball of ice, and the next he was transported. It was like his probing mind had inadvertently found a small crack inside the fragment's reluctance to share. Or, like he and the fragment had suddenly reached some kind of common ground, some shared link. Or—*something*. There were no words. There were only perceptions and sensations for which there were no words, no concepts. The bottom of the universe had opened up and he fell through, past all rules and natural law.

But it didn't hurt anymore, and it didn't drive him to the brink of madness. Everything just washed over him; it just *was*.

And then Wally saw a figure, both impossibly far and frighteningly close. It was the only thing he had perceived that bore any relationship to the structure and substance of the universe he knew. It was dark, maybe black, and it was vaguely humanoid in shape, encased in armor that reminded him of the chitonous plates of an insect or crustacean; its big, almond eyes in the flattened sphere of its head were intense and staring and burned into his consciousness. It wavered in and out of his perception, fighting to retain a recognizable shape in his brain. It broke into meaningless nongeometry, and then shimmered back to solid structure. It fought to maintain this form of contact they had made. It struggled to speak, its eyes burning into his. Wally caught the distinct impression of two words that had no place here:

Iris West.

Iris West—Iris *Allen*—was his aunt, and meant the world to him.

Panic clutched at his heart.

And then the figure disintegrated into a swirling madness of brain-twisting unreality, as if its effort to communicate had proved to be too great. And for the briefest of eternities, Wally gleaned something even more incomprehensible, even more horrifying than all else he had encountered within the object.

Glaring hatefully out at him from the void left by the armored figure's disintegration, he saw his own face.

Wally staggered and dropped the fragment. Superman, standing nearest him, caught it before it hit the ground. Wonder Woman and the Lantern, he realized, were suddenly supporting his slumped, limp body.

"What? I'm okay . . . let me go . . ."

Diana and Kyle gingerly released him. Whatever trauma he had suffered had been short-lived, and his physical control quickly returned.

"What happened, Wally? One second you had the fragment in your fingertips, the next you're convulsing like a epileptic on amphetamines." Kyle's concern came out creatively explicit. "You sure you're all right?"

Wally tried to sort through all the layers he had encountered in that instant of time. "It all happened that quickly, huh?" he offered, weakly.

"A fraction of a second." Superman got to the point, "You were able to see it, weren't you? You broke through . . ."

"*Perceive it* is probably more accurate, although what I perceived I've got no words for." Wally slowly shook his head. "You're going to have to trust me— it's going to take me some time to figure out a way of articulating this. At the very least, this thing is one mother of a hallucinogenic."

Wally had already decided he wasn't about to say anything concerning the little he perceived that he could describe: the dark figure, his aunt's name, his own face. Those things just seemed too—personal. He realized, he feared, that they were most likely images he somehow projected from deep inside his own psyche. Why, he didn't know, but any other explanation was impossible. They *couldn't* have any real connection with the hurtling menaces from far beyond Earth, Wally reasoned.

"What I can tell you is that the phenomena are not from anything we recognize as the universe. They are not of themselves responsible for the event, and . . ." Wally hesitated, wishing he could offer logical support to what he had to say, ". . . there is some direct connection with Earth. Those fireballs did not appear in near-Earth space strictly by chance."

The others looked to him expectantly.

"I'm sorry. That's all I've got for you now and, believe me, I can't offer a solid reason why I know that much. Just give me some time to sort things through—there was a hell of a lot . . ." He faltered.

Diana clapped him on the back. "Then that will have to be good enough."

Over his protests, the team insisted on giving Wally the field version of a League physical, to insure his nervous system hadn't suffered debilitating damage. While he seethed inside, impatient as he was with any delay he saw as coming from himself, Superman performed a full-body X-ray, Green Lantern created and executed a makeshift ring MRI scan, and Wonder Woman manipulated his power points, using her Amazonian healing skills. The Manhunter requested his permission to perform a complete Martian mind scan, which the others enthusiastically endorsed. Wally saw their point; maybe there was something he'd absorbed below the conscious level that the Manhunter could ferret out; but he unambiguously let them know that that probe would have to wait for another time. He was in no mood to allow any telepath to go rifling through his rampant subconscious just now. *Iris West, for God's sake. . . .*

A squall had descended on the ridge below the peak of Mt. Khalatsa. Wally suddenly realized that he was standing calf-deep in drifting snow.

Satisfied that his teammate was fit to travel, Superman indicated to the Manhunter that O'Brian at the Watchtower should be alerted that they were ready for teleportation home.

"We need to get both you and our fragment under the scopes as soon as possible," the Kryptonian informed Wally. "If you're right about the Earth connection, this will happen again. And we may not be so lucky next time."

Wally winced. The last thing in the world he wanted was to sit still for more tests. If only he had some excuse. . . .

Unexpectedly, the Manhunter turned to him. "I was just in the process of hailing O'Brian, and I received an emergency transmission—for you." The Martian's face showed surprise.

Wally nodded and the Manhunter linked his mind. Immediately, the psychic impression of an unmistakable voice filled his head like a living vapor.

West . . . I don't like interrupting a JLA mission, but I'm afraid I've got bad news . . .

There was only one person whose telepathic voice carried such velvety dark, commanding shades.

It was the Batman.

I know you and the team have your hands full, I know you've got important business out there . . . The Dark Knight, even when not physically part of a League action, was always kept informed by his own mysterious means.

. . . But I thought you'd want to know as soon as possible . . .

If the Batman was taking the time to contact him personally, it had to be very bad . . .

. . . There have been six people murdered in the last two hours in Keystone City . . .

Keystone. Wally's city.

. . . Individually, but using the same method, same pattern.

Serial murder. In his city. The Batman always believed in taking care of hearth and home first. So did Wally.

I thought you'd want to know.

The Flash wouldn't be teleporting to the Watchtower tonight.

CHAPTER 2

Criminal Science

Wally could have run all the way to Keystone City if he'd chosen, but that would have entailed the consumption of a good deal of energy—especially as concerned the treadmill foot action necessary to skim the ocean—and he was already feeling a bit low after his exertions climbing the sky. And although he might not admit it, his unfathomable experience with the fragment had taken another kind of toll on him. His mind felt heavy and tired and off-kilter.

He could have had O'Brian teleport him directly home, but that was not what he wanted, either. He chose to be placed down on the shore of the East Coast of the United States, in a stretch of pine barrens about equidistant between Gotham City and Metropolis. He had almost half a continent to cross on foot before he reached the twin cities of Keystone and Central, but he could do that in a few minutes at no more than his equivalent of a comfortable jog.

This would give him time to think, to clear his head.

The point of his reintegration was wild and isolated, but to the north he could see the reddish glow of massive urban light pollution as it reflected off the night sky's low cloud banks. That would be Gotham.

He did a quick mental calculation: It had been somewhere in the neighborhood of 4:00 A.M. back in the Caucasus; here it must be about—what? Eight the previous evening? Wally didn't carry a watch; time on the scale kept by human society had little relevance to him. Without really thinking about it, he assumed that a guy with his powers should be able to play catch-up whenever necessary; he had no real reason to hold to conventions when it came to keeping a schedule.

Which is not to say that Wally was lackadaisical, or unconcerned with time. On the contrary, he was *very* concerned with time and his extraordinary ability to utilize it. He figured that a man who could think and move as fast as he—relative to the norm of human culture—had a certain responsibility to use his powers to maximize that time. In effect, he expected himself to accomplish a great deal very, very quickly.

A spare minute for Wally was a chance to turn the world around. A wasted second was a lost eternity—a betrayal of his extraordinary gift, of the hero's responsibility to public service.

Wally felt he could never do enough. There was no problem too distant, no situation too complex, that would keep the Fastest Man Alive from stepping on the accelerator and *getting things resolved*, and he hated it when he occasionally glimpsed his limits.

So the Flash was forever busy filling up his time, with all the best intentions in the world, always thinking he could fit in one more noble task. And as a result, Wally West more often than not was late when it came to his civilian appointments and responsibilities.

Which his wife Linda quite understandably found irritating.

She found it a little sad, too.

If anyone had been there to see the Flash materialize in the piney woods, they would have had a second or two to absorb a tall figure clad in body-hugging scarlet material, accented with yellow boots, a decorative lightning zigzag pattern belting his waist and forearms, and a yellow lightning bolt over white circle chest insignia. His cowl, worn solely to provide environmental comfort, as it was no secret that Wally West and the Flash were one and the same, left the lower part of his face, from the nose down, uncovered. On either side of his head, the cowl sported tiny golden devices; sleekly designed wings that symbolized for all the Flashes their ancient, guiding spirit Mercury, the messenger of the gods, swift as thought itself. It was an elegant costume, brazen and simple; an emblem of speed in the service of humankind, both beloved and feared worldwide.

Wally himself, as would be expected of one in his profession, was muscular and well proportioned. He did not carry the hugely overdeveloped muscles of his confederates whose powers revolved around brute physical force—Superman, Captain Marvel, and their ilk. Speed, and the momentum it built, did much of his heavy lifting for him. Nor were his thighs as massive and his upper body as whip thin as one might expect of a power runner. There were obviously other forces at work in defining the Flash's shape. His lean, hard frame was beautifully proportioned, and perhaps most closely mirrored the overall suppleness and economy of line seen in a triathlon athlete. His every physical feature looked necessary and conservative, coiled and prepared to do its job.

For just a couple of seconds after materialization, Wally lingered, set and still in space. He found his bearings, a sometimes tricky task after the intrinsically disorienting experience of teleportation. He located Gotham, caught a whiff of cool salt air mixed with the scent of pine tar breezing up off the unseen ocean, dug in a toe, and was off.

And, with a strobe of blurred crimson and an instant of yellow witch fire, he turned invisible to the eye, leaving only a spray of sandy soil and a track of boot prints that faded and disappeared within twenty-five feet of their starting point.

For Wally, who hated more than anything else the time lost standing still, this was perfectly natural. From the instant he had materialized, his mind had started to gear up to its accelerated state, in preparation for the velocity jump it was about to initiate. The couple of seconds it took him to orient himself, and for his senses to adjust to their new environment, were leisurely and more than adequate from his point of view. Then he was all motion, the thick, corrugated soles of his boots providing the traction for the purely muscular push needed to begin his transformation to something faster than possible; something that would not be turned to jelly and then vaporized by the very speeds it would attain.

Wally set a comfortable pace for himself, and briefly considered a side trip through Gotham. He didn't kid himself; one of the reasons he asked to be dumped in this specific location was because of its proximity to the home of the Batman. In less than a minute he could do a thorough tour of the city's streets, and maybe satisfy his curiosity as to the whereabouts and activities of the detective. Wally was realistic about his chances, and knew full well that he wasn't about to actually run into the notoriously secretive crimefighter. But it drove him crazy that the man would have learned of a murder spree in far-away Keystone City even as Wally knew the Keystone Police Department would be clamping an investigative lid over the incidents. The announcement of the horror would come soon enough that day, but for the first couple of hours the cops would have done their utmost to keep the investigation clean and unencumbered and entirely to themselves.

To learn of a crime, exceptional though it may be, in a distant city, maybe even before the investigating officers themselves understood what they had on their hands, spoke of a far-reaching intelligence network deeper and more effective than any other crimefighting organization on the planet. Beyond that, it spoke of the Dark Knight's obsessive and frightening genius.

Yes, Wally was not embarrassed to admit, *frightening*. Anyone not a little afraid of the Batman's almost supernatural ability to ferret out secrets was a fool.

But the Batman's unnerving skills also made Wally incredibly curious, and not a little competitive, too. If he did detour to the dark labyrinth of Gotham, it would be against the astronomically bad odds that he might stumble on some hint of the trail that led from Keystone to Gotham, before that trail grew cold.

In the end, Wally decided against it. There was very little to gain and much to lose, especially as there was little chance that the Batman would not somehow detect his brief appearance and then someday, somewhere, remind Wally of the indiscretion. There would eventually be hell to pay.

Wally's cryptic associate in the League had decided to give him a generous if annoying heads-up, he told himself, so why look for trouble?

Keep your head in the game, Wally. Clear your mind and get your scarlet butt to Keystone. He couldn't allow his tendency to keep adding on more and more quickly achieved but time-devouring tasks to distract him from his objective.

And although he hadn't consciously returned to the subject for some minutes now, his mind was still reeling from the figures and the face inside the fragment. And Iris West Allen. None of this was helping his ability to stay on task.

Clear your mind. Good Lord, you'd think you had ADD.

That might not have been far from the truth.

*   *   *

Wally skimmed across the country, carefully picking his way along deer paths and dirt farm roads and gleaming highways, always taking the course that offered the fewest obstructions. When he came to a body of water he accelerated, leaped, and pedaled through space until he cleared the far shore.

If he passed close enough to another human being, that individual might catch an instantaneous blur of red out of the corner of his or her eye; a bright flash that was gone long before it registered in their consciousness. If it entered the conscious mind at all, it would be dismissed as a freak refraction of light.

To Wally, the world he passed through was one of perfect stillness, of sculpted light, and low, keening drones. The people and animals he casually loped past were statues. Those posed in a snapshot instant of interrupted movement, teetering in the unbalance of a half-completed step, or a perilously cantilevered lean. Birds hung suspended in midair and midflap. Automobile exhaust and smokestack plumes and clouds petrified to ivory pillars, supporting the sky. He plowed a tunnel through suspended curtains of jewel-like raindrops somewhere just west of Philadelphia, and weaved between more substantial obstacles.

Everything appeared compressed, flattened from the norm in the direction in which he traveled. The faster he traveled, the greater the distortion. He knew this was just an illusion, a visual side effect turning on his mind's ability to cope with his great speed; Wally had learned to compensate as needed. Distance, too, was strangely compressed; his strides seemed to eat up vast chunks of territory.

Colors were impossibly vivid and tended toward a kind of three-dimensional high contrast that bleached out the middle ground in the hues, giving the impression that all darks were darker and all lights were lighter, more brilliant. Wally found that while accelerated, the focal lengths of his eyes were extended far beyond what they were in a state of normal consciousness; everything, near and far, assumed a sharpness and definition usually associated with either precision optical lenses or dream states.

Smells, unfortunately, carried as they were by molecules, blew by too quickly to make any impression in his nostrils. Sound was distorted to a long, low wail combined with a somnambulant buzzing as of a hive of sleepy bees. Occasionally, a high-pitched interference crackled through; Wally was never sure from where that came. *The music of the spheres,* he told himself.

Through most of his jaunt, Wally did a good job of sticking to his agenda, of getting to the sister cities of Keystone and Central without delay. But on the metro outskirts, with the 474 Expressway under his tread and leading him toward the heart of Keystone, his discipline cracked and he found himself racing through gridworks of residential blocks, and twisting through industrial netherworlds in a ritualistic patrol of his hereditary turf.

In spite of his best intentions, Wally took the time

to forestall numerous industrial and traffic accidents, thwart an amateurish convenience store robbery, scare the pants off a playground bully, lift twelve packets of street-grade heroin from the hands of uncomprehending dealers in the midst of their sales, give a novice metavillain named Trash—whose low-level power somehow involved foul odors—second thoughts about following a criminal career, make a perimeter check of the Keystone City Penitentiary (commonly known as Iron Heights), and rescue a family cat from a backyard tree.

As a result, he arrived at Keystone Police headquarters three minutes later than he had planned.

Detective Jared Morillo slouched down in his swivel chair and tried to shift his heels onto the old oak desk in front of him. He was exhausted and feeling mean; it had been a long brutal day with no end in sight, and now he could find no comfortable resting place for his feet in the midst of the piles of clutter overrunning his blotter.

The fingers of his partner, big Fred Chyre, clattered over the computer keyboard, creating more of a racket than should have been possible. This did not sit well with Morillo.

"You're not going to find anything helpful there."

Chyre continued to work through the file marked UNSOLVED MAYHEM—HEAD TRAUMA. "We won't if one of us doesn't look," he mumbled flatly.

Morillo expelled the air in his lungs in a long, exaggerated sigh. "Damn it, Chyre, you're getting on my nerves. We're *not* going to get anywhere in this case unless we sit down and give ourselves time to think. We're *not* going to find any answers to what we saw today in any old police files. We *are* going to have to start thinking outside the box on this one. But right now I'm just too tired. . . ."

Chyre muttered something vicious under his breath, swiveled abruptly away from his workstation, and commenced to stare out the office's dusty double-hung window. He pointedly avoided any eye contact with his partner, feeling just as frayed and raw. Both of them knew that they were in no shape to get any more serious work done tonight, although they also doubted that either would be able to sleep. Not after what they had seen this day, and what they knew was yet to come.

Partners in a productive, if obscure and misunder-stood, department of the Keystone Police, the two men could not have been more dissimilar in shape or manner. Chyre was all bleached driftwood and dusty iron, the hulking end result of generations of KPD beat cops, born and resigned to a blue-collar exis-tence. In contrast, the younger, slighter Morillo was dark and exotic, an immigrant from the coast whose attitude and sense of style spoke of upscale longings. Chyre's jeans were faded and frayed; Morillo's pressed slacks still looked as fresh as they did when he began his tour that morning.

Chyre finally broke the stony silence. "Did you put in a call for him?"

"Just five minutes ago. He's out of town. Probably

JLA related. Maybe something to do with that big-ass meteor shower over Russia. That's the kind of work *they* do." Morillo, massaging a throbbing temple, shifted his tired body again.

Chyre sat stiffly in his chair and ran a big hand through his gray buzz cut. "I hate it when we can't give him any more than this. I hate relying on him. We're the goddamn Keystone Police Metahuman Hostility Department and we're forever calling in a goddamn metahuman whenever the going gets rough."

"Metahuman Hostility" referred primarily to supervillain activity. Metahumans were those persons who manifested strengths and powers beyond the normally human as a result of their genetic makeup. Most metahumans probably kept their freakish powers undisplayed. Some chose to use their powers to aid their fellow man, and became super heroes. And, unfortunately, some slid down the criminal path.

The two normal human detectives' involvement in the shadowy world of outrageously powered megalomaniacs was fraught with extraordinary danger, and high-strung and frustrated outbursts were one of the unavoidable side effects. They were par for the course, and the detectives were usually careful to give each other space, but tonight Morillo had about all he could take of Chyre's attitude. Tonight was not the night to go picking at anyone. The smaller man was about to explode in a tirade that he knew he'd regret in five minutes when a gust of air blew through the open door of their office, strangely enough carrying the faintest scent of salt water and pine.

There followed a vibration that lightly shook the entire room, and was felt deep in the two police detectives' chests, and then the Flash was standing before them, leaning casually against an ancient file cabinet, witch fire flickering ghostly under the cold fluorescent light.

"Judging by the expressions on your faces, this has not been a good day. Even by your standards." Wally spoke from experience—he had worked with the two ill-matched partners long enough to tell when their famous unease with each other was running even higher than usual.

Morillo ignored the jab, choosing instead to be amazed yet again by the Flash's *promptness*. "Jesus, Wally. I just put the call in to you maybe five minutes ago. I thought you were on the Moon, or over Russia . . ."

Wally wasn't about to further upset them by admitting that, actually, he'd been alerted by a source outside the KCPD.

"I'm good. You ought to know that by now." Always keep the mystique alive, he figured.

Chyre, just as amazed as Morillo but less willing to show it, lashed out reflexively at the show of self-confidence. "If you're so damn good, how come there are seven dead citizens on your turf?"

"Seven? Not six?" Wally asked without thinking through the consequences of revealing just how much he knew. The Batman had told him six.

Both Morillo and Chyre looked at him with new interest, their sullen, tired eyes suddenly gone all predatory.

"Huh. Did you hear differently?" Morillo smoothly shifted to interrogation mode.

Wally mentally kicked himself. His mind was still accelerated; he wasn't thinking patiently. *These guys are too good to ever get lazy*, he reminded himself. *You know they are world class. Now they have an inkling that you got information from somewhere else.*

He tried to recover, but knew it was weak. "I really don't know that I heard any number. I just was surprised that there were so many . . ."

Morillo chose to let him off the hook. There was a lot about Wally West and the network of metahumans with whom the Flash consorted that the detective would have liked to learn more about, but this was not the time. "Well, the body count keeps rising. At first it was an individual, then we got calls on three more, then it's up to six. Fifteen minutes ago we're told there's another."

Chyre, in tune with his partner as to just how far they would trust the Flash, picked up the thread. "Homicide is out there right now with the latest. I say latest, and what I mean by that is the latest *reported*. Because it's looking like every one of these whack jobs was perpetrated at just about the same time. With the same method, or power, or whatever you want to call it, employed in each case."

"So what we have is either a gang of sadistic freaks with highly disciplined timing and execution . . . or one really fast son of a bitch," Morillo concluded with his eyes locked onto Wally's.

Wally calmly returned the gaze. "I wish I could

vouch for every speedster out there, but you know I can't. And if you think I'd cover for any of my own kind, think again. You ought to know—"

"Don't get all defensive on us. You ought to know us, too. We're not out to give you any grief."

But you aren't about to hold anyone above suspicion, either, thought Wally. *I do know you. Just doing your job, and damn well at that . . .*

Wally threw the dozen packets of heroin he had confiscated on his street run onto Morillo's crowded desk.

"Right . . . and, by the way, here's a gift for Vice, if you'll see it through the system, please. Courtesy of two confused dealers on Ninth and Carmine. So you're telling me there's no question this is metahuman hostility?"

Morillo studied the packets noncommittally. Wally had a flair for dramatically reminding them that they should remember how helpful he could be, but right now neither he nor Chyre felt like pretending they were impressed.

"In no uncertain terms. Homicide wouldn't have asked us pariahs to the dance if they could have avoided it. It was a rotten, long day to begin with, and then we get called into this. Now we're well into our second shift with no real idea what the hell is going on. We're hip deep in dead bodies and maybe getting deeper." Chyre's frustration and concern shined bleakly through his exhaustion.

Morillo interjected, "Wally, this is real ugly business, and it's happening all over town. We've been running our asses off the last two hours trying to keep up with the body count. Nothing to go on, just trying to keep ahead of the game. You know the chief's got to hold a press conference soon, and the mayor's going to want us to be able to offer some assurances— it's going to be a panic out there. But we've got *nothing*."

"Have you taken a look at this seventh crime scene yet?"

"Didn't you hear? We just learned about that fifteen minutes ago. Pardon us for not keeping up to your standards."

Flash checked his retort, reminding himself that Chyre, always surly, was exhausted and at the end of his tether, and deserved credit for caring so much about the job.

"All right then, let's get out there and take a look. I need to see for myself."

Morillo and Chyre nodded silently, solemnly. They were dead on their feet and embarrassed to admit they needed help, but they would do their jobs.

While Morillo and Chyre drove to the scene of the latest murder, Wally did an exterior inspection of all seven sites. The detectives had given him the addresses in exchange for his promise that he would respect police protocol and not enter any of the crime scenes under cover of speed; not that Wally would have compromised his reputation by sidestepping procedure, no matter how great his impatience. Besides, the Keystone City cops were all well aware by now of the telltale signs that indicated a superspeed-ster in their midst: the unexpected breezes and sud-den shifts in air pressure, the vibration felt most prominently in the chest. The Flash was not com-pletely undetectable to those who knew what to look for, and he held enough respect for the skills of the rank and file cop to ever challenge them unnecessar-ily. He contented himself with his fruitless inspections outside the yellow tape, and then for the remainder of the twenty minutes it would take Morillo and Chyre to arrive on the scene he stayed out of sight, trying to settle his racing mind down to a state that could deal analytically with the cold, ugly information he knew he would soon receive.

Morillo and Chyre made good time through the evening traffic, and pulled their unmarked Crown Vic-toria up to the open space in front of a fire hydrant. The old brownstone beyond was surrounded by a crowd at the base of its porch steps; eager reporters and camera crews were held in abeyance by a team of stoic blues.

This was one of Keystone's recently gentrified neighborhoods, known locally as the Spanish War dis-trict for its streets, named long ago after the heroes of that conflict. It had recovered from the hard times of the fifties through the eighties to recently become a fashionable haven for urban professionals.

Keystone City's Metahuman Hostility Department pushed irritably through the gathered press, who themselves were none too happy to be kept so long in the dark about something they all sensed was growing into something extraordinary. The policemen guarding the steps curtly nodded Morillo and Chyre through, and the two detectives passed the tape barricades and entered the vestibule of the building, to be greeted on the stairs by the Flash.

Chyre glared. "I thought we'd agreed you were to wait for us outside."

"Don't worry, I haven't looked at anything inside. If I'd followed your instructions to the letter, the press would know I'm here. You want them to know that before you're ready?"

Morillo began to walk up the stairs and motioned the others to follow. "Never mind, you two. Let's get to work."

Two floors up they came to another line of blues outside apartment 2F and were motioned inside.

Wally would remember till the day he died what he saw in that room. He had encountered terrible things before, and would certainly see terrible things again, but the grisly absurdity of the Hurst apartment would always remain with him.

The room was crawling with the constant, methodical actions of a team of crime scene analysts who scraped and dusted and fluoresced and bagged, stopping only occasionally to talk with the three homicide detectives who were present. The room was long and its purpose divided midway, with a living room arrangement to the right and a small library to the left. Wally's eyes traveled to the center of activity, the living room area, which was set with sleekly modern furniture, and accented with tasteful postmodern pottery and Oceanic folkcraft. A flat-screen, cinema-proportion theater system filled most of one wall. The TV was turned on; Wally vaguely noted one of those annoying reality misadventures was in progress. In the center of the living space, facing the TV, sat a leather couch. Seated in the couch's center, Dockers-clad legs crossed, still lightly holding the latest issue of *Sister Cities Living* magazine in his cold hands, was a man with the top of his head blown clean off.

The seated figure looked as if he could have still been contentedly relaxing after a hard day at the office, except for the fact that there was nothing to his skull starting about an inch over his eyes. And all around the room, all over his precious and carefully chosen artifacts and treasures, lay a fine haze of his own blood and brains.

Wally was no forensic specialist, and he had certainly never seen anything like this before, but it seemed apparent that the man's head had *somehow* exploded from within, and that the force had been so powerful and so rapidly deployed that bone and tissue had practically vaporized as it shot outward. Despite the explosive violence evident in the gore splattered across the room, the edge of the wound itself was remarkably clean, almost surgically so, the bone not splintered or chipped below the decapitation line.

A fat, gray homicide detective, who looked as tired as Chyre and Morillo, sidled up to the three newcomers. "Hey, Wally. Guess I win the pool. It took seven bodies before Morillo and Chyre pulled you in."

"Screw you, Jodarski," Chyre offered with little hostility. "What you got for us?"

"What you see is what you get, unfortunately. Meet Mr. Alvin Hurst. His death doesn't appear significantly different from the six others." Jodarski turned from the corpse and jabbed a thumb toward a hallway leading off the living room. "Mrs. Hurst is in a room down there talking with one of the female officers. She's still pretty much incoherent. All we know is she came home shortly before eight, found the apartment locked, and her husband sitting here as you see him now. Started screaming and the neighbors made the call. You want to talk to her?"

Both Chyre and Morillo shrugged indifferently. "Not yet."

Jodarski pulled a pen from his rumpled shirt pocket. "Check this out, Wally. And remember, it's consistent with all the other victims."

The homicide detective tapped the pen on the edge of Alvin Hurst's skull. "This edge of the wound—the margin—it's *melted*. It's cauterized. Just the very edge. The trauma that caused this generated a damned high temperature. So high and so brief that just the margin was effected. No damage beyond, I dunno, a micron, maybe. No fusion beyond that. That cauterization extends throughout the entire remaining bowl of the skull. Look at the nose, the ears; no leaking, no blood. And his eyeballs; the whites would have gone all bloody with ruptured capillaries if everything connecting his brain to the rest of his body wasn't burned shut."

Wally indicated the gore sprayed over the walls

and ceiling. "Looks to me like the force that did this must have generated inside Mr. Hurst's head."

"Certainly looks that way. Also consistent with the other victims. And if that wasn't strange enough, I'm sure your escorts already told you that everything indicates that all seven of these poor suckers bought it at close to the same time. Hell, I don't know, maybe the *exact* same time. That's why Chyre and Morillo and you are crowding the room. This has got to be metahuman work."

Wally did not necessarily like that it appeared the KCPD had already decided a metahuman was responsible for this spree, but he continued the line of thought. "Any ideas why? Any connection between these folks and metahuman activity or crime?"

"Absolute zilch. Nothing we know at this time links Hurst or any of the six others to anything that would put them in this condition. All check out with nothing more extraordinary between them than a few traffic scofflaws and a case of tax evasion. But Morillo and Chyre apparently think you can help lead us through this." Jodarski looked skeptical.

Chyre walked off to talk with Mrs. Hurst. Morillo began questioning Jodarski about forensic specifics and Wally drifted out of the conversation. His attention returned with morbid fascination to the empty socket of Alvin Hurst's skull. He moved around the back of the couch and bent over the back of the corpse, angling himself to get a good, close look into the man's ruined pit.

There was a slight odor of burned flesh, and not

much to look at but a black, charred, oddly slick surface inside the skull. *Sort of like sand melted to glass and formed into a bowl*, Wally thought to himself.

Then, for a moment, he felt dizzy. He felt he was losing himself in the darkness of the bowl and was suddenly reminded of his experience forcing his attention into that weird fragment. For a moment it all came back very clearly; the dark alien figure, his hateful self . . . Iris West.

Wally gave himself another swift mental kick for allowing his thoughts to drift. The clarity of those fragment memories frightened him.

"Wally, you want to see the victims' specifics?" Morillo was calling to him.

The detective handed Wally a battered spiral notebook; Morillo still liked to keep his notes handwritten.

There was a column of names down the left-hand side of the page to which Morillo had flipped:

Thomas Lundgren
Dr. Julian Bibby
Beverly Schull
Benjamin R. Smith
Kimberly Chermenko
Louis Graziul
Alvin Hurst

Accompanying each entry on the right side of the page were the individuals' specifics, tightly packed by Morillo's cramped script into the remaining space. The ages varied from seventeen to sixty-nine. Addresses placed the crimes in neighborhoods all over the city, from here in the Spanish War district, to the China Flats, to River Bluffs South, to Krenkel Park, to right downtown. Five were done in their homes, one at a Kaiser Steel office at that company's Basin Street mill, one in a Toyota Camry at the City Bank ATM drive-up at Cardiff and Market. Upscale neighborhoods, working-class ghettos, industrial and business zones, automobile: Wally could see no pattern to the killings, no obvious connection between any of the victims. Could it be that they were all chosen randomly? By some sick punk with extraordinary powers flexing his muscles experimentally?

Morillo had also briefly noted the victims' professions—auto mechanic, medical internist, printer's assistant, stock broker—absolutely nothing tying them together here, either. Wally resisted the growing notion that these killings must have been random because that train of thought led to nothing but failure. There had to be something to dig into, some pattern, or else there would be no point, no hope of ever reaching any justice. He fought hard to reign in his impatience, the growing desperation that was beginning to eat at his cool, and whisper, *Wally, this may be it, boy . . . this may be the time when you can do absolutely nothing . . . this may be the time you stand revealed . . .*

There had to be something. Morillo and Chyre had brought him into this expecting that he would provide the key. He fought to stay focused, to keep his mind from racing with the specter of failure.

Wally returned his attention to Morillo. "Jared, all

the victims were found like Hurst here? I mean, with no sign of a struggle? Like they didn't see it coming?"

Morillo took back his notebook and flipped through several pages. "Let's see. Okay—most, it was like they died in their sleep, happily unaware. Like Mr. Hurst here. But Smith and Chermenko were apparently in motion when they died; walking, or maybe running or struggling. When they fell, they knocked over objects, like you might expect. But there might have been brief struggles. Crime Scene is still working on it. Far as I know, there's been no physical evidence of the perp—blood or hair or prints—found yet."

Morillo flipped another page. "Hey, here's something maybe you should hear. Lundgren—he was the first reported—he had someone in the room with him when it happened. We're basing the time of these events, six-fifteen, off this witness. Name's Mrs. Barbara Kovel, and she's Thomas Lundgren's personal secretary at Kaiser Steel. Understand that, like Mrs. Hurst here, she was understandably pretty hysterical—not exactly one hundred percent reliable, in my opinion."

The detective lifted his gaze from the notebook and looked directly at Wally.

"She told us that, like, seconds before the event, Lundgren, who was sitting behind his desk and not in her direct line of sight, complained of dizziness, and a buzzing or ringing in his head. Then he was quiet and she figured he'd gone back to reading his reports until she hears this loud *pop* that made her ears hurt, like a rapid air pressure change in an airplane, and she felt like an ocean wave had hit her in the back. She looks around and there's blood all over everything, herself included, and Lundgren is slumped in his chair with no noggin, much as Hurst here. That's as close as we've got to an eyewitness."

When he heard Morillo mention Kovel's report of Lundgren's dizziness, and the buzzing in her boss's head, Wally's thoughts shot back to his experience with the fragment . . . and the dark figure . . . and Iris . . .

His Aunt Iris had mentioned something to him once, when they were talking family.

"Let me see your victims list again."

Wally tried, once again, to clear his mind and just focus on the seven names. *Forget everything else, just look at the names.*

There was something here he was missing; somewhere in his impatient, chaotic brain, there was a memory. Iris said . . .

Beverly Schull.

That name was vaguely familiar, wasn't it? He remembered a time when Aunt Iris had been trying to get him interested in their extended family, and hadn't she mentioned a Beverly Schull?

"Jared, I think . . ."

Wally reconsidered his tack.

"Jared, I think you want to have the DNA on all your victims run by S.T.A.R. Labs."

Morillo raised his eyebrows. "S.T.A.R. Labs is very expensive. It would take some serious arm twisting to convince the chief we need to take our investigation outside the department. I'm going to need a strong argument . . ." Morillo's expression urged Wally to continue.

Wally avoided eye contact. "Sorry, but no can do at this time. You're going to have to trust that I've good reason, and if we find what I think we might, I'll explain then. Tell the chief I've got no interest in wasting the city's money; my wife and I pay taxes here, too."

"You're not making my life any easier, Speedster." Morillo shook his head skeptically. "But I guess we've trusted you this far. . . ."

Wally knew that one way or another, Morillo would get the tests run at S.T.A.R.

Wally left the the Hurst apartment shortly after that. He'd seen as much as there was worth seeing, pending the dreaded discovery of another victim. He realized he'd been up and running around since seven that morning, had put in a full day of city patrols and minor skirmishes before the call up to the Watchtower and the League and the whole disturbing situation with the spaceborn phenomena. And now this mess. By the time he decided to check out, it was close to eleven, and he felt as tired as Morillo and Chyre looked.

He loped home at a speed that would not take his mind too far into its accelerated mode. Too many times he returned home to poor Linda Park all revved and edgy. His wife deserved better than that.

Their apartment building rose up along Monacacy

Avenue, not far from the university. Wally could have surged a bit, climbed the exterior wall to their twelfth-floor flat, and let himself in through the outside-latched slide window he'd devised for quick access. Instead, he determined he'd keep his velocity and mind in low gear and glided invisibly up the twelve flights of steps in the fire well. As he climbed, Wally effortlessly dissolved his scarlet costume into free molecules and stored them as kinetic energy within his body—a neat trick he'd discovered through varying the vibrational field surrounding his body. At the same time, he pulled his similarly stored street clothing into molecular shape and, as he exited onto the twelfth floor, his appearance was that of any well-built young man dressed for spring weather. Although everyone knew who he was, Wally didn't like to flaunt his super-hero status in front of the neighbors. It just didn't seem like the thing to do in one's own home.

He keyed himself into the apartment. Coming directly from the expensively appointed Hurst living room just seconds ago, Wally was struck at how his familiar quarters suddenly looked plain and shabby. He hadn't really noticed before, but the walls were dingy, the carpet was frayed, the stereo and television set were long outmoded, and the sofa had definitely seen better days. Far from skid row, but a reminder that no one got rich playing the full-time adventurer.

Wally found Linda where he suspected he would: hunched over the kitchen table, pounding away at her laptop. Her back was to him, her lustrous, coal black mane flowing over her shoulders. Engrossed as she was in her work, she had not heard him enter. He tiptoed up to her and gently ran his fingers down and through her hair; he loved its thick silkiness. She gave only a slight start; living with a speedster prepared one for the unexpected approach.

"Hey, sweetie. Long day, huh?" She yawned and stretched, lithe as a cat.

Wally sat down next to her, continuing to toy with her hair. "Don't I surprise you at all anymore? What good is it being the Fastest Man Alive if I can't sneak up on my girl?"

Linda shrugged good-naturedly. "None at all, I guess, you big loser. Man, you look as tired as I've ever seen you look without a physical beating."

"Yeah, that sounds about right. And you look as beautiful as ever, even though I bet you've been cracking books all day." She did look lovely, even in a ratty old Peanuts sweatshirt and boxers.

"Why, you dog. I think you're looking to get lucky, you're so charming. As a matter of fact, this was my busy day at school. *And* I had anatomy lab, yuck." Linda still was having a tough time dealing with cadavers. "*And* I've been working on this endless diagnostics paper all evening, except I did manage to make some dinner. Yours is in the fridge, just pop it in the microwave."

Wally suddenly realized how hungry he was. He hadn't eaten since at least noon, and he'd burned a lot of energy pounding through the upper atmosphere. No wonder he was tired.

There was a time when Wally had been convinced that he needed to consume unholy vast amounts of calories in order to maintain his metahuman strength, back when he was operating under the assumption that his speed derived somehow from simple muscular power. He'd fallen in with a sort of fad diet, shoveling gobs of the highest-calorie junk down his gullet. As it turned out, while he never actually gained excess weight from the binge, he did find that his stamina suffered somewhat, and his disposition got downright cranky. He eventually came to realize that his power did not depend on caloric input, but that didn't mean that he still didn't get hungry as hell running around all day.

He pulled the plastic container out of the refrigerator, lifted a corner, and peeked inside.

"Meatloaf and mashed potatoes and Korean cabbage. My, my—you *have* been busy today."

"Well, we hadn't had it in a long time."

Wally stuck the container in the microwave, set the timer, popped open a beer, and sat back down. He sat across from Linda this time, so he could watch her dark almond eyes as she went back to pecking at the keyboard. He still couldn't believe how beautiful she was. How unaffectedly beautiful. And quick. And thoughtful. It took a special kind of individual to put up with the daily trials and anxieties of living with a super hero. Wally imagined life with him must be part aggravation and part sheer terror. Linda handled it all unbelievably well. She knew when to question him and when to let things ride. She trusted that he would come home at the end of every adventure, of every battle, even though she knew he was putting his life on the line each and every time he stepped outside.

And she always managed to put food on the table.

Linda had been a successful television reporter, fast rising through the Sister Cities' news hierarchy, on a course for an anchor's position on the evening broadcast. She was the golden girl; she had the looks and the charisma and the news savvy that probably would have led her in a few more years to a network position. But she didn't enjoy dealing with the attendant career grooming, or the unspoken expectations that she become more of an entertainer and less of a journalist.

She was also very good at hiding her frustrations, so it came as a surprise to her station when she announced one day that she was walking away from it all and going back to school. To medical school. Pediatrics, eventually. Linda had never been afraid of a challenge, and now she was old enough to know what she really wanted. Or so she told herself.

Hers and Wally's income had taken quite a dive after that. Linda was a full-time student and Wally's career as the Flash did little to contribute to the family coffers. Luckily, Linda had saved well during her prime contract years at the station, but even that had to be spent judiciously, spread over the seven years they figured it would take her to become a certified doctor. Still, Linda had never asked Wally to consider a career change to something more lucrative. He loved her for that, too.

Linda understood. Some things were more important than money.

Eventually she would complete her studies, start a practice, and then, Wally figured, then . . .

He'd think about then, then.

Right now it was enough that she supported and loved him, despite the fact that she was juggling fifteen credits and a part-time job, and that he sometimes disappeared into thin air for days at a time and could offer no explanation when he returned. Right now, relaxed in the moment, focused so completely on her, he had an understanding of just how lucky he was.

Then the microwave sounded. Without thinking, Wally accelerated. Halfway through sliding his warmed-over dinner onto a plate, he remembered that he hadn't wanted to do that. He hadn't wanted to shift up, because that tuned up his consciousness, however slightly. Now his mind would be racing when he had wanted it to stay nice and low and at Linda's speed. Now, until his mind found its way down, he would have to fight hard to keep from seeming edgy and impatient.

Of course, Linda noticed what he'd done. She'd heard the microwave and looked up immediately to see Wally sitting across from her, starting to chow down on a dinner that seemed to have magically appeared. She wished he hadn't done that.

Linda made a halfhearted effort to return to work, but found herself quietly watching her husband with eyes veiled under long lashes. Wally began to eat quickly—normal time quickly—but then sat back in his chair, tapping his fingers on the table edge. She could tell he was having a great deal of difficulty slowing his mind this time; something had happened today that had unsettled him. She didn't often see him this keyed up, but when she did, experience had taught her it meant trouble.

Wally's fingers began to tap faster, slightly at first, then faster and faster until the staccato rhythm became a rolling vibration. They blurred into invisibility and the entire table took to trembling. Linda knew her husband was completely lost in thought, oblivious to the supersonic action of his nervous fingers and to the commotion he was causing.

Deciding she had worked long enough for one day, Linda reached across the table and snapped her fingers under Wally's nose.

"Hey, Slowhand . . . a penny for your thoughts."

Wally blinked and glanced at his fingers, an odd expression in his eyes. Linda knew he would be disgusted to realize he had lost control of a body part.

They both watched in silence as his fingers slowed and stopped, all very gradually, like they needed time to properly decompress.

"Can you talk about it?" Linda asked.

Right now Linda was thinking that Wally looked fragile, which anyone else might think was an odd way to view one of the most physically talented humans on the planet. But she had lived around him long enough to know that his particular talent levied a heavy toll.

It was not surprising that they should have met. When she had been a reporter she'd covered the metro crime beat. The Flash had shown little aversion to being interviewed, especially by her. A mutual respect grew quickly into mutual attraction between the two public figures, and he had chosen to reveal his civilian identity to her personally before going public. When he did make the big announcement, she was at his side. To them, it all seemed very natural; he was excitement and romance, and she was stability and order. They complemented each other.

Not that they were exactly a balanced team. Falling in love with an indigent super hero cost Linda a lot. She paid the bills, she bought the groceries, she was the couple's support system, and she was well aware of that. Super heroes did not take pay, they did not accept rewards, they were not for hire. Linda thought there was probably even something in the Justice League's bylaws proscribing financial gain acquired through the exercise of superpowers.

Where the other heroes got the wherewithal to keep body and soul together, Linda had no idea. Maybe they were independently wealthy. She doubted they all had altruistic others covering their personal expenses. She only knew that Wally had made a commitment to serving as the Flash full-time, and she had willingly accepted the challenge of supporting what she strongly believed was a noble cause. It was her contribution to the big picture; she was insuring the solvency of a man who had, on occasion, assisted in literally saving the world.

Linda did it, too, because she loved him and secretly knew that it would be impossible for Wally to do anything other than be the Flash. That was what he did, that was what he knew, that was who he was. Her insight, however, didn't mean that their circumstances and their relationship were not without difficulties.

But she did have a strong sense of herself, as well, and when it came time to drop the television posing and make the move into medicine, she did so without hesitation. It would be tough times for many years, going full-time to med school while supporting them both, but she was very smart with money and with her time.

Linda shut down her laptop and closed the lid with a snap. Her husband's mind was still speeding somewhere else, and she tried reaching him again. "Wally. What's on your mind, honey?"

She saw him struggle to decelerate and focus on her.

Finally, Wally spoke, slowly and deliberately. "Linda, when was the last time we saw Iris?"

"Iris? Your . . . ?"

"Yeah. Aunt Iris. West . . . or rather Allen. Why do I keep thinking of her like she was before she married Barry?"

Linda thought that that was curious. "I don't know. It's been a while since we last got together. Maybe a year or so. I seem to remember we had dinner while her forsythia bushes were blooming. Why?"

"I don't know, I . . . I'm just thinking that we

should stay in closer touch. We've kind of drifted apart."

Linda was very aware of the tremendous influence Iris had had on the young Wally West. He regarded her with a kind of fierce loyalty and awe that was generally reserved for someone who had saved your life, or so it seemed to Linda.

"Well, we're all way too busy these days. She's not sitting home knitting sweaters, either."

Wally chewed his lip, trying to decide how much of the day's events he wanted to reveal to Linda. He desperately wanted her council, her feedback, but he knew full well it wasn't going to do any good to get her involved with his business when all he had were questions and fears.

He finally resolved to keep silent until he had a better idea of what was what. Bouncing all his confusion off her would make him feel better, but it wouldn't help solve anything. So why frighten her unnecessarily? They would both be better off if he kept his mouth shut. Wally just hoped she would always be as patient and understanding with his evasions and mysterious half truths as she had in the past.

"Iris was trying to tell me, I guess it was several years ago now, about that side of my family. Her side, my father's side. My mom and dad never stayed in close touch with relatives, so I don't have a very good idea as to what I've got in the way of cousins, or second cousins, or whatever. Anyway, a few years back,

Iris decided that it was a shame that I didn't know any of my extended family and she began filling me in. She gave me names and their relation to me, family tree stuff. But I guess I wasn't much interested at the time, because nuts if I can remember any of it."

"So, um," Linda tried a quick mental check of her brutally overloaded calendar, "let's give her a call and see if we can't come up with a time that works for all of us to get together."

"Yeah. Sooner rather than later." Wally's eyes had grown distant again. "Real soon."

Linda sighed and stood up. "Wally, you're a lost cause tonight. I'm sure you have your reasons for bringing up Iris and your family tree, but it's late and I'm too tired to try to pry it out of you. Love you, kid, but I'm packing it in. You should, too."

Wally gazed down at the table and was surprised to see his dinner lay half-eaten, his beer untouched. That was a rare occurrence; he'd thought he was hungry.

He suddenly realized he was worried. It wasn't the amorphous, general anxiety he'd been feeling ever since his encounter with the unearthly fragment; this was something specific and directed.

He knew Linda was right—he should hit the sack—but . . . "Hon, I'm going to make a few calls before I turn in."

"At this hour?" Linda called back from the bathroom. "It's almost midnight."

"I know, I know." Wally lowered his voice and mumbled to himself, "But I've got to or I'm never going to be able to sleep."

He dialed Iris's number and, as he expected, got her answering machine. Iris was her own woman, and did not suffer fools or late-night calls gladly. Even from her favorite nephew. He was sure she was in bed and wouldn't hear the message. "Aunt Iris, it's Wally. I know it's late, but it's been too long and I was thinking of you. If you're not picking up, give Linda and me a call in the morning, okay?"

With nothing more to say, he hung up, but it felt like an unfinished job. Maybe he should scoot over to her house just to be sure.

Don't let yourself get obsessive, Wally.

Next, he called his parents out in Blue Valley. His father picked up, and was understandably unhappy to be awakened by a call with no real point, as far as he could tell.

"Yes, your mother and I are fine. No, nothing unusual. What's up? Someone making threats against your family?"

Wally told him no, not really, he was just feeling uneasy for no particular reason. As with most interactions with his father, the conversation ended with Wally feeling like an annoyance. Still, it was better that he had called.

Who else? He remembered the name from Morillo's list that had struck a distant chord: Beverly Schull. Iris had talked about Schulls—he was sure she had. There were Schulls that were somehow related to the Wests.

Wally pulled out the battered phone directory from its cubbyhole next to the refrigerator. He thumbed through the volume until he came to the listings for

Schull, and ran his finger down the six entries. Thankfully, Schull was not a particularly popular name in the Sister Cities.

He found the deceased Beverly listing, confirming it against the address. A few lines below, he came to *Kevin Schull, 1028 Crawford, Brksvlle.* Kevin in Berkittsville, a suburb to the north of Central. It seemed like he might be someone Iris had mentioned.

Wally shrugged; he wasn't going to get any rest if he didn't try. He dialed Kevin Schull's number and the phone on the other end was picked up almost immediately.

"Yeah?"

"Uh, my name is Wally West, and I'm trying to reach Kevin Schull . . ."

"You've got him." The voice was alert and even. Wally was relieved that Kevin Schull did not seem to be upset despite the hour. In the background, he could hear a television blaring.

"I'm sorry to be calling you so late."

"Not a problem, but if you're trying to sell me something . . ."

"No, no . . . um . . . I got your name from a relative, Kevin. Actually, I'm calling because I think we may be related."

"Oh, Christ! This is about Lori and her damned paternity claim, isn't it? You bastards. I've been cleared and—"

"No, Kevin, listen . . . please. I don't know any Lori. I think we're distant cousins. I think the Schulls and Wests are related."

"Oh, yeah? Sorry. I got a crazy ex-girfriend. Y'know, I do think we got some Wests in the family somewhere. Hey, you said your name was Wally West? You're not the same dude who's the Flash, are you?"

Wally had been hoping that Kevin Schull wouldn't put his name together with his famous alter ego, but he wasn't about to lie, either. Then, before he could acknowledge Schull's deduction, a quickly rising wave of static rolled out of the receiver, loudly obscuring what could have been a sharp, wet *pop* coming through from the other end. Wally stood, confused for a moment, as the static receded as rapidly as it had come. He could again hear the tinny sound of the television, from over at Kevin Schull's residence. A deep dread began to spread through him.

"Kevin? Hello?"

There was no answer. Only the television spoke. The line was open, the phone was working, but Kevin Schull had ceased to answer.

Wally felt sick, deep in the hollow of his chest.

CHAPTER 3

The Presence

Wally did not remember much of his wild dash to 1028 Crawford Street in Berkittsville. He remembered yelling an apology to Linda that probably came out unintelligible. He remembered the sick feeling in his chest and fighting the clutch of panic, but he was too stunned to be fully conscious of the route and passage that brought him to Kevin Schull's so quickly that windows banged and leaves were sucked off trees in the vacuum of his wake.

Something in the back of his unconscious must have recalled the street layout of the tiny working-class town of Berkittsville, because before his thoughts could catch up he found himself racing on to Crawford Street. Then there was 1028 right in front of him, a small, ordinary bungalow that probably was looking its best obscured by the night. Wally tore into the front yard, past bald lanes in the grass where a shackled dog must have once patrolled, and did not slow down as he approached the front porch.

He knew he was taking a terrible chance if he was right, and facing embarrassment and public outrage if he was wrong, but he didn't see where he had a choice. This was a judgment call. This is what heroes did.

He accelerated up the porch and was literally levitating over the wood plank surface when he set his entire body, every single molecule, vibrating to a higher frequency.

He amped his racing body to this state by a combination of intensely precise concentration and total control. As Wally understood it, he was forcing his molecular structure to oscillate to a rhythm completely out of tune with the physical world surrounding it. He didn't bother to think further about the science, but the result was that Wally could pass through solid objects without injury to himself.

Injury to the object penetrated was another thing, however.

Wally slid through the thick oak front door with no more difficulty than a radio wave and stopped on a dime inside the vestibule. But the door behind was left a smoking ruin, much to Wally's chagrin.

This was the one speedster trick he hated to pull, because it was the one he could not seem to master. Barry Allen, the previous Flash, had spent countless hours teaching him, working to refine his technique, but to no avail. Other speedsters—Max Mercury, Johnny Quick, even the young Impulse—all were able

to easily pass through solids without inflicting catastrophic damage. Wally's speed and control far
eclipsed them all, except in the case of this one particular skill. When it came to this, he was just plain
clumsy.

Regardless, he had accessed Kevin Schull's house
in the absolutely fastest manner possible. From the
time his mind had wrapped itself around the potential situation on the other end of the phone line till the
moment he pulled up in the Schull entrance hall,
barely fifteen seconds had passed.

Wally hesitated just long enough to absorb his surroundings, then cautiously accelerated again and
moved toward the room ahead. The bluish flickering
of an unseen television provided the only lighting,
partial and unsteady. The broadcast sounds he had
heard over the phone less than a minute and an eternity away now boomed off the walls. Wally moved
around a corner and into the living room at a speed
something just under Mach. The room and its furnish-
ings heaved out of shadow under the ghostly, now
frozen light of the cathode tube, which Wally duly
noted was tuned to a late-night talk show. There was
a slight odor of burning hair.

It took a moment for him to acclimate his vision to
the wan, cerulean glow. Then he found what he
feared he would. There was a figure, sprawled in a re-
clining lounger set very close to the television. It
slumped a little to one side of the chair, which was
fully extended into its horizontal posture. In the faint
lighting, Wally could not discern details, but he could

hear the insistent electronic bleat of an active phone coming from near the figure.

Wally moved a bit closer, his eyes growing more accustomed to the light. He stared unblinkingly at the top of the lounger, where he knew the figure's head should be.

Then he saw it. It was unmistakable. It was what he'd already seen once that night. It was clear now that the figure was a man and the top of his head was gone.

Wally moved slowly closer, filled with an almost superstitious dread. The wound, the details, he now recognized, were indeed identical to those he'd seen on Mr. Hurst. The top of the man's skull and his entire brain were gone. There was no seepage, no blood flowing from the fresh carnage. Wally shifted his eyes to the surrounding walls and ceiling and thought he could dimly perceive a broad, dark stain circling the surfaces of the entire room like a wheel, with the dead man seemingly at its hub.

Like a Milky Way of blood, thought Wally, as the sick feeling in his chest grew worse.

He returned his attention to the scooped-out remains of the man's head. He assumed the poor guy had to be Kevin Schull, but until that was confirmed, he'd refer to the corpse impersonally. He bent closer, squinting for a clearer view in the soft, dull light. Looking right inside the black bowl . . .

. . . And felt a presence.

A tangible thing, a psychic weight, an invisible malignancy, somehow centered in the man's skull cavity.

Wally became dimly aware that the sick hollow in his chest was more than a symptom of fear and despair. There was something physical, something right in this room, affecting him.

Then the assault came.

It was like the atmospheric pressure permeating the space surrounding him had suddenly crashed, leaving him nauseous and struggling to breathe, aching in his joints and chest like a case of the bends. He felt a buzzing, a *ringing*, in his skull.

Innate survival instinct screamed for him to leave—*now!*—but before his accelerated reflexes could respond, a surge of blinding pain washed over his mind, stabbing like a burning knife and crippling his ability to reason. More pain followed, rolling up like waves smashing into a beach, each one worse than the previous.

Each seemed to scream, *It's coming! It's coming!*

Strobes of brilliant red light began to burst before Wally's eyes, even though they were squeezed tightly shut in a grimace of raw agony. Through the haze of the hammering pain, Wally was vaguely aware that the capillaries in his brain were about to explode.

He began to shake uncontrollably, but not spastically, not in a full-body heave. Rather, his molecular structure was convulsed by something that did not vibrate in a pattern that had anything remotely in common with anything in this universe.

That realization, hit upon by Wally's pain-wracked, chaotic mind, even as it began to shrivel and die, saved his life. That, and the fact that a scant second earlier he had consciously set his own body vibrating out of harmony with this world as he passed through the front door.

With an enormous effort, part instinctual, part blind panic, part desperate cunning, Wally forced his remaining consciousness back to the state he had so recently invoked, and called on his molecular structure to again dance to a different tune. If his mind had not so recently executed that shift, it would have been extremely doubtful that Wally could have made the jump under such horrible circumstances.

Even under ideal conditions, the maneuver called for delicate execution. But Wally's willpower was nothing ordinary. He reacted pitch perfect. His finely tuned body responded as if on cue, and as a result he cleanly shifted to the alternative field of vibration, surviving the onslaught.

Wally found himself in a strange place. He had never found it necessary to maintain the state of alternate oscillation for more than the briefest of instants; the object previously had always been to get quickly through an obstruction. In this situation, however, his life might depend on keeping his molecules in this forced state for some time.

The world around him had become a hazy, distant mirage. He saw the blue gleam of the television and the bulk of the brainless corpse in its chair, the gore-stained walls and the shadows that hid everything else. But it all seemed infinitely far away, although perspective told him he could reach out and touch anything he wanted.

Part of his mind, the part that maintained the level of concentration necessary to keep his molecular structure in this state, also kept his legs treading in a constricted, precise cyclical motion. This served to keep him suspended in the air that now seemed thick and sticky relative to his structural resonance. If he had remained in contact with the floor, gravity would have eventually pulled him down through the house and theoretically, thought Wally, straight to the center of the Earth.

Most important, the pain was gone. The devastating, blind-side attack had ended as quickly as it had come, and this was incentive enough to keep Wally tightly focused on maintaining the alternate oscillation state.

The wave of panic had passed, too, and with the return of calm came a clear-headed appraisal of his bizarre situation. Scanning the room carefully, Wally could still feel it. The presence was still there.

Then, miraculously, it seemed to drift into focus, seemed to descend out of nothingness, and allowed Wally to glimpse it. Suddenly, it was in front of Wally, half the room away, observing him, scrutinizing him.

Or so Wally somehow intuited. He had no clear sensory impressions to support this.

The presence was curious, Wally understood. It had never encountered anything like him before, had never been presented with a problem of this sort. Maybe it had ceased its attack because of just this.

The presence was cold, and analytical. Wally had no doubt that it felt no more empathy toward him than a human being would to a microbe under the microscope.

Despite the terror of the powerful unknown confronting him, Wally, too, felt curiosity for this thing that apparently moved in and out of the world at velocities even higher than his. He stared back at it and tried to define its shadowy form in his mind.

It was . . . it was . . . a black seething horror. A vacuum surging out of a void. A roiling thunderhead blotting out the night sky. A gaping, sucking maelstrom that sometimes phased into something *else* inside a misshapen, anthropomorphic outline. It was the smell of sulfur and ozone, cold brass and death. It was the sound of a hive of bees inventing electricity, a hurricane at sea, the still heart of a dead galaxy. It was all sticky and prickly with subatomic static. It was all these things and none of them.

The presence was completely and unknowably alien, and yet it had an intelligence that Wally felt could be comprehended in human terms. And it was ultimately malicious; hatred and contempt flowed over Wally like waves of heat.

What in the hell is *this thing?* Wally was questioning his sanity more than anything else. There was no time for comprehension.

But the thing seemed to wordlessly reply to him, *I am everything you are not, and more than you can hope to be. I am so much more powerful than you.*

The presence and Wally regarded each other for an eternity of nanoseconds, like two gunfighters sizing up the strengths and weaknesses of their opponent, each hesitating to make a move until he better understood the nature and soul of the other.

For Wally, who understood nothing of his opposite, it seemed that the presence was hesitating. This confused him; it seemed clear that the thing was more than powerful enough to outmaneuver and destroy him with very little effort.

But that line of thinking wouldn't do, he berated himself. He carried no fear for his physical well-being, but the fear of failure, of failing those who would become the thing's future victims, was overwhelming. If this monstrosity was going to give him the chance to crawl up off the carpet, then he was going to press that advantage.

That was his only chance, he realized. He had to hope the thing had no idea he could and would attack. He had to count on the element of surprise.

A plan sprang to his mind, followed almost instantaneously by action, as Wally launched himself at the presence without hesitation, fearing that his nemesis would sense his intention if he delayed.

Wally maintained his alternate oscillation rate and lunged straight for the presence's midsection. Although there was no way to be sure, he was hoping that it was in some manner a physical being, because that was the only way his plan could work. If the thing had some material substance, no matter how tenuous, his molecular vibration could disrupt it as it had the entrance door.

Wally accelerated as powerfully and as quickly as the space between him and the presence would allow, and his skill and coiled strength were such that by the time he reached it, he was moving at close to half the speed of light.

He had planned to burrow himself deep within the thing, and hold there, hoping his otherworldly vibrations would tear it to atoms.

He was well aware that this could be his last act on Earth.

But the thing dodged his furious assault easily, almost casually, like an accomplished prizefighter dodges the bull rush of a barroom bully. Wally couldn't say exactly how the presence accomplished its maneuver—it was there and then it wasn't. It was very, very quick.

Wally, caught off balance, twisted and accelerated awkwardly, shifting gears in an attempt to avoid the expected counter blow. But none came.

The presence was still studying him, collecting information, perfectly calm and conceited. Perfectly confident that it could annihilate him whenever it chose.

With a start Wally suddenly realized he was no longer maintaining his state of alternative oscillation. At some time during his offensive action, he'd lost concentration without recognizing it. Things were happening too fast, which was an unusual sensation for Wally.

But the pain had not returned, and the presence still floated somewhere before him, an undefinable concentration of malignancy.

I interest it. It tolerates me because it's decided I offer no threat.

His blindly conceived stratagem had not worked, and the thing was giving him another chance.

Wally briefly considered an attempt to flee the scene, to regroup and seek assistance. But his nature found running from *anything* far too repugnant, and the very real possibility that the presence would kill again if not countered now kept him rooted in Kevin Schull's crepuscular living room.

Think, Wally . . . think . . .

It couldn't read his mind, Wally was reasonably sure of that, but it did seem to have a pretty sharp understanding of his technique and tactics. Wally had not been able to catch it by surprise.

He doubted he could match the presence in a race up the velocity ladder. It was frightening to conceive, but Wally was starting to form a picture of where the thing's outer limit abilities might reach. Wally had a top speed limit; if he hit the speed of light, he knew from experience that he would be absorbed and transmuted into another state of being, into something the speedster mystics called the Speed Force. Once there, he would be out of the game, cut off from all contact and influence in this world. That way wasn't an option, because what Wally had seen so far led him to believe that the presence might somehow be able to circumnavigate the Speed Force and surpass the speed of light, leaving it free to continue while Wally was trapped.

For the Fastest Man Alive to admit that his opponent was even faster, that was the ultimate slap in the face.

But, maybe, if he did the unexpected: if he took things *down* the ladder . . .

Wally began to decelerate in a smooth, gradual descent toward normal time. A *very* gradual descent. Even though he was holding relatively still within the context of the room, his atomic frequency would signal the change in his body's PSF, his Potential Speed Factor. He was counting on the presence's ability to perceive that.

As Wally slowed himself, his view of the already indistinct thing grew even more clouded as his decelerating frame of reference found the higher speed factor of its corpus harder to discern. Then it suddenly appeared to him to shift back to its original focus, and Wally allowed himself a grim interior laugh. It had taken the bait, and was decelerating with him, presumably to better observe its subject's mysterious actions.

Wally continued his gradual descent, eyes calmly locked onto the shapeless thing. He watched for any deviation in its focus or rate of movement, but saw none. It was carefully matching his slowing time, keeping itself in uncanny synch with the object of its interest.

Down the Mach scale slid Wally's PSF. Past Mach 100, Mach 50, Mach 25, 15, 10, 5 . . .

The presence kept pace. Kept precise time. Kept observing him.

Down below the speed of sound. Down to speeds to which normal human beings could almost relate.

Wally thought he could see the presence becoming

somewhat more . . . *material.* It appeared the anthropomorphic aspect of its nature was more prominent, more readily visible. As it slowed itself, the thing was becoming all the more horrible for this tendency toward something more human.

Nine hundred relative feet per second . . . 800 . . . 600 . . . one half Mach speed . . . Now.

Wally slammed on the mental brakes, threw himself out of reverse, and sprang the clutch, thrusting himself forward into acceleration mode with all the power he could muster.

This time the thing was an infinitesimal moment too slow. Wally's extended fists drove simultaneously into the region that would be called the chest in a human. He felt grim satisfaction as they sank deep into a soft, dense mass that sent prickling shocks down his arms. Wally had been right: he had seen the thing take on more physical substance as it had decelerated.

The thing roared a terrible, unearthly howl of pain and hatred that seemed to come from deep within Wally's own head. It might be stunned, but given another instant, Wally knew that it would recover and destroy him.

Wally had to react more quickly, and he did so, continuing the attack with rapidly accelerating speed.

Up the ladder: Mach 20, Mach 50, Mach 200, Mach 800 . . .

Wally slammed a flurry of savage haymakers into the presence's nebulous head. The thing continued to reel, apparently dazed. It was recovering its speed, but it lagged well behind.

He had to keep it stunned, had to put it away *now*, before it caught up with him. Hopefully the headlike shape he pounded was the seat of its consciousness.

Smashing his fist again and again with trip hammer force into the spongy, prickly mass, he realized it was changing. Now it felt more like he was punching holes in a viscous liquid, and then through sticky, electrified smoke.

Wally's heart sank as he realized that he had failed. Despite the punishment it had received, the thing had managed to accelerate back up to speeds where its substance became less material. Wally could no longer hope to stop it with brute force.

The presence suddenly rocketed past him, accelerating at a rate the Scarlet Speedster could not match. The game was over; he had tried and failed. A pulse of laser-intense hatred drove home like a spike to his brain. A tidal wave of engulfing pain washed over his convulsing body. The red explosions returned to the insides of his eyes, and his body went into a state of shock as it prepared to wither and die.

Then, strangely—even at this height of black, rending agony—Wally became aware of a tone in the back of his head. A familiar alert from long ago and far away. A psychic tug, a telepathic phone ring . . .

The pain had stopped.

Wally floated, unable to move or form a coherent thought. But he was aware that the presence was listening, was examining the tone in his head. Except . . . except the tone was in the presence's head.

In the presence's head. Also.

He sensed doubt in the presence. Confusion. What was this psychic tug in its consciousness?

Why . . . ?

Wally? Wally? May I come in?

The Manhunter. In his mind. In the *presence's* mind.

He was hammered by a blot of rage and frustration so intense it felt physical, and then the presence was gone.

Released from whatever grip held his limp, nerveless body suspended, Wally slumped to the floor, slipping into unconsciousness.

At first there were red tendrils snaking through sparking blackness, then they lifted like a veil, the universe fading to a wash of pale sapphire. A second or an infinity later, Wally realized he was looking at blue cloth. A blue shirt. He shifted his gaze with no little pain and numbly realized that the shirt belonged to a figure close over him. A police officer.

There was a cop kneeling over his prostrate body, who carried a look of deep concern in his strangely familiar eyes. The ringing and the static were receding now and he could sense a distant, *Wally? Wally?* from somewhere behind his inner ear.

But the officer wasn't moving his lips. Wally slowly moved his eyes over the man's face, down his uniform, searching for information. He found it on the name tag pinned above a chest pocket: Officer Jon Jones.

Jon Jones. A play on J'onn J'onzz, the Manhunter's Martian name.

The Martian Manhunter, chameleon supreme.

Wally tried to force a telepathic reply to the alien hero, but found that effort even more excruciating then tensing his eye muscles. Something was not right in his brain. The notion that he may have had a stroke brought the sharp prick of fear back into his awareness, and then it all flooded back: where he was, why he was there—the presence—the battle . . .

The Manhunter had somehow known he was in trouble. And after his encounter with the empty horror of the presence, the JLA member from Mars, the being who usually filled him with such unease, seemed downright familial, even comforting. *Everything is relative.*

Wally parted his lips and began with great effort to speak. Haltingly.

"Did . . . you . . . see . . . *sense* . . . it?"

"I don't think so," the Manhunter replied. "We can talk about that later, Wally. Right now we've got to get you to the Watchtower and some medical attention. I did a quick scan of your body functions and I'm getting some weird readings."

Wally slowly shook his head. "No, J'onn. I'm getting . . . my wind back. Shock . . . I'm in a state . . . of shock . . . I think. Tell me . . . how did . . . ?"

"I was trying to contact you. I'd sounded the link tone and you didn't open up. But then I picked up on some alarming thetawave fluctuations coming off your mind. Frightening, actually, and I took the liberty of forcing my way into your head a bit—and I apologize for that, but I thought that circumstances warranted my move. I could only see a little—whatever you were up against created some extraordinary psychic interference. So I fixed your coordinates and had myself teleported down. I was worried. I wouldn't ordinarily interfere in your home field business . . ."

"No . . . really. Thanks. I think your call saved my life. I think you confused . . . frightened it off. It was somehow linked with my mind and when you called . . ." Wally's dazed thoughts shifted. "I've got to get in touch with Morillo at the KCPD . . ."

The Manhunter shifted his gaze from Wally and looked into the murk of the room, still lit by the flickering light of the television. "You've got quite a situation on your hands, haven't you? What is this thing you're dealing with that shaves off a man's skull?"

Wally could finally feel the strength returning to his limbs and clarity spreading through his mind. He gingerly lifted himself to his elbows. "You tell me. I just had a pretty good go-round with it, but damned if I know any more now than before it beat up on me."

The disguised Martian examined the dead man.

Wally searched his memory for any information he might be overlooking. "All I know is that, whatever it is, it's fast. Very fast. In fact . . . it's faster than me."

The Manhunter cocked an eyebrow. "That's frightening. And, I thought, physically impossible . . ."

"I know. But it *had* to be moving beyond the speed of light. Somehow. Jeez."

"So this is another good reason to get you up to the

Watchtower. You can access the crime and MO files after we've done a full examination and—"

"No, J'onn. Eventually, yes, but right now I've got to stay with the investigation already in progress. I think I'm going to hear that there were other attacks, all about the same time. I've got to get in touch with Morillo."

"Well, I can hear the local police coming up the street," the Manhunter offered. "I'm surprised it's taken them this long; that must have been one big bang when you came through the front door."

Wally gave the Manhunter a wry look for a reply. He was on his feet now, a bit wobbly, but considering what he'd been through, he was happy he could keep his balance. He caught a glimpse of his scarlet-clad form in a decorative wall mirror across the room and was relieved to visually confirm he was still in one piece.

"What time is it, anyway?"

The Manhunter glanced at his illuminated watch. "Twelve twenty-seven. You should sit down."

"Nuts. I must have been out almost half an hour . . ."

"Probably. I've been here with you about twenty-five minutes."

"Jeez, J'onn. That was decent." More than the time spent by the Manhunter, Wally was impressed that the alien hadn't chosen to cart his unconscious body from the battlefield. The Martian had assisted, but kept his interference in Wally's affair to a minimum.

Half an hour, though. That was a long time.

Now Wally could hear the Berkittsville Police cruisers pulling up to the house. He glanced around the
room. There was nothing he could detect to indicate
that there had been a terrible battle fought here in the
wake of the murder. Only the murder and the ruined
front door.

Wally made a decision with which he was not entirely comfortable. "J'onn, I'm not staying for the police. There's nothing I can tell these guys that's going
to make any sense to them and, to be honest, the circumstances and my presence here do not add up to
good news for me. I'm pulling out and telling my
story directly to my contacts in Keystone. They're already on the case."

"But won't that open a can of political worms?"

"You don't know the half of it. But this thing is
growing bigger and bigger, I'm afraid. They'd all better learn to cooperate on this one."

"You sure you're going to be all right?" The Manhunter eyed Wally doubtfully.

"Once again—thanks for saving my ass. Now go
and mind your own business."

"Smile when you say that, partner," the Martian
deadpanned.

A thought suddenly occurred to Wally. "Hey—why
were you trying to contact me in the first place? If
there was a League emergency, you wouldn't be
here . . ."

"No emergency, just information. Thought you'd
want to know that our observatory network had just
picked up another mass anomaly outside Pluto's

orbit. Well outside. No threat to any of the inner planets this time, but very similar in nature to our phenomenon last evening. Oh, and that fragment I recovered from the fireballs—it's gone. Evaporated."

Then he turned and walked to the house entrance, greeting the incoming officers who would never know that it wasn't one of their own who announced that he'd already surveyed the grim scene, although in none of their reports could they ever quite remember which officer that was. The Manhunter's deception would delay the Berkittsville night patrol's entrance just long enough for the Flash to gather himself and disappear.

"Really, Wally, you do look like hell."

"For crying out loud, if I hear one more person tell me that . . ." Wally had just finished giving Morillo and Chyre a detailed twenty-minute summation of the previous few hours, from his phone contact with Kevin Schull to his explosive entry into the Schull residence to his discovery of the body to his battle with the presence. Wally did not include the Manhunter's appearance at the scene in his report.

"I just can't recall ever seeing a super hero looking this messed up before. Maybe when you guys roll out of bed, but in public?" Chyre stared at Wally with unabashed fascination. *He's pushing it*, groused Wally to himself. No—more probably the lack of sleep was making the big cop stupid. If it was at all possible, all of their eyes were even redder and baggier than they had been four hours earlier.

Morillo and Chyre sat across a speckled Formica table from the booth seat into which Wally slumped. Wally's cowl was flung back and he and the two detectives gulped black coffee.

After slinking out of the Schull residence unnoticed, Wally limped back to the apartment in a spectacularly slow two minutes plus, and every step of the way hurt. Home was just a pit stop again; he only stayed long enough to leave a message on Morillo's cell arranging a meeting, slam down a handful of ibuprofen, and let Linda know he was okay but would have to go back out. She wasn't happy; she could tell, even in the dark, that he was hurt, but he assured her he wouldn't be mixing it up again tonight. The truth was, he wasn't in any shape for another battle.

The rendezvous point was a greasy spoon at the south edge of downtown named the Blue Moon Diner. It was one of the few establishments this side of the interstate that still stayed open twenty-four hours. Wally had to wonder why. There seldom was anyone but him and his police contacts in the joint, which made it an excellent unofficial spot to exchange information. This 2:00 A.M., he and Morillo and Chyre sat alone in the red vinyl booths, a waitress behind the bar and an unseen fry cook the only witnesses, and disinterested ones at that.

"We all look like hell." Morillo sounded as impatient as Wally felt, his mind locked into low-level acceleration mode for hours now. Wally could tell the detective had something to say, was trying to figure how much to spill to the crimefighter who was, technically, not police personnel.

"Cripes, Morillo, just tell him. You don't think he hasn't figured it out already?" Wally was surprised Chyre was giving him that much credit.

"Yeah, c'mon, Morillo. I gave up everything I know to you two. I didn't have to; you never would have known I was involved."

Morillo fixed Wally with his dead-tired eyes. "Don't kid yourself, fancy feet. You called Schull from your apartment. You don't think we wouldn't have traced the last call the poor son of a bitch got? Don't you think Berkittsville is doing that right now?"

Wally had to admit they would have had him regardless. "I only left because there's no time to deal with cops I don't know jacking me up. Now, tell me—there were more murders, weren't there?"

"*Tell* him, Morillo," Chyre growled.

Morillo relented. "Yeah. Many more. And all executed in the same manner."

Chyre butted in. "After you split the Hurst apartment, three more headless wonders were reported, all apparently whacked during that initial six-fifteen cluster. All were in Central City—the goddamn CCPD were sitting on their situation tighter than we were, but now both departments are reciprocating. That's ten simultaneous six-fifteen deaths that we know of."

Chyre glanced at Morillo, who picked up the thread. "Then at about midnight, we get hit with a *second* round. Eight reported so far. All the same. Only two in Keystone this time, three in Central, and three in outlying boroughs, including your Kevin Schull."

"I was afraid there'd be more. In multiples."

"It's turned into a goddamn bloodbath out there. Nine in Keystone, eighteen total."

"So far," chimed in Chyre.

"Yeah. So far."

"So, Wally, this thing you encountered, this is it, right?

"I'm sure of it. I've no doubt it was about to pop my head, just like the others."

"So why didn't it?"

"Like I already told you, I got a telepathic call from the Martian Manhunter. A Justice League communiqué. Somehow, the thing picked up on it—I could tell. Then it bolted. That's all I got."

"So, according to you, we've got a . . . a *ghost monster* in the city popping heads at the speed of light. That . . . that is a hard sell, my friend."

"That's what I got."

"Is it metahuman?"

"I don't think so. I'm not sure. I don't know."

"Okay. So whatever this is, is going to continue. It's going to murder at will. We don't know why, we don't know when, we don't know how. It's just going to off unrelated people in bunches for no good reason."

"Well, I told you I called Schull because I thought he might be related to *me*. And it's looking like I was on to something, given that the thing *did* whack him."

Chyre looked unimpressed, but a gleam of comprehension suddenly lit Morillo's eye.

Wally nodded at him. "Just get the DNA run on as many of the victims as you can, as fast as you can."

Wally trotted home after that, since there was nothing else to be done. If the thing chose to strike again, there was little he or anyone else could do to prevent it. All they could do was wait and hope that more information would be forthcoming. Wally would hate every bit of the waiting, too. Much as he had always feared, he had not measured up. Fast as he was, he had not been fast enough. For the life of him, he couldn't stand waiting.

Before he and Morillo and Chyre had ended their meeting, all had agreed that the best they could do at that point was get some sleep and let the graveyard shift cops do their jobs as best they could. Morillo had warned Wally of what he could expect, given his phone call to Kevin Schull. It was an unnecessary heads-up, but Wally was impressed by the detective's concern.

"Of course, this looks bad for you. Some folks are going to want an arrest real quick. The time element points to a speedster. There's going to be pressure to put you on the hot seat."

Which was exactly why he had needed to avoid the Berkittsville Police. They didn't know him like Morillo and Chyre knew him.

The questions would come soon enough, regardless. Morillo had told him that a decision had been made, immediately after the second cluster, to go public. Keystone and Central Police public relations would hold a joint news conference for the press, already in a frenzy, at six that morning. The media would be screaming bloody murder in a few hours, and then, with no progress in solving much less explaining the ghastly crimes, city efforts would have to turn to panic control.

Chyre had added that there was a rumor from the mayor's office that a state of emergency might be called, that the National Guard might be brought in.

They all felt defeated and unnerved, waiting for the hammer to come down again, and they weren't worth anything to anybody in their current states of exhaustion. Sleep or the attempt to sleep was the only good option.

Wally flopped into bed at close to 3:00 A.M. The wracking pain he had accrued in his battle had receded to nagging aches, but the extraordinary velocity efforts he had performed that day had left him bone weary. Linda barely stirred. She'd wake up soon enough to the horrific news on the radio.

Wally fell asleep immediately and chaotic images of nebulous sucking pits of darkness blurring into insect-plated figures blurring into Aunt Iris swirled across his inner eye.

The phone was ringing.

He cracked open a gummy eye and saw that it was suddenly eight-thirty.

The light was low and gloomy in the bedroom and there was a patter on the window. Rain today.

The phone continued to ring and he heard Linda

pick up. Beyond her voice he heard a news broadcast. He knew what she was listening to.

She came into the room carrying the phone, trying to look calm, but unable to hide the fact that she had been shell-shocked.

Like the entire city, thought Wally.

She handed the phone to Wally, looking at him with eyes that said she could not begin to comprehend the horror in which she knew he surely must be involved. He wanted to hold her.

"It's Morillo."

Didn't the man sleep?

He took the phone reluctantly, fearing what he might hear.

"Don't you ever sleep, Jared?"

"Wally, S.T.A.R. Labs pushed through the first batch of DNA analyses."

"*Already?*"

"They're in emergency mode. They can move when we ask them to."

"And . . . ?"

"You guessed right, Wally. All the victims tested positive for the metagene. All were potential super heroes."

CHAPTER 4

Metagenics

Before he met Linda, the only two people with whom Wally had ever felt comfortable were Barry Allen and Iris West Allen. Not coincidentally, those two were also the biggest influences on the young man's life. Barry, of course, was the Flash, Wally's boyhood hero and later his mentor and partner. He molded Wally's sense of identity and gave purpose to his life.

But Iris meant something more primal to Wally. Iris had saved his life.

It's said that children often resemble their grandparents more than their parents. Wally, uniquely, took after his father's sister. For as long as he could remember, he and Iris had been soul mates. Born to two joyless people plagued by depression and personal demons too dark to shake, Wally came alive only when Iris visited his world. She had been well aware of the troubled nature of her brother's household and had shown a special interest in her nephew. Wally's parents were not bad people. They did not abuse him. They saw to his physical needs and his schooling, but they had no business being parents. They were desperately unhappy people too crippled by their own emotional turmoil to ever properly nurture their precocious only son. No doubt Wally would have slipped down the same drain they were circling had it not been for his aunt's instincts and intelligence.

Iris took to Wally, however, out of something more than familial concern. There was a tie between the two, an intangible shared quality that drew them together as co-conspirators within a larger family from which they stood apart. Their personalities, their enthusiasm for life, their senses of humor and attraction to adventure, were one and the same and not shared by the greater West family. They were born best friends, despite the age difference, and that was all there was to it as far as they were concerned.

Iris and Wally spent time together whenever possible. She introduced him to museums and comic books and baseball games and the Beatles and Mexican food. She shared her enthusiasm for things both great and small; the vault of the night sky and the armored labors of the insect world engaged her equally—the whole ball of wax, she would say—and that interest ricocheted on to Wally. He was the child she never had and she was the mother he needed. They filled a void in each other that the rest of their family could never supply.

Of course, the young Wally had never thought of

his and Iris's mutual attraction in terms that specific.
A child has no frame of reference outside his family.
All Wally knew was that Iris was the greatest, coolest
person in the world, the sunshine in an otherwise
gray existence.

But Wally lived in Blue Valley and Iris was all the
way down in Central City, ever since she got her
dream job reporting for the big-city paper. She could
not possibly visit often enough to suit Wally.

Then, in the summer of Wally's tenth year, she
threw out a proposition to his parents. She thought it
would be a good experience for Wally to come stay
with her in Central City over his summer vacation.
The time spent there would broaden his perspective a
bit, introduce him to new worlds. Wally's parents really didn't need convincing and for once the family
was in accord; they could not wait for Wally to get out
of the house, and Iris would be the perfect guardian.

That was the summer that changed Wally's life.
That was the experience that lifted him up and gave
him direction and saved him from slipping into another directionless pattern of despair. Not only was
Iris the best aunt in the world, not only did she open
his eyes to a way of living that didn't begin each
morning with dread but, unbelievably, *she knew the
Flash*. The *Flash* . . . Wally's favorite super hero since
he couldn't remember when, the fastest, slickest man
alive, was on speaking terms with his very own *aunt*!
Nothing could be cooler.

Except *meeting* the Flash. Dear Aunt Iris had
arranged that, too, and the unimaginable joy of hav-

ing the Scarlet Speedster show a particular interest in
him more than offset the hours of tedium spent in the
company of Iris's fiancé, the unsurpassingly boring
and chronically late Barry Allen. Barry was actually
pleasant enough, in his own sedate, academic way. He
worked in the Central City Police Department laboratories—but didn't even carry a gun, for pity's sake—
and on occasion helped the Flash in his crimefighting
endeavors.

Iris met the Flash through Barry; that was reason
enough for Wally to stay civil to the boyfriend, fighting to stay awake through interminable dinners
where Barry jawed on endlessly about obscure police
procedure and Iris remained inexplicably fascinated.
Why, thought Wally, *why oh why does she spend so much
time with this nerd when she could be with the Flash?*

Long after that, well after the Flash had taken him
on as an apprentice and begun to shape him into an
eager crimefighting weapon, well after Iris had become Mrs. Barry Allen, Wally learned that Barry and
the Flash were one and the same. In retrospect, that
disappointingly explained the Flash's initial interest
in him, but Wally's mind still grew dizzy when he
considered the myriad coincidences that brought
them all to the relationship they shared for years—
greatest of all being the freak laboratory accident.

One stormy day that summer, while in the company of the Flash at Barry Allen's private lab, Wally
had stumbled against a shelf containing huge beakers
of various electrolytes and enzyme solutions. The
beakers had smashed as the shelf toppled, soaking the

embarrassed Wally in their contents. Immediately, as if preordained, as if part of some strange conspiracy between the chemical elements and electricity, a bolt of lightning had flared out of the rumbling skies above and struck the building square. The fire from the heavens seemed to concentrate almost knowingly on Wally; it was like he had suddenly become the world's most attractive lightning rod.

Then it was gone and Wally sat in the center of the charred laboratory, stunned, smoking slightly, emitting an eerie yellow glow that lasted for hours. He was otherwise unharmed, something anxiously confirmed by the Flash and a battery of medical tests.

But the bolt of Wally-seeking lightning was not the most amazing thing. The far greater coincidence was the fact that the very same set of circumstances had happened to Barry Allen years earlier. That weirdly identical incident had proven the catalyst to unleashing Barry's latent superspeed, and now Barry looked at Wally with a suspicion he was afraid to voice. Coincidence is one thing, Wally would later think, but this showed the hand of something bigger. Something with a plan.

Soon enough, Barry's suspicion was confirmed, as Wally began exhibiting the early indications of superspeed. From that time on, Wally's future was set and the balance of influence in his life shifted.

Iris had been the tutor who had shown her pupil what the world had to offer. The Flash was the master, under whom the student apprenticed toward his place in life.

Through the remainder of that summer, Wally had spent every moment free from Iris's direct attention developing his nascent powers under the critical, watchful eye of the encouraging Flash. Then, far too soon, the summer was over and Wally was returned reluctantly to Blue Valley and endless gray desolation. He had promised the Flash he'd keep his powers under wraps, and he did try hard to please his hero, although his record wasn't perfect. That autumn, winter, and spring were hell for Wally.

The following summer, which could not come soon enough, brought another offer from Iris. Apparently, she was very pleased by the paternal interest Barry was showing in the kid—her boyfriend had done nothing but encourage her to bring her nephew back to their sphere of influence as soon as possible.

So the pattern was set for the next six years, during which time Iris and Barry married and Iris became privy to their secret metalives. Then, when he was seventeen, Wally moved for good to the Sister Cities and the Allens became his family full-time.

And, as Kid Flash, crimefighting became his life full-time, and the only occupation he'd ever hold.

Up until he had met the Flash, Iris had been the undisputed center of Wally's universe. After his life-transforming chemical electroshock, the Flash/Barry Allen became his focus.

Not that Iris exactly lost her importance. Her place in the order of things just became less obvious. Like the Sun, she was still the center, the heart of the matter; but like the Sun, she was more often taken for granted.

Despite Barry's best efforts, Wally would develop the crippling impatience—with both himself and others—that was the personality hallmark of so many speedsters. Barry had hoped that careful training in deep meditative techniques would allow his young charge to control the lag that kept his mind accelerated long after his body had come down, and to avoid the attendant difficulties of communicating with normal-time minds.

Unnoticed by either of them, however, was Iris's subtle influence on Wally regarding his impatience. Unlike her husband and nephew, who almost instinctively relied on movement as the solution to all problems great and small, Iris was still and unhurried. Despite the flurry of meta-activity that surrounded her world and was the distinguishing characteristic of the men in her life, Iris kept deeply, mysteriously immune to the seductive nature of speed. But she always *knew*.

She was always there for either or both of them. She was grace under pressure and the perfectly calm, collected heart of a hurricane. And somehow her example mitigated Wally's impatience, or at least allowed him to understand that there was another way.

The three of them had years of adventure together before Barry had passed on and Wally had graduated from novice to adept, from Kid Flash to the Flash.

Eventually, Iris's broken heart healed and she got on with her life and Wally found his own Iris. Linda and he began their life together, and Iris and Wally gradually and subtlely began to drift apart. There was no break, they continued to live within ten miles of each other, but the previous closeness, the need to be a part of each other's daily routine, was no longer there.

Or so Wally had thought.

Iris was still on Wally's mind when he reached the Science and Technologies Advanced Research Laboratories. She had called back, just as Wally knew she would, that morning while he was still dead to the world. He hadn't heard that ring; Linda must have picked up quickly. Later, as soon as he had finished talking with Morillo, Linda had filled him in on Iris and her conversation: how they had exchanged impressions of the breaking story that was all over the news. How, as two old news hounds, they shared their studied opinions on the media coverage. How both knew that Wally was in for some kind of hell and how both felt that veteran, modulated fear they always felt whenever their boy headed into the unknown.

Then, Linda told him, they had promised to get together soon. As soon as this thing was over.

Maybe before, thought Wally.

S.T.A.R. Labs' Keystone City facility was a gleaming cluster of glass-and-steel cubes and hemispheres next to the old Karsh Mills district. Built in the early eighties, it seemed to glow with a silvery architectural optimism in keeping with that era of economic boom. Surrounded and contrasted by grimy, rusted mills, with their dusty patina of age and wear, the Labs stood particularly removed from the soul of a city built on the back of the first Industrial Revolution. The hi-tech economy that the Labs beckoned may have transformed cities like its corporate home, Metropolis, but it would be a long time before that trend took root here in the Rust Belt.

S.T.A.R. Labs was known by the general public for its development of advanced technologies, supplying everything from military satellites to hydrogen automobile engines to improved in-vitro fertilization processes. Less well known, and less obviously lucrative, was the Labs' dedication to research into the nature and practical understanding of the metacondition. They were vanguards in the development of a relatively new science. They were the go-to institution when a metahuman developed a disease associated with his genetic makeup, or a metavillain proved too intractable to be dealt with by conventional methods.

Morillo, on the phone that morning, had asked Wally to meet him and Chyre at 9:30 at the Labs, in the offices of a Dr. Pradash. Wally had an hour to kill till then, and the way his mind was racing he knew it would seem an eternity. He felt—maybe—incrementally better than he had before he'd hit the sack. However, he still ached, although now it was more of a stiffness, which was disturbing—Wally was not used to a reluctance on his body's part to move. His head didn't hurt now so much as it felt foggy, slightly disoriented. The rainy gloom didn't help, either.

A shower and shave—Barry had drilled into him the firm belief that nothing looked more seedy than a super hero with stubble—took no time at all. Neither did breakfast, although he was ravenous now and packed away plenty of carbs. He tried to sit quietly and talk with Linda before she left for the university, but couldn't settle his mind enough to be much company. His thoughts tumbled out faster and faster until his words were indecipherable. He kept catching these unintentional accelerations, but found it impossible to prevent them from recurring. Linda was patient at first—as she always was when he was cranking like this, like the world's most accomplished speedfreak. Eventually, however, her eyes glazed over, and Wally noticed. Embarrassed, he stopped cold, realizing that what he'd meant to sound reassuring was more likely frenzied. He had probably verbalized nothing she could understand, but his distressed state of mind was communicating plenty, he was sure.

Everything suddenly seemed hopeless. *Why does she put up with this crap? Why can't I just talk to her? Why can't she keep up with me?*

Wally apologized and Linda told him it was all right. She asked him repeatedly to be careful today, kissed him, and left for school. After she was gone, Wally sat motionless for a full minute.

He spent the remainder of the time before his meeting jogging through the city. This cost him no significant energy and limbered his stiff joints. He had set a pace that would allow him to cover every highway, avenue, alley, mall, and pedestrian pathway in an efficient pattern that would bring him around to the Labs by 9:28, with a conservative amount of time factored in for interventions. The crime business, however, was all but closed down this morning. The news of serial decapitations had thrown the illegitimate, as well as the legitimate, back on their heels. So Wally kept moving and watching, dodging raindrops and skimming puddles, trying to clear the unmoving bank of fog over his brain and thinking about Iris and the murderous presence and even back to the weird phenomena from space, until 9:28 rolled around.

Wally walked through the S.T.A.R. Labs public entrance. If he'd chosen, he could have cased the entire complex in the blink of an eye, locating Dr. Pradash's office before any sensor alarms sounded, before any cameras recorded his presence. But that would not have been polite. Wally had a good sense of what normals needed in order to feel comfortable around him and went out of his way to establish trust. Just because he could find his way through the Labs and into Pradash's office long before the receptionist could direct him was not reason enough to flaunt his gift. Just because he could was never an excuse. Barry and Iris had both hammered that deep into his moral fiber. Not everything required or benefited from speed, no matter what his accelerated thoughts might tell him.

The receptionists and security staff stared in ill-concealed surprise. Even though the Labs dealt regularly with metahumans, few came in through the front door. Wally stated his business at the reception desk and received clearance and a visitor's badge from security.

After passing through a battery of detection devices—"Not that they really apply in your case," a security officer remarked without smiling—he was escorted through a labyrinth of corridors and atriums by three armed guards.

If you must, thought Wally.

After passing through two more security check points, and as many ID-only lockdowns, they arrived in an area designated simply GENETICS, META. His escorts motioned Wally into a side room and departed.

Morillo and Chyre were already in the simple, utilitarian room. A conference table filled most of the floor space, around which were crowded a dozen plastic chairs. The two detectives were seated with coffee mugs in hand, still wearing their raincoats, poring over sheaves of printed matter spread across the table. They glanced up casually as Wally entered.

"See you came the conventional route," Chyre noted.

"I'm a player. This isn't an office. I thought we were meeting a Dr. Pradash . . ." Wally sniffed the sharp, antiseptic air. This facility, for all the good things it had brought to Keystone City, reminded him of death and always made him a little anxious.

"No. It isn't an office. We were told at security we'd be meeting Dr. Pradash here instead." Morillo's expression was bland, but Wally could tell he was unhappy.

"And that's significant?"

"Any time a meeting with a professional type gets switched out of his office at the last minute, it usually means somebody's changing their mind about something," Chyre broke in, speaking with the conviction of the experienced.

"Somebody's hesitating . . ." Morillo cut himself short as he heard shoes clicking down the hall.

Two men turned into the room. The lead was tall with a neatly trimmed beard and darting eyes. He wore an expensive, carefully tailored suit. *Hong Kong*, Wally guessed. Following the suit was a slight, dark-haired young man in a white lab smock and thick, horn-rimmed glasses.

Smock had an open, unseasoned look to him, while Suit's expression was closed and polished. Regardless, Wally thought they both looked nervous. *What did they have to be nervous about?*

Suit spoke. "Detectives Chyre and Morillo, Flash, I'm Samuel Metz, head of bio research and development."

He gestured to Smock. "This is Dr. Luk Pradash. He supervised the analyses of your DNA samples." Pradash bobbed his head and waved a tentative hello.

"I see you have the results. What else do you need to know?" Metz's tone was clipped and aggressive. He was obviously used to controlling situations.

This was not the reception that Morillo and Chyre had hoped for. They remained seated, fixing Metz with noncommittal stares for a couple of seconds before Morillo responded.

"I'm confused. Your attitude—I'm getting the impression you consider our presence here a nuisance, Mr. Metz?" The detective's tone was mild, but direct.

"Not at all, of course not. I just don't know how much we can add to the report. Dr. Pradash is at the end of a long shift—I'm sure he's tired and wants to go home. And it's *Doctor* Metz."

"I apologize, Dr. Metz." Morillo did not sound like he was sorry. "You know, we have an extraordinary situation in progress. We're trying to get a handle on it and we think S.T.A.R. Labs can help our understanding. We won't take any longer than necessary, I promise you."

"Actually, *Dr.* Metz," Chyre interjected, "It was Dr. *Pradash* who we set this meeting with. Why don't we move things along and include him in the conversation. Hmm?

Metz shrugged. "Of course, but I'll be staying right by him. It's S.T.A.R. Labs' policy that a department director monitors all interviews for inappropriate—"

Chyre appeared to reach the end of his patience. "And it's police policy that we decide what's best for the interview. Jesus. Do you want us to drag you and your employee down to the station? We could do it that way."

Pradash paled, his mouth twisting into a sickly, silent groan. Metz smiled quickly and raised a placating hand.

"Please, detectives. I'm not here to cause problems. It's just my job to help guide Dr. Pradash—he's new to this country. I promise, I won't impede—I'm here to facilitate." Metz was looking to Morillo, who at that moment appeared to be the more amenable of the two cops.

"That'll be fine, Dr. Metz." Morillo nodded agreeably to the deflated executive. Wally admiringly watched the interplay of the two detectives. For as poorly as they meshed personally, they were a great working team. They had knocked a potentially obstructive public relations flack into acquiescence with very little effort.

Wally was suddenly aware that Pradash was staring at him. He caught the doctor in his open expression of wonder and smiled at him. Pradash may or may not be acting hinky for good reason, Wally decided, but he didn't look like trouble.

"How you doing, Doc? I'm the Flash—please feel free to call me Wally if you like." He figured there wasn't any harm in putting the guy at ease.

"I've never been this close to a super hero before. I'm sorry—I don't mean to stare." But the scientist's expression didn't change, and Wally got the queasy feeling that his starstruck fascination was tempered by a morbid, if professional, curiosity.

He'd like a real live metahuman to work on, I can just tell. He'd like to cut me open to find out what makes me tick—but I bet he'd do it with the utmost respect.

Wally liked the guy in spite of his reaction. "Hang out here in Keystone long enough and you'll get over *that* attitude."

Morillo seemed to approve of the direction in which Wally had taken things. He motioned for Pradash to sit down. "The Flash is involved with this investigation—he'll be asking questions, too. Please respond to him as openly as you would Detective Chyre or myself."

Pradash slid into a chair across the table from the detectives, but kept stealing glances in Wally's direction. Metz sat stiffly beside the scientist, marginalized and obviously uncomfortable.

Wally alone remained standing, arms folded across his chest. No one asked if he wanted a chair. His stance seemed appropriate for the situation; the Flash represented something apart and above.

As was the partners' usual tactic, Morillo took the lead. "Dr. Pradash, first thing we need to ascertain—and forgive me if I'm asking idiot questions—is there any chance of error in the test results?"

Pradash became much more focused, much more relaxed, now that the conversation had turned into his backyard. "Absolutely no, sir. The truth is, we tested and retested all eight samples. Because the initial results were so surprising, that is. We have never tested such a batch of multiple samples, all of which were positive."

"So all eight samples were from different persons, and all eight tested positive for the metagene."

"That is correct. It is amazing."

Morillo glanced over at Chyre and then to Wally.

"Now, Dr. Pradash—and again, I apologize if these questions are very basic, but we need some background here—how common is the metagene in the human race?"

Pradash adjusted his glasses and furrowed his brow. *He's on his home turf now*, thought Wally. *He's getting comfortable. Here comes the lecture.*

"The metagene—ah—the existence of the metagene

was discovered relatively recently, you know. We do not yet have a wealth of statistical data. We have only been able to map a small portion of the human race. A very narrow demographic. So far, we have only had the opportunity to study broad samples from populations in North America, western Europe, and a bit of the Pacific Rim. But the incidences we have seen of the metagene in those select populations indicate wide variations in the percentage within geographically specific populations. So, you see, Detective Morillo, there is no simple answer."

Chyre drummed his fingers against the table while Morillo stroked his chin thoughtfully before pressing on. "So, okay, I take your meaning. Is there any way you could, um, *extrapolate* what the percentage of people carrying the metagene in our *immediate* geography might be?"

Pradash's eyes lit up. Morillo had struck his particular passion. "Well, the Sister Cities are part of a larger area of study that encompasses much of the central United States. This Midwest region is my field of expertise. I have been compiling statistics based on population studies done here since graduate school."

"Then I guess we're talking to the right man." Morillo smiled encouragingly.

Pradash continued. "To answer your question then, based on the partial evidence we have so far accumulated, my guess is that the metagene appears in no more than point-fifteen percent of the population of this region."

"Wow. That seems to me to be a pretty small percentage. What's that translate to? Something like one in every thousand?"

"One in every six hundred and sixty-six."

Chyre grimaced and shifted noisily. "Naw, that doesn't add up—there aren't even near that many metahumans floating around."

You'd be surprised, thought Wally. But Chyre's observation was essentially true, and he knew enough on this subject to weigh in. "That's because not every metagene carrier actually manifests. Not every carrier develops metapowers."

Pradash bobbed his head enthusiastically. "That is it, precisely. Genes are units of DNA that transmit our hereditary characteristics. They determine what we look like, how we sound, how we smell, as well as many health factors. Maybe even personality itself. But not every gene we carry develops into a characteristic. Some are what we call recessive—essentially they lie dormant. Detective Chyre, you, for instance, may carry the gene in you for brown eyes, and that may someday be passed to your children. In you, however, this trait is recessive, dominated by your gene for blue eyes. Therefore you have blue eyes."

Pradash became more animated, warming to his audiences' visible interest. "The metagene, in most carriers, is recessive. The recessive metagene does not have the potential to develop and manifest as a superpower. Perhaps you, Detective Morillo, carry the metagene. While it may remain recessive within you, someday a descendent of yours may inherit your metagene, and in her it will manifest as a great power."

Morillo looked uneasy with that notion.

The scientist continued. "Actually, let me be clear about this . . ."

Wally began shifting his weight. *Well, Morillo wanted background information.*

"Many of us studying the metagene believe it may be what we are calling *latent*. Meaning that we believe the metagene does not begin to manifest—metapowers do not develop—without the presence of a catalyst, or a catalytic incident."

Pradash nodded toward Wally, again fixing him with that overeager stare. "Flash, if I understand your history correctly, you are an excellent example. Your childhood was normal. You showed no manifestations of your superspeed until an accident involving a combination of chemicals and atmospheric electricity apparently activated your previously latent gene. Of course, without scientific testing, this all remains speculative. But, such an amazing coincidence . . ."

Morillo tried to get the interview back on track. "So only a fraction of those carrying the metagene will actually develop superpowers, like our speedy friend here. Do you have a percentage for that?"

Pradash spread his hands resignedly. "That is impossible to say. As you in your profession well know, metahumans tend to be extremely secretive. We here at the bio labs seldom see a power-positive metahuman unless he or she is experiencing health problems. I cannot even begin to guess at the percentage who manifest. The Flash here is a rare exception. His public openness regarding his identity and his history have given us one of our very few glimpses into the development of metapowers."

Pradash's enthusiasm got the better of him. "Mr. West, I would very much like the opportunity to run a few tests on you," he said, the words spilling out.

Wally suppressed a frown as Chyre jumped in. "Maybe someday, but not just now. Let's keep focused and get you off your shift, Doc."

Wally's curiosity, however, had been engaged. "Dr. Pradash, when you look at a DNA sample and see metagenes, can you tell from those particular metagenes what that individual's powers might be? I mean, is the metagene just kind of generic, or does it specify the power?"

"That is a very good question, and the answer is *maybe*. I wish I knew the answer but, as I say, we have only begun to scratch the surface."

Morillo looked at the Flash curiously. "What are you thinking, Wally?"

"I'm wondering if there might not be a metagene specifically for superspeed." Wally had noticed in the past that the area of the country around Keystone City and Central City seemed to produce more than its share of speedsters.

The atmosphere in the room changed with Wally's last words. Pradash shriveled and glanced nervously at Metz, as if unsure of himself. Metz stared ahead with opaque eyes, then spoke in measured tones.

"Dr. Pradash was part of a team studying superspeed, actually. It's S.T.A.R. Labs' policy to not discuss findings until a study is complete, but—as this is a matter of public security—we will be happy to offer whatever information may be of help. Answer their questions, Dr. Pradash." Metz spoke almost mechanically and all but audibly sighed at the conclusion.

Morillo's and Chyre's eyes gleamed hawkishly at the signs of distress. Wally, too, could easily see that there was something the two scientists were gingerly dancing around. Something in what Wally had said had struck too close to a nerve.

With a quick duck of his head, Chyre urged Wally to continue. It was obvious to the cops that Pradash wanted to please the metahuman.

Wally cleared his throat and chose his words carefully. "Let's just speak hypothetically, okay? If there is a metagene specific to superspeed, how might it be identified?"

Pradash looked confused. "I do not understand. There would of course be a specific base sequencing . . ."

"No, I'm sorry—what I mean is, how might the *carrier* be identified? Could there be a physical, an observable, trait that would tell you that I was a speedster, maybe even before I developed my speed? Something I'd share with other potential speedsters?"

Pradash slowly shook his head. "Of course not. There would be no reason . . ."

Wally suddenly had a notion and decided to go out on a limb. "What about the brain? Would there be something about the brain? Maybe some unique wave pattern an empath or a telepath might discern?"

Pradash's eyes began to shine again. "Not the brain, but the pineal body, perhaps."

"The pineal . . . ?"

"The pineal body. It is a tiny organ surrounded by the brain. It helps control our circadian rhythms—our bodies' reactions to night and day. A quite mysterious little bit of tissue, and for a long time there has been speculation that it is responsible for many other functions, as well. Based on the experiments we have conducted on carrier cadavers . . ."

There was a moist sheen forming over Metz's forehead and he cleared his throat. Pradash didn't notice.

" . . . Our team is forming a theory. The pineals we've autopsied have been absolutely loaded with metagenetic material. We—*I*—think the pineal body may in some way be responsible for activating or controlling metagene development."

Metz interrupted. "We encourage our researchers to give their imaginations free reign." He smiled with paternalistic pride, but his breathing was a little too heavy. "You should understand, Dr. Pradash is speaking very speculatively."

No one paid attention to the disclaimer. Pradash continued. "That is what some of our research indicates. Other research, elsewhere, has suggested that the pineal may serve as a sort of antenna for mind-to-mind communication. So when you ask me about the possibility that someone with telepathic talent might recognize an individual with unmanifested speed power by specific genetic factors within that individual's pineal body, I must tell you that, as a scientist, I can confirm nothing. Yet there are some intriguing possibilities. You see?"

"Um—I see." Wally thought he did.

Morillo seemed satisfied with the path the interview had taken. The Flash had touched upon something that made the S.T.A.R. Labs science boys squirm. The detectives had come here looking for nothing more than a better understanding of the DNA results, but inviting Wally along had paid unexpected dividends.

"All right, listen to me," Morillo interjected. "We're going to put our cards on the table now—all of us—because we don't have time for any more cute word games. There are people dying out there, so if there's any information you need to give us, you had damn well better give it now."

The detective paused for effect before pressing on. "We'll show our hand first. The eight DNA samples were all from victims of this murder spree that's all over the news, but I think you've guessed that already. No doubt we're going to see more coming our way, too, and I'm willing to bet here and now that every victim carries the metagene. Who or whatever is responsible is targeting metagene carriers, of that I no longer have any doubt."

He paused again. "The Flash is asking about the brain for a specific reason—all the victims experienced massive head trauma. The tops of their craniums are missing. And their brains appear to have been exploded—*out*. Every one. Every last one. *Eighteen in all*. By something that can either exist in multiple locations at once—or is moving at superspeed."

Chyre took the ball that Morillo had started rolling

and leaned his massive frame across the table. "Does this make any sense to either of you? Because we have every reason to believe there are going to be more casualties, and if there are, they could just as well be your wives or your children as anyone else. So unless you've already determined that none of your loved ones might happen to have this metagene in them, you've got a personal reason to hope and pray we can put together some insight into this monster."

Morillo closed. "So there—we've spilled. This is what we're all up against. Now, is there anything else you can think of offering that might prove relevant?"

Pradash had gone white as a sheet. Wally had noticed him inhale sharply when Morillo had connected superspeed to the crimes. The slight man seemed to shrink into himself as he turned his worried, hollow eyes to the director. Metz himself, for the first time, looked shaken.

Pradash barely whispered. "He has done it, has he not?"

Metz jerked his gaze around, level at the startled Pradash. "Leave us, Dr. Pradash."

"It is harvesting. It is following its first imperative."

"*Now,* Dr. Pradash."

Chyre began to protest. "No one goes until—"

Metz raised a silencing palm. "Let him go. It's me you need to talk with. I can help you. *Go,* Dr. Pradash."

Pradash scurried out, looking torn between horrible fascination and relief. Morillo and Chyre did nothing to stop him.

The department director, who had moments ago oozed arrogance, now slowly pulled an unsteady hand over his damp forehead and stared blankly at the table, as if resigned to some unpleasant fate he had failed to bluff his way past. Wally took this as a sign they were about to get someplace.

Morillo and Chyre sat patiently, apparently content to allow Metz the next move. The director looked up at them suddenly, focused and resolved.

"There was no reason to involve Pradash any further. There's no reason why he should be involved."

Morillo nodded agreeably. "Okay, so we won't involve him."

"What do you have for us, Dr. Metz?" Chyre prompted.

Metz stood up and motioned for his three visitors to follow. "In for a dime, in for a dollar, I guess. I need to go to my office—you might as well come with me."

Morillo and Chyre exchanged quick expressions of surprise as they followed Metz out into the hall. Wally purposely hung behind them, wanting to have proper positioning if an opportunity to go exploring arose.

Metz lead them down the corridor, in the opposite direction from which Wally had arrived. At an intersection he turned left into an alcove, at the far end of which stood a massive door of gleaming metal. META-GENICS SECURE AREA was blocked in big red letters over its upper third. The director swiped his identification card through a laser recognition lock and, after a second of bleeps and grinding noises, the door slid open smoothly, disappearing into a pocket in the wall. Metz motioned them through.

Wally carefully kept to the rear, all the way into the secure area. With all his visitors through the door, Metz bent to a small keyboard control and began punching in the command to resecure. Both Morillo's and Chyre's attention were pulled momentarily to Metz's action, and this gave Wally the opening for which he had hoped.

He accelerated. Upon entering the area, he had done a quick survey and insured that there were no other eyes to witness their arrival. With Metz, Morillo, and Chyre distracted, he had the fraction of a second he needed to gear up to a speed that rendered him invisible to mortal eyes. Of course, there was always the possibility that a hidden surveillance camera would record a visual hiccup in its taped continuity, allowing the reviewer of the tape to infer his move, but that was a risk he would have to take.

Wally figured he had a quarter of a second to act. Any more time, and his absence could conceivably register with Metz and the detectives and he did not want anyone to know of this action that was inspired purely by a hunch. Metz had given him an incredible opportunity—access to the heavily secured metagenics research area. Wally could never have cleanly accessed this on his own—and he had seen enough in the behavior of Pradash and Metz to overcome any misgivings about the ethics of taking full advantage.

While Morillo, Chyre, and Metz stood like statues, Wally skittered through the secure area, absorbing as much visual information as possible. His first impression was of the construction material used throughout the facility; every wall, ceiling, and fixture was fashioned of the same shining, silvery metal as the entrance door. Perhaps for hygienic reasons, perhaps for temperature control, Wally speculated. The high-ceiling corridor onto which the entrance had opened was lined with a series of laboratories off its left wall and offices and a record storage room off the right. Wally nosed his way through each and every room, like a mouse carefully and thoroughly inspecting new quarters for any evidence of food. Except that Wally didn't know what he was looking for, exactly.

He went down the line of labs first. The initial lab was crammed mostly with computers and peripherals—equipment for analysis and statistical compilation. Several white-smocked men and women sat seemingly frozen, hunched over their consoles, oblivious to their fleeting observer. Wally glanced quickly over every active monitor, which to his accelerated perception glowed and pulsed with startling clarity. Nothing he scanned jumped out at him; all was an indecipherable jumble of numbers and decimals and obscure abbreviation.

The three labs following offered no more insight. These were what Wally considered more appropriately *real* laboratories—meaning that they contained rows of test tubes and beakers, as well as centrifuges, incubators, spectrometers, and miles and miles of plastic tubing. And a wealth of other bizarre apparatuses for which Wally had no names. Gangs of technicians and specialists stood suspended in each room. There were plenty of scribbled notes and neatly printed labels, but nothing that meant a thing to Wally.

At the end of the corridor there was a set of double doors, painted with big diagonal yellow stripes spaced evenly over the shiny metal. Small, square windows set with thick panes of glass broke the surface of either door. Wally peered through one of the slightly misted windows into a small room furnished with steel benches and hooks on the walls. On some of the hooks were hung what looked to be heavy, insulated containment suits, like those used by chemical firefighters or hazardous waste clean-up crews. On the opposite side of the room another door was opening. A figure outfitted in one of the containment suits, on the far side of the door, was frozen in the motion of pulling it open by its massive handles. Wally craned his neck to see around the figure, into the space beyond. He couldn't see much through the narrow opening blocked by the bulky figure, and whatever was in there was lit only dimly by a low, greenish glow. A cloud of frozen vapor further obscured the interior; this space was kept refrigerated. But beyond the opaque steam, Wally could detect vague hints of a tall structure with a crown of thick conduits octopusing out into the dark. The image of an old-fashioned coal furnace sprang to his mind, perversely enough.

Wally eyed the simple lock mechanism on the doors before him, but quickly decided against an attempt to enter the airlock. It might be very worth-while exploring this mystery further, but there were just too many unknowns, all things considered. *Play it smart, Wally—stick to the game plan.*

He moved down the line of offices next: All were remarkably similar, except for the few personal details each occupant had allowed him or herself. There was no time to pour over all the stacks of printouts and reports covering the desks and shelves—all he could do was skim, and nothing made an impression.

The final room was the record storage facility, which, like the first room, was jammed with computers and monitors. The back wall, however, was lined with a room-length table divided into workstations. Above each station was a wall cabinet. At one of the stations sat a tech, leaning over a pile of small vials sealed in clear vacuum bags, jotting onto a small notepad. Above her motionless head, the cabinet was open, and neatly filed within were rows and rows of other similar vials in their bags. Wally bent close and read a large label on the vacuum bag in the line of the tech's vision. Over a jumble of numbers and enigmatic technical terms was printed a name: *North, Roberta Jean.* Wally glanced at the tech's notepad. Sure enough, she was in the process of copying the information from Roberta Jean North's label.

Wally moved to the next workstation. There was another pad sitting on that table surface. Like the one being updated now by the tech, this notepad was also filled with a list of names and data. Wally quickly scanned the unfamiliar names listed.

He moved to the pad placed at the next work space, and had leafed about a third of the way through it when a name popped out at him.

Rudolph, Carson Polk.

That seemed vaguely familiar, and his thoughts were once again flung back to Iris's lecture on the extended family. If only he'd paid more attention at the time.

Wally continued and the listings ended about halfway through the pad.

He flipped one more page, just for the sake of being thorough. Unexpectedly, he found one last entry scrawled across that bit of lined paper. His blood froze as he read the single word.

Allen. Written in large, emphatic letters, underlined, and followed by an exclamation point—*Allen.*

Nothing else. Just *Allen.*

Wally shook his head in an effort to dispel the shock. *Don't lose focus here!*

He had hoped to find something of value on his little fact-gathering expedition, but this was somehow more than he'd expected. It told him nothing specific, but it implied so much.

Allen. Somehow they'd obtained a DNA sample of his predecessor.

Barry, for crying out loud.

Wally ratcheted up his speed a bit and did a search through the labeled vials in the cabinet above. Sure enough, *Rudolph, Carson Polk* was tucked away inside, along with vials for all the other corresponding names. All except Allen—there was no vial for Allen.

The things these bastards could do with the Flash's genes.

Wally looked carefully at the Rudolph vial. Inside was a tiny amount of clear liquid. That was all. He stood indecisive for a relative moment and then placed the vial back in its slot in the cabinet. His self-allotted window of opportunity was about to close.

Hurrying back to Morillo and Chyre and Metz at the entrance, Wally did his practiced best to simulate the pose he had stood in when he had accelerated, and geared down. *Maybe a shade over a quarter*, he reviewed, *but that shouldn't be a problem.*

As Wally decelerated, the detectives and Metz appeared to swing back to life. Metz finished punching in the secure door code. Chyre turned to say something to Wally, but stopped himself with his mouth half-opened. His bland expression had turned to surprise.

"Jesus, Wally, did your dog just die? Where'd the sour puss come from?"

Wally was embarrassed to find he'd done so poorly to hide his reaction to his discovery. Now Morillo and Metz were looking at him, too. He smirked, trying to cover. "Maybe I just figured my dog's got metagenes. So I'm a concerned pet owner—what about it?"

Chyre shrugged his "crazy metahumans" shrug. It wasn't worth pursuing as far as he was concerned, but Morillo's squint was more considered, like he had an idea that Wally had been up to something. Had he felt a slight, recognizable vibration in the center of his sternum?

Wally began concentrating on bringing his mind down. *Keep focused. Forget what you found for a moment. Don't obsess. Stay with these guys. Get into their rhythm. Stay with them.*

It wasn't easy, however. He saw too many angles, too many awful possibilities, and his mind wanted to filter through them all.

Metz led them silently to his office, the surfaces of which Wally had already examined in detail. The director walked behind his desk and turned a small key in the lock of the central drawer. Opening it, he pulled out a piece of paper without looking, which, Wally thought, was impressive, given the state of confusion that appeared to reign over the top of his desk.

The director fingered the paper and looked squarely at his guests across the desk.

"You know, there *is* a high percentage of metahumans that come from this region. My wife is from here and, yes, I've had her tested. She is a carrier. Just in case you wonder why I'm doing this."

He paused before continuing.

"Understand that once I give you this information, I'm most probably gone. I won't be able to assist you from the inside any longer. What I'm doing breaks my confidentiality agreement."

"Dr. Metz, you're cooperating with a police investigation."

"That doesn't matter, Detective Morillo. Don't get me wrong—I'm not trying to make S.T.A.R. Labs the bad guy here. This isn't the company's fault. This is my fault. I let things go too far. I've put the company in a position of liability. I'm only asking that you keep Pradash and the rest of the department out of this. Pradash is a good man, a fine geneticist. He only got involved because he was doing what he was told."

Metz paused for emphasis. "Remember that you only talked with *me*."

Chyre leaned forward, impatient. "Give us what you've got, Doc."

Metz licked his lips and continued. "Up until recently, the department was spearheading a priority program dedicated, as Dr. Pradash alluded, to exploring and understanding the nature of superspeed. If we managed to crack the genetic code and develop our own speedsters, the hope was that the physicists would be able to figure out the mechanics—would be able to finally understand the contradictions.

"I mean, look at you," Metz gestured to Wally with a pained expression. "How do we explain your physical condition? You're undeniably flesh and blood, yet you easily attain speeds that should splinter human bone. Then you reach speeds that should reduce you to jelly and then vaporize you. Whatever it is that makes you work, it's beyond biological science. You can see why Dr. Pradash couldn't resist asking if he could test you."

Wally was reevaluating Metz. Even though his personality was cold and off-putting, the man clearly cared. On the other hand, those vials . . .

The director continued. "If we could understand the physics, then maybe it would have technological applications."

"Military applications," countered Morillo.

"Of course. For starters. The Labs will need to make back its enormous investment, but after that, who knows?"

Metz swallowed and blinked repeatedly, as if in an effort to return his focus to bitter reality. "Anyway— the program was headed up by a brilliant man who I think—I *fear*—you'll want to find. I say find, because I can't tell you where he is. I don't know. None of us knows. He was dismissed almost a year ago and all I've got is this." He held out the piece of paper. "It's an account number at the Union Bank of Keystone. Royalty monies for patent licensing—monies owed him. He gave us this account number for deposits."

Metz suddenly fell silent, lost in his thoughts, until Morillo softly spoke. "What's his name, Dr. Metz?"

The director, steeling himself, exhaled.

"Upchurch. Jonas Upchurch. He was dismissed . . . he was dismissed because . . . because I let him go too far. I should have acted sooner. Upchurch is brilliant—he headed up the superspeed program for five years and much of what we've learned about the metagene and superspeed goes right to his credit. However, he became obsessed with some questionable experimentation. His intentions were honorable, but he went too far. There were too many ethical . . . too many safety questions."

Morillo continued to press. "What was this Upchurch doing that got him dismissed, Dr. Metz?"

"He was trying to . . . was trying to . . ." Metz paused, breathing deeply. "He believed he could use metagenetic material to create life. He wanted to build his very own speedster from scratch, and from what you've told me today, I'm afraid he's succeeded on his own."

Samuel Metz looked from Chyre to Morillo to Wally. "And your murders—do you see? His speedster is trying to reproduce."

CHAPTER 5

Strategy and Tactics

Superman slightly tensed a big blue biceps and even from one hundred yards away that minute action was intimidating. *He wants to psyche me out,* Wally marveled. *God knows why, but he's not taking me for granted.*

Wally stood a football field across from the Kryptonian in the middle of the great domed chamber the Justice League used for physical training and personal combat simulation. They each toed a line on the floor, set opposite each other, and carefully eyed the other's slightest movement. Wally centered on Superman's eyes, but tried to keep his peripheral vision relaxed and prepared to pick up any indication of intent betrayed by a limb's positioning. The twitch of the biceps had yanked Wally's focus from Superman's eyes to his arm just momentarily, but Wally knew that that nervous action told Superman that Wally was spooked. If he felt any satisfaction—if he felt any disappointment—the Man of Steel did not show it.

Son of a gun, Wally. Don't make this easy for him.

Wally shifted his weight back and forth, high on the balls of his feet. Superman gazed at him with apparent disinterest.

A bell tone sounded from somewhere unseen, and a second later the dodecahedron smoothly descended from the dome high above. The five-inch object radiated a dull, silvery glow and stopped its fall five feet from the floor. It hovered there, motionless, precisely midway between the two super heroes.

From Wally's distance, the geometrical solid could easily be mistaken for a sphere, but Wally knew from experience that its twelve flat surfaces made for a prize much harder to grip than any ball. Actually, its shape worked in Wally's favor. The difficulty in handling it somewhat nullified Superman's far superior physical strength.

But the most important commodity here was speed.

It was, in essence, a child's game, probably known by a hundred different names in fields and on playgrounds around the world. Wally grew up calling it Steal the Bacon. Two children faced each other behind designated lines with the bacon—an old sock, or a stick—lying on the ground between them. At a signal, they were free to advance to the bacon. The goal was to grab the object and get it across your home line before your rival got it. The trick was to get it there without being tagged by your rival. If you were tagged with the bacon, you lost—the bacon was stolen.

With few variations, this was the game that Wally

and Superman played, a fine tune-up for those who
relied on blinding speed and split-second decision
making.

A second, sharper bell tone sounded and the dodecahedron's color instantly shifted to a deep, angry
red.

That was the go signal. The game was afoot.

For several seconds, the two teammates stood stock
still, giving no hint that they realized they could now
cross their lines. In fact, they were studying each
other for any hint of the other's intended strategy.
Their mutual goal was to catch their opponent back
on his heels and then to move forward before the
other's balance would allow him to react. Or to lure
the opponent into a rash grab at the bacon, followed
by a successful steal.

Wally feinted a couple of times in rapid succession,
tapping a toe to the floor like a racehorse pawing the
earth behind the gate. Superman, however, wasn't
buying.

*He's very patient today. He wants me to make the first
move. But, he's not going to get what he wants.* Wally determined that it wouldn't be he who made the first
mistake.

But what seemed like an infinity of minutes
stretched by and Superman still had not moved.
Wally felt an internal spring winding tighter and
tighter; even his breath grew constricted. *How can he
just stand there, wasting time? It's only a stupid game and
he's acting like we've got all day.*

I . . . will . . . not . . . break . . . first . . .

Wally's patience failed him. Maybe two minutes had passed since the go signal, but the itchy voice in Wally's brain was yammering that it had been forever. Superman's calm, unconcerned expression had not changed one iota.

With an unspoken curse aimed at the time wasted and his own stupidity, Wally broke for the dodecahedron. Body and mind accelerated smoothly, precisely, and in less than a millisecond he was closing his fist around the twelve-sided prize, all the time keeping one eye on Superman, who had launched himself forward a microsecond after Wally had made his move.

Wally had the sinking feeling his impatience had undone him. Superman barreled toward him, all muscle and mass and grim willpower.

Carefully cradling the slippery prize in his fingers, Wally wheeled and pushed off with a thickly treaded foot, aiming for home. When it came to raw speed, he was still faster than Superman. *If* he could complete the turn and overcome inertia quickly enough.

Too late. Wally felt a yank at the ankle of his trailing leg; his opponent had caught him. His balance gone, Wally smacked headlong onto the floor, the dodecahedron popping free from his grasp. The preprogrammed object sped through the air back to its default position midway between their home lines. Wally threw himself up off the ground, knowing that Superman would already be turned and speeding to the solid.

In desperation, he flung himself backward in a tight, overhead flip that he had to land by pure concentration and calculation; he did not have time to look. The gamble paid off and he hit square and balanced on the balls of his feet, opposite the dodecahedron from Superman, whose hand was in the midst of a grab for the prize.

Superman hesitated, withdrawing his hand. Wally had been too fast. For the briefest of instants, the Man of Steel flashed Wally an expression of admiration that clearly said, "You got me, buddy—slick move."

Don't get caught up in that, Wally—he's still trying to skunk you.

They danced around the center, each an arm's length from the dodecahedron, again guessing and second-guessing the other's next move. Sweat dripped into Wally's eyes, making him blink. Not from exertion, but from nervous strain.

This time Superman lunged first—it was a ruse, a feint, but Wally bit and shot his body past the dodecahedron and to a spot where Superman should have been had he committed. But he hadn't, and Wally flailed against thin air.

With Wally out of position and heeled over, the Man of Steel snatched the prize, cradled it in two hands, and darted for home. Too late, Wally realized that his opponent had made his move only once he had circled to a position that placed him facing his home line. Superman had a straight line home—he wasn't going to lose any speed negotiating a turn.

Wally recovered, wheeled, and launched himself, but Superman was already crossing his line.

A third tone sounded. Game over. *Damn it!*

The dodecahedron, released by Superman, soared back to its repository in the ceiling.

They walked across the floor to a bench along a far wall. Wally threw back his cowl, disgusted with himself. Sweat drenched his face. Punching a panel in the wall, a towel popped out for his convenience.

I'm faster than him. He shouldn't be able to beat me.

Superman sat down on the low, simple bench, even here with all the grace and command of a king assuming his throne. In spite of this, the Kryptonian looked perfectly affable and relaxed. Like them all, Superman was extremely competitive. He just never allowed that to show.

"It's like chess," he offered, as if reading Wally's mind. "You need to train yourself to think three, four moves ahead."

"I don't play chess."

"I could teach you."

"Really? You don't have that kind of time."

"Aha, that's the other thing. You're still intimidated by me. I beat you at speed and reflex exercises mostly because you're still worried about what I think of you. We're teammates, Wally. We're going to be in some nasty scrapes together. I need you to most definitely not be intimidated by me."

Wally sat silent and began tapping his toe rapidly.

Superman casually noted his junior partner's nervous action. "Oh, and that's the *other* thing. Patience. I had you beat from the get-go. You couldn't wait. You've got to learn to be more patient. You're fast enough to give *anyone* the first move and still recover in time to dominate the situation. Remember that. I'm the only being in this world that comes close to your speed and you could beat me every time, if you'd just relax and think ahead."

Yesterday, Wally would have agreed unreservedly— while there were other speedsters on the Earth, none could match Superman, and Wally's potential trumped the Man of Steel. But events since then had convinced him otherwise. Given the way the last twenty-four hours had gone, his attitude had pancaked. Even his admiration for the Kryptonian felt strained. Intimidation or no.

"Okay—so I'm a lousy strategist, you intimidate me, and I'm impatient. Anything else?"

"Well, you're in a bad mood, so long as you ask. But *that* can be made to work to your advantage."

"Sorry I asked."

"Don't be. What's bothering you?"

Wally was a little surprised by the blunt turn in the conversation. Maybe that was Superman's intent.

The last thing Wally wanted was to draw Superman into his problems. In his present state of mind, asking the JLA for help with his home situation would be an admission of failure. Besides, what *could* they do?

"It's been a bad day. Unresolved murders back home. I'm working on it."

"To be honest, Wally, J'onn told me. He also mentioned the shape he found you in this morning. I don't think I would have risked waiting for you to come around."

"You weren't there. As you can see, I came out all right."

"We could be more sure of that if you'd consent to some scans."

Wally shook his head. "I'm not going to be spending that much time here. I know my body—I'm working okay."

Superman stood up, stretching his arms wide and flexing his fingers with the nonchalant ease of a waking tiger. He continued to nudge Wally, even though his tone remained conversational.

"Sorry. I just thought maybe you came for some feedback. Why *did* you come up here today, anyway?"

Here was the Watchtower, the Justice League's headquarters in the great crater Copernicus, on the Moon.

Instead of waiting for an answer, the Kryptonian continued, "Listen, I need to stop up in Control. Why don't you come with me."

Superman walked to the pneumatic elevators, set in an alcove off the training chamber, and Wally followed, not quite sure why. They stepped inside a waiting tube and Superman punched in their destination request. With a rush of pressurized air, the transport rocketed up to the Control Deck.

Good question, thought Wally. *Why* did *I come up here today?*

After he and Morillo and Chyre had finished business with Metz, Wally had found himself with nothing of consequence to do in Keystone. There was literally nothing he could do at that point to further the hunt for the decapitating metagene killer. Not until Upchurch was located and checked out, anyway.

In the parking lot outside S.T.A.R. Labs, Wally and the two detectives had briefly discussed the information Metz had offered. They all agreed that Metz, although one hinky duck, was trying to be cooperative. Morillo and Chyre were not altogether sure of the validity of the scientist's suspicions concerning Dr. Jonas Upchurch and his supposed artificial creation, but with nothing else to go on, they figured that time invested in locating the man was not unwarranted. "Any port in a storm, or something to that effect," Chyre had mumbled.

Morillo had turned a searching eye on Wally and asked if the Scarlet Speedster had anything to add. Anything he might have observed on his own.

Wally put on his best blank expression and offered nothing.

After the detectives departed, Wally had shot like an arrow to Early Street and Iris's house. As he suspected, she had left for work. In another instant he was outside the low office complex on Allegheny that housed the pharmaceutical company where she did administrative work. He zipped up the side to the second story and, through a window, saw her on the phone, absently flipping through a neat stack of paper on her desk.

Still beautiful. Still perfect. Still his Aunt Iris, as he saw her as a boy.

She was safe right now. That's all he needed to know. That's all he could hope for. He didn't linger—

something nagged at the back of his mind, pushing unnamed fears forward. He was worried for Iris. If this thing had targeted metagene carriers, then he had to assume till proven otherwise that any blood relation of his was in danger. But what frightened Wally equally was the fact that Kevin Schull had been attacked at the same time he had contacted him. Probably just coincidence, of course. But on the outside chance that there was something more to it . . .

Stop thinking like a superstitious old woman.

But the vision in the fragment had said *Iris West*, and had shown a hateful reflection of himself.

He had to talk to Iris sometime. But not now. Not yet.

It had been over ten hours now and the thing had not struck again. Maybe it wouldn't. Maybe it had been, as Morillo had suggested, frightened away, and was now wreaking bloody havoc in some other unfortunate corner of the universe.

Wally didn't believe that. He *wanted* to believe it— because his experience had taught him there was nothing he could do to prevent it from taking any person it wanted—but he didn't.

Wally had left Iris and, out of habit, continued his patrol of the Sister Cities. He kept the comfortable pace he had set before his meeting at the Labs, the relatively low rate of which would have actually allowed an alerted citizen, for a fraction of a second, the glimpse of a red streak cutting a zigzag across their line of sight.

The rain had continued in a steady stream and a

chill depression hung over the world. Wally still had the streets practically to himself. It was a workday, but the traffic jams that habitually snarled Keystone's antiquated thoroughfares had not materialized. People were staying indoors, the weather offering a convenient excuse for avoiding mingling with a suddenly poisonous world.

Suspicious of the uneasy quiet, Wally had even checked in with his friend the Pied Piper, a reformed supervillain whose past connections with the underworld had many times proved invaluable. But the Piper's sources revealed nothing remarkable. Mark Marden, the Weather Wizard, was on another drunken binge, and Lenny Snart, aka Captain Cold, had sunk into one of his frequent black dogs. With its two prime instigators incapacitated, it wasn't surprising that Keystone's foremost criminal metagang, the Rogue's Gallery, was inactive.

But Wally had kept moving, kept running the blocks, despite the calm. It was better than standing still. At least when he was was running he could tell himself he was moving forward.

No metacrime, no petty crime, no drug deals, only one or two preoccupied pedestrians wandering into the paths of unobservant motorists. Fear of the unknown certainly made for a well-behaved populace, Wally noted with chagrin.

Eventually, having covered his territory many, many times, even the calming effects of ritual failed.

So what to do on such an uneventful day?

His first choice was not going to happen. Linda would be at school all day.

That left the Justice League, and it might do him some good to get away from Keystone. Maybe the view from Luna would offer some perspective.

The view from Luna offered no perspective.

Wally called for League transport and had been teleported almost immediately to the Watchtower, but his thoughts refused to come with him.

From his arrival and verification by the Batman's fiendishly ruthless security and log-in program, to his pickup game with the unusually accessible Superman, Wally's thoughts had remained anchored in Keystone City, jumbled and itchy and foreboding.

He and Superman stepped from the pneumatic tube onto the Control Deck, high into the upper reaches of the tower. A full, marbleized planet Earth greeted him, shining and huge through the vast viewing port, set against the silky nothing of interplanetary space. It was beautiful and distant and he could not resolve in his mind the fact that this transcendent jewel held his home, his life, and his problems. It was too abstract, too unreal. Even super heroes, despite all the inexplicable and the awful that they encountered, sometimes found it hard to wrap their heads around the notion that they could stretch their tether to Mother Earth so far as to see her reduced and exalted to a luminous disk.

Yet there she was, infinitely far, yet big and bright

enough to touch. A physical manifestation of his dislocated, contradictory thoughts.

J'onn J'onzz, the Martian Manhunter, was working a science station along the curving console boards that ringed the Control Deck, entering data for God knew which of his countless personal research projects.

It took Wally a minute to realize it but, of course, the shapeless scarlet sheet draping a padded chair and extended over the controls of several adjacent monitoring consoles was Plastic Man, relaxed and in position to respond to any computer emergency with the least amount of effort on his part. His uniform's black diamond insignia, distorted but still recognizable, had been the tip-off. *Lazy, efficient rascal,* thought Wally, enviously.

The Elastic Marvel did not react to their entry, zoned as he seemed into another state of consciousness to match his form. The Manhunter, however, quickly glanced up and motioned him over. Wally immediately felt the impression that he had been manipulated—or at least guided—here by Superman. Suddenly, nothing seemed to be happening by chance. Superman and the Manhunter were here for a reason.

J'onn J'onzz continued entering his data. Wally leaned against his console, folded his arms in an unconscious defensive gesture, and watched the numbers fly from the Manhunter's dark green fingers into the monitor. Formulas were entered and processed faster than his limited understanding of calculus could comprehend.

Wally grew tired of waiting. "What?"

The Martian didn't look up. "I'm sorry. Just give me . . . one . . . more . . ."

Idly scanning the room, Wally noticed that the Man of Steel was over by Plastic Man, rousing the xenomorph from his meditations, bending low to talk to him. Poor O'Brian, low man on the JLA totem pole, pulled more than his share of monitor duty. Sometimes the monotony of the job got to even him, Wally knew, leading the chronic clown into uncharacteristic reticence. Now he was pulling himself together into a shape vaguely bipedal. As Superman patted him on the shoulder, Wally could see the rubber man say something—no doubt rude—before glancing across the room at Wally and settling back down to duty, this time in a more stiffly conventional posture. Superman glanced across the room toward Wally.

Everybody's stealing a peek at me, Wally groused to himself. *Something's up.*

Suddenly, J'onzz was finished and, yes, staring at Wally, too. Superman was right there, as well.

What? What the hell is this all about? I think I'm about to have two founding fathers leaning on my scarlet ass.

Superman, now all serious, exhibiting none of the affable looseness he had on the contest floor, began. "Wally, could we talk?" He motioned toward a side room. "In there?"

Wally nodded and moved with his two seniors into the small conference room. The air throughout the Watchtower was dry and sterile, and in here it seemed even more so, flowing sharp into his nostrils. He tried to breathe measuredly, in order to keep check on the annoyance he felt at having been led like a schoolboy into an arranged meeting with parent and teacher. Superman hit the wall touch and the door slid closed behind them.

"We think we may have a situation in the making," Superman began, getting right to the point. "We're not saying we do, but we want to stay on top of things."

"We always want to stay on top of things." Wally fought to keep his temper. "So why the big deal?" *Don't play games with me.*

The Manhunter cleared his throat, an earthly affectation he had picked up recently. "Working with the astro-observational network, I've been able to pinpoint some times. Precise times for the appearance of the—*phenomena*, the anomalies. The extraordinary visitors from—um—*wherever.*"

Impressive, that even the Manhunter still didn't have a good word for the things—the occurrences.

"For our purposes, I'm translating the two incidents from sidereal mean to a terrestrial point of reference: Central Standard Time—Keystone City time.

"The first phenomenon—the one we met over Asia—manifested yesterday at eighteen-seventeen and forty-nine seconds, or six-seventeen and forty-nine seconds P.M., if you prefer. Blew out of some infinitely small point of nowhere and expanded to Earth-threatening mass in microseconds."

6:17:49. Oh, God. Wally felt that sick ache in the hollow of his chest return. The other shoe was about to drop.

"The second episode—what we *think* was an anomaly close in nature, if not identical, to that of the first, although the fact that it occurred far outside the solar system has limited our observations—we've pinpointed that moment of manifestation at . . ."

"Eleven fifty-eight P.M." Wally filled in the blank.

"Twenty-three fifty-seven and twenty-two seconds, to be exact. Do you see?"

Wally saw. The twin anomalies had appeared at the same times—maybe the *precise* same times—as the KCPD had determined the two sets of multiple murders had been committed.

"I don't suppose we allow for coincidence?" Wally knew his question was only rhetorical.

"Once is coincidence," Superman stated flatly, "twice is pattern. There's something connecting the murder spree on your turf to what seems to be a much more *transterrestrial* danger."

Wally didn't bother to ask how they happened to know the unreleased police estimates for the time of the murders. The Batman, maybe. Or the Manhunter in human guise, again. It didn't matter.

"I'm on top of what's happening in Keystone and Central. I can handle it. I don't have the lid on it yet, I admit, but this isn't a League matter, I promise you." Wally listened to his words roll out, in all their defensive posturing. He wasn't exactly happy with his position, but he didn't see any other stance he could take.

Besides, don't you see that there's nothing the League can do in this case?

Superman and the Manhunter exchanged a look.

You know, I can see you doing that.

"Look, the thing I encountered—it's faster than I am. *Much* faster. There's nothing any one in the League is going to be able to do until I figure a way to get a handle on it. Me—the Fastest Man Alive."

Wally found himself growing more and more irritated. Part of him knew there was no good reason for a hostile response, but most of him felt so frustrated by circumstances that all he could focus on was the fact that he was sick and tired of being stuck on the second tier, relegated to B-team status, and treated like a dull child.

He'd reached his limit, even with Superman.

The Man of Steel was conciliatory. "No one's suggesting otherwise, Wally. League policy is that we stay clear of each other's homefront situations unless invited in. That's not an issue. There is a broader issue here, however. J'onn?"

The Manhunter stepped in, immediately pulling Wally's attention back to him. Wally suddenly had the briefest flash of unexpected insight. The situation in the room felt oddly familiar. *Morillo and Chyre,* Wally thought. *They are going at me the same way Morillo and Chyre would—back and forth. Because—because this is how they keep me off balance. This is how they keep me from getting the chance to stay one step ahead. They fear that if they don't keep me disoriented, they'll never be able to control my accelerated thoughts.*

The revelation passed through his mind in an instant, and then he was refocused on the Manhunter's words, but with a new sense of self-awareness.

"The issue is, your boogeyman may be doing more damage than just the taking of human life in your neck of the woods. It may be responsible for somehow upsetting basic physical laws. It may be affecting our reality. And that *would be* a League matter."

Wally was sobered by the new perspective.

"Yeah, I guess if that was true, it would be. But—what have you got, really? What evidence do you have? Even if we—okay, let's *say* we accept it as true: This thing committing murders in one little corner of North America is also responsible for throwing down some big, damn weird cosmic crap. So where do we go from there? What's our next move? As far as I can see, there's no predicting the next occurrence. Can you tell me otherwise?"

Despite his best efforts, Wally had allowed himself to become defensive again.

Superman remained annoyingly calm. "Slow down, Wally—we don't know. We don't know if we have a League problem at all. However, you know perfectly well that proactive prevention is part of what we do. We appreciate that Keystone and Central are yours, and we're going to respect that. But if we find any concrete evidence that supports our concern that this may have wider ramifications . . ."

Wally calmed himself with a tremendous effort of self-reason. He knew he was overreacting. He knew his mind, his emotions, were jagged and raw and unfocused and coloring his perceptions. He deserved their attitude, this intervention.

"I know. And I would never risk lives in my cities,

or anywhere else, if I thought there was any chance
League support could help."

Superman and the Manhunter stood silent, giving
Wally the chance to take the conversation forward. He
did so with a note of resignation.

"All right—what can we do?"

The Manhunter didn't mince words. "You can
allow me to perform a complete, in-depth mind scan."

Exactly what Wally had expected. He began to
slowly shake his head. *Uh-uh. No way.*

The Manhunter continued patiently, knowing
Wally's resistance wouldn't easily be broken. "Wally,
you're the only connection we have to this phenomenon. That's the other reason we think the space anomalies and the Keystone killer are connected: You and
only you have been able to interact with—to perceive—either of them . . . and survive. Somehow you
are connected with them. Your mind has been
touched by both. I think there may be information regarding the nature of all this deep inside you. Information I may be able to tap."

J'onn J'onzz carefully pressed his case home.
"You're all we've got, Wally. The fragment I gathered
from the fireball—that strangely elusive bit of matter—
it didn't make it through teleportation to the Watchtower. It went in with me, but it didn't come out. I
don't think its molecular structure could be reassem-
bled because the programs couldn't *recognize* it. In fact,
I think we might have been lucky that the teleporter
didn't freeze up, leaving us all in limbo. This is some
very, very weird stuff, Wally. I don't need to tell you

that. All we have now is you. You've got to know you might help provide us with some real insight."

The realization of actually having come to a point where there was no longer any intelligent, responsible excuse for denying the Martian's mind scan terrified Wally. This was not something he could ever reason away—this squirmy fear and hatred of allowing anyone into his memory, his inner world.

"Your feelings are understandable," said the Manhunter.

Wally knew he'd have to submit. It was his duty. Superman and the Martian were right to have confronted him this way.

But it was not going to be pleasant.

Just then a tone sounded from above. Wally barely heard it.

O'Brian's voice came over the intercom. "Hate to break in where it's been made clear I'm not wanted . . ."

"Go ahead, O'Brian," Superman responded. "No unnecessary commentary, please."

"What you call unnecessary and what I find crucial in the ongoing battle against crushing boredom are—"

"O'Brian, not now."

"Sorry—*sorry*. I've taken a call for a Wally West? Might he be in there with you? From a Detective Morillo? He requests Mr. West's immediate presence regarding a pending police action. Concerning a Mr. Upchurch. He says Mr. West will know as to what this regards. *Thenk yew.*"

*   *   *

The first thing Wally smelled upon deceleration was the heavy tang of cordite. The rain had stopped while he had been off-Earth, but leaden skies kept a cold, damp pall locked over the city streets. The damp magnified the smoky odor of gun.

Police sirens screamed in the distance, getting closer. The street and aged, cracked parking lots surrounding the old prison were already jammed with police cruisers, flashing a galaxy of revolving red-and-blue strobes. An army of Kevlar-jacketed cops manned makeshift battlements behind their vehicles, armed with pump-action shotguns, as well as standard-issue revolvers. The KCPD SWAT team was on the scene and apparently in command. Wally had noted the barrels of semi-automatic weapons poking over the rooftops of two neighboring buildings. That meant Lieutenant LaTour of Tactics, now huddled behind the team van with Commissioner Jewett, was calling the shots.

Every eye was focused on the decayed stone relic that was the penitentiary, its tiny defensive loopholes, and the vacant black inside them.

Morillo's call to Wally, patched through to the Watchtower by League communications satellite, could not have been better timed. To Wally it was the Seventh Cavalry, the bell, the governor's pardon, and the improbable eleventh-hour rescue all rolled into one. His duty to submit to the mind scan justifiably delayed, Wally felt guilt at his relief, but the circumstances were not of his making. Just as he and Superman and the Martian Manhunter knew he had no choice but to submit to the scan, so, too, did they all acknowledge the greater importance of his immediate response to the call of his protectorate.

Even so, Wally was positive he saw a fleeting expression of chagrin cross Superman's face, but the senior member quickly waved him out. The Manhunter had voiced a hurried "Godspeed," and then Wally was through the teleporter and back in Keystone.

He'd rocketed straight for police headquarters, where the desk had directed him to the stand-off situation at the old Quaker Penitentiary on Endicott, down in Old Town. Two officers were down. This was not what he'd expected. He'd parted with Chyre and Morillo that morning with the understanding that the detectives would contact him when they got a line on the mysterious Dr. Upchurch, only to return to a lighted powder keg.

Wally quickly located Chyre and Morillo in the confusion of various police departments attempting to coordinate strategy. They had been pushed to the rear; metahuman hostility apparently did not figure in this.

The two detectives noted Wally's usual instantaneous appearance without comment. Nearby cops, less experienced with the Flash and keyed by the circumstances, glared uneasily.

"The desk said there were two officers down . . . ?"

Morillo growled, "They didn't make it." Wally's heart sank. Chyre deflected any further conversation along that line with a jerk of his massive head toward the ancient penitentiary. "Who would have guessed you could make so much money on patent royalties?"

Wally stared. "The Quaker Penitentiary—Upchurch?"

Morillo explained. "We took the deposit number we got from Metz to the bank and got them to agree to open the account. You wouldn't believe the kind of money this guy was getting in the way of royalties from S.T.A.R. Labs. If that's his cut, I shudder to think what the company's making on his discoveries. But to the point, there were ungodly huge withdrawals, as well. Under a number of aliases, Upchurch is financing something very, very expensive."

The detective continued. "He's sneaky, but he screwed up when he used a bank service to help locate the penitentiary here. Apparently, he needed a sizable facility for whatever it is he's dumping money into. The place has been empty since at least the fifties, and he was able to purchase it quietly from the Society of Friends, ten months ago."

Wally had, of course, passed the old jailhouse regularly on his city patrols, but had noticed nothing to spark a close examination of the facility. The exterior looked undisturbed. One of the drawbacks of superspeed was the infinitesimally small amount of time it allowed Wally to spend in actual observational contact with his city. He patrolled frequently, but each patrol was usually completed in seconds. That left enormous blocks of time in which the city evolved unobserved.

In his haste, Wally had missed the recent occupation of the Quaker Penitentiary. That did not sit well with him.

"We figured Upchurch had started up his own lab here." Chyre picked up the narrative. "Makes sense, right? So we come up here with a street patrol. Martinez and Albers go in first—we had to jimmy the lock on the entrance—and as soon as we're all in the main foyer or whatever they call it, they start unloading on us. A goddamn crossfire. Martinez and Albers went down and we're damn lucky we could drag them outside without taking any more hits."

Morillo was a tough customer, but Wally could tell by a slight hitch in his otherwise stoic cadence that he had been badly shaken by the ambush. "They've got heavy ordnance in there. Military stuff. Concussive shells. Stuff developed by the S.T.A.R., I'm guessing. There's at least half a dozen men in there. Maybe a lot more—we really couldn't see anything. They're loaded for bear."

"And Upchurch?" Wally asked.

Morillo shrugged. "No sign of him, but there's your money well spent—a damn cadre of killers armed to the teeth with high-caliber prototypes. These guys were organized—prepared and efficient. And it explains the multiple simultaneous killings."

Wally shook his head. "It doesn't explain what almost killed me."

Morillo shrugged. "Right now, I've got to say, these crazies are looking more and more like the explanation. I don't know what you think you encountered at the Schull scene, but synchronized attacks by trained terrorists can be *explained*."

That last insinuation infuriated Wally, but he kept his calm. Now was not the time to pick a fight.

"Sorry, Morillo, but the notion of a wealthy scientist bent on creating an artificial metahuman *and* funding and housing a terroristic hit squad doesn't exactly add up in my book. What do you say I go in?"

Chyre and Morillo glanced at each other uneasily. They knew Lieutenant LaTour would not cede control of the situation to the Flash under the current circumstances.

"What's the status?" Wally asked.

"There was a fire fight at first," Chyre answered. "Now, apparently it's a standoff. There's been some talk, but no negotiation—whoever's talking inside says they regret the shooting, but there's no way they can surrender."

Wally grimaced. "So no progress is being made. Come on—people are going to get hurt. Give me a chance to diffuse the situation. Let me go in."

The Metahuman Hostilities detectives had no authority in the matter and Wally would never point to them as an excuse for his actions. But he needed their okay for his own peace of mind.

"Just to reconnoiter . . ."

Chyre barely moved his lips: "Do it."

Morillo nodded.

The Flash was gone, and just as suddenly a series of blinding bursts of light lanced out of the penitentiary's loopholes.

CHAPTER 6

Penitentiary

Wally loped through the masses of police locked in stasis behind their vehicles, the glare of the light bars casting frozen patterns of blue and red over tense faces. Accelerated, he no longer caught the pungent smell of gunfire, no longer felt the weight of humidity.

Once inside the police line, Wally circled the stone walls enclosing the prison. He tried to recall all he knew about the ancient edifice. It had been built in the midnineteenth century, he thought, by the Society of Friends in their efforts to create a more humane penal system. It was built strong to refute fears that prisoners were more likely to escape a Quaker institution than a state facility, surrounded by eighteen-foot-high walls of granite and mortar, many feet thick. Unused since the 1950s, weeds and small trees now pushed out of accumulated dirt along its ramparts. Despite the wear and tear of time, the old penitentiary could well withstand a long siege.

Wally knew he'd been inside once, as a boy. Maybe on a tour with Iris. He remembered that the rows of dark, vaulted halls lined with cells basically followed the exterior walls, leaving a courtyard space open in the center.

That was where he was headed.

Wally drove with his legs and scaled the exterior wall, easily finding fingerholds in the protruding stone blocks to aid his balance. He was surprised to find the parapet walk deserted—he had expected to see at least a hidden observer or two stationed there.

Wally glided over the roofs of the cell blocks, choked with low, pioneering vegetation. No one was manning the prison's upper reach. At the edge, facing the courtyard, he hesitated to carefully scan below. It was clear, although the scuffed and trodden dust on its paved floor gave evidence of recent human activity.

Wally heaved himself over the ledge and churned his legs rapidly, creating a cushion of air that canceled what would have been the crushing effect of gravity on anyone moving earthward at such a speed. Landing gently, he quickly noted the open doors breaking the surrounding courtyard walls. Within a couple of the dark doorways, he could dimly see human figures, frozen in normal time. They all were clad in some unfamiliar body armor, hoisting big firearms, wearing bulky, goggled headgear.

He moved forward confidently—one step, two steps . . .

He felt something light as a spiderweb break against his shin.

Three steps, four steps, five steps . . .

The world went painfully white and vacant. The blinding strobe had flashed so quickly, even he had been unable to avoid the full brunt of its awful glare. Wally was blinded, his brain shocked and uncomprehending.

Even so, his instincts served to protect him, his body unconsciously fighting to regain balance, his legs shifting direction, and launching him horizontally on a path at right angles to the one he had been on.

At the same time, Wally struggled to shut the numbed lids on his scorched eyes. But another blinding, agonizing light strobed at him.

Then another, and another.

Stabbing, stabbing, stabbing him. Disorienting, blinding.

His body slammed against the hard pavement and skidded painfully. By chance, the angle of his head turned his eyes down and the impact carried his face into his upturned arms. Momentarily protected from the constant barrage of the strobes, Wally squeezed his eyes shut.

It was a booby trap, his stunned brain finally acknowledged. A sequence of extremely rapid strobe lights set to disable a speedster. And he had stepped into it very neatly.

Then, horrified, he realized what had to be the aim of the ambush. Dazed, he had dropped out of superspeed. He was lying there blind and vulnerable to any normal with a weapon.

Wally began to roll even as the concussion shells slammed into the paving stones beside him, shattering them with deafening thunder cracks. As he rolled, he picked up speed, an uncanny sense of direction carrying him straight toward the nearest wall. He kept his eyes squeezed shut, fearing the light barrage might still be continuing, knowing his dazzled eyes would not be of any help.

His hours and hours of athletic training paid off with a neatly executed tuck and tumble, which carried him from a roll to a full run. His course stayed true even when he felt the air pressure shift as a gruesomely huge projectile shot past his cheek. He was still in terrible danger, but he was gaining speed.

The question was, could he gather himself, stunned and blinded—could he *concentrate*—and bring his body up to that necessary molecular frequency before he dashed his silly brains out against the stone wall.

He had done it in the Schull house, in the face of the presence. He could do it here.

There was a sticky thickening about him, and then a crashing and an exploding and the world seemed to be caving in about his head.

Then, silence nearby and shouting out *there*.

He gathered his senses as he tensed his numbed body, now quivering and cold as if it was wracked with fever. The air was cooler and damper here. He realized he had phased through the wall—just barely, he guessed—leaving probably a very large portion of it in smoking ruin.

His momentum had carried him deep into a prison block, and relative safety. But now he was decelerated again and very weak.

He cracked open his eyes, cautiously. There was no glare, no light, only inky black. Either he was completely blind, his optic nerves burned out, or he was surrounded by darkness.

He chose to believe that the latter was the case.

Regardless, he was in no position to return to superspeed. Even if he had the strength to maintain it, without a fix on his surroundings he'd quickly bash his brains out on some unseen obstruction.

Outside, muffled by the tons of masonry that must have crashed into the breach he'd blown through the wall, Wally heard angry curses and confusion. Maybe a note of panic.

He heard nothing inside, except the occasional clink of rubble settling and a soft scurrying.

Rodents—*rats*.

Dragging himself up from the floor, he acted more on the instinct to seek shelter, to get his back up against a wall, than any conscious plan. But as he moved, his mind cleared further, and he began to assess his situation.

He was in a bad strait, but it seemed he had bought some time. Maybe the men who had attacked even thought he was dead under the collapsed wall. He couldn't count on that, but it didn't seem like this hall was occupied.

His attackers had been prepared for him. The strobes would have effectively disabled anyone, but they had been set to flash in very rapid sequence. They had been very cunningly and expensively rigged to confront eyes looking in any direction.

There had been batteries and batteries of extremely high candlepower flood strobes positioned around the courtyard, set at a frequency and irregular pattern expressly configured to catch a speedster. And the armored figures, they had been wearing very special goggles that no doubt protected them from the strobes.

Wally knew he had been incredibly lucky. Stunned by the onslaught of light, he had come within a hairbreadth of catching any number of explosive shells.

Whoever these men were, they were well-armed with elaborate defenses and they fought with a desperate efficiency for Jonas Upchurch.

But why?

Wally felt his way to a wall and followed its rough brick surface till he came to a set of vertical metal bars. He had guessed right: He was in a cell block, in a long hallway lined with barred cells.

Suddenly he became aware of a faint gray blob set against all the black. Looking up, there were dim gray shapes somewhere above. With great relief he realized that he was not blind—at least not totally. There were windows set high up in each of the cells and a dirty smudge of light filtered wanly through each.

The lights were mere blurs, his eyes no doubt still impaired. In any event, they did nothing to illuminate his surroundings. He was still going to have to rely on touch to navigate.

Wally moved gingerly down the hall, his fingers guiding him along the repeating pattern of brick wall followed by metal bars, followed by wall, followed by bars.

Something else caught his attention: The rustling and scurrying that he had recognized earlier was increasing. There were lots of rats here, an army of vermin unused to human intrusion. They scuttled nervously around him, leaving a wide berth, but the place sounded thick with them. They were agitated and they were growing more and more frantic.

What at first seemed of little direct consequence began to concern Wally. *Rats deserting ships—they say rats know before a ship goes down.*

Wally jumped as a metallic clang sounded from down the hall behind him, unbelievably loud and shocking in the Stygian silence.

An equally loud thud followed and then distant shuffling. His attackers had found a door into this cell block and had popped the lock. He saw no lights coming up behind him; the fancy headgear they sported was no doubt equipped with night vision.

Wally didn't know how far their vision would extend—could they see him at twenty feet? At fifty? Now?

He guessed they were, at most, three hundred feet down the hall. The soft shufflings and measured treads, hard to hear over the increased scuttling of the rats, were ever so slowly growing louder.

Wally imagined that there must be a gang of armed warriors, carefully sweeping up the hall, checking every cell as they came. Every so often he heard a rusty metallic groan, indicating a barred door had swung open.

Gulping hard, he fought down his fear. Sooner or

later they were going to find him, no matter if he did
try to hole up in one of the ancient cells. Any noise he
made would just bring them in faster. They'd always
have the tactical advantage of seeing him before he
could see them.

Wally knew he had no choice but to resign himself
to desperate measures. Although he'd probably wind
up killing himself in the dark, he was going to have to
step up to superspeed, bum rush the searchers, and
hope for a miracle. If it happened that he smacked
into one of them, and captured a night vision goggle
device before their shots hit him, he would have a
fighting chance.

Most likely, though, he would end up smashed
against a wall without having come close to any of
them. Game over.

Wally began to steel himself for his action, wrapping his fingers around a cell bar to steady his still
shaking body. He tried to separate the various hushed
noises filtering through the dark and focus on the approach of one particular set of shuffling steps.

But the scuttling and now the thin, high squeaks of
the rats drew his attention.

His body was vibrating, he suddenly realized. He
was unconsciously keying himself up—revving his
engine, so to speak—as he stood there, tense and
coiled, hanging onto the cell bar. And he was sending
a constant, steady vibration through his fingers and
into the cell door—and from there probably right into
the cell block masonry . . .

. . . Because it sure as hell seemed like the rats were responding to that vibration.

Wally concentrated and increased the frequency of the vibration and, sure enough, the sounds of rodent distress increased. *That* was what was irritating the legions of rats: The unconscious vibrations his traumatized body had been emitting ever since his poorly executed phase through the cell block wall.

Wally had heard of bees and worms driven to frenzies by electromagnetic frequencies introduced into their environments. Why not rats?

He tried to imagine the floors and walls and the writhing, spasming carpet of greasy fur and glittering black eyes that must be covering them.

Just as glad I can't see, he shuddered.

Then he decided to gamble and amped his vibrations—just slightly. Careful to maintain a consistent frequency, his body resonated powerfully, the results sending the cell door, the floor, and the walls quivering to match.

As he had hoped, the rodents were driven to frenzy. The thousands of sharp, tiny scramblings combined into a stampede as the panicked creatures careened away from his position. The invisible horde washed down the hallway, desperate to get away from the maddening vibration, heading straight for the approaching searchers.

Through the dark, a curse and an unsteady gasp of fear rose above the din. The gasp escalated to a panicked howl and Wally allowed himself a fierce grin.

He'd hoped at least one of the searchers suffered from a fear of rats.

More curses followed. More gasping, more horrified groans.

Then, a gun shot. And another, roaring like a cannon up the barren corridor. It was chaos down there. Another blast and a sickening, gurgling moan. One damn fool had shot another.

More curses and screams. Someone was yelling something that sounded like, "Don't do it! Don't do it!" and then there was a brilliant flash of light and an ear-splitting roar. The entire cell block shook with a paroxysm that threw Wally to the ground.

Wally began to scramble up, dazed by the concussive force, and stopped cold.

He could see.

For a split second, the blurry scene before his blinking eyes seemed fixed and stationary, even though Wally's mind was working in normal time. About a hundred and fifty feet down the curving corridor, lined with its dank, barred cells, the men stalking him lay stunned, knocked off their feet by the explosion that had torn a huge gap in the high ceiling between them and Wally.

A gray, ground-hugging cloud was disappearing into the darkness beyond the men: the army of rats was moving on. The confused creatures couldn't get away fast enough, but they had done more than Wally could have hoped.

Curtains of pulverized masonry swirled through the enormous shaft of daylight pouring through the hole in the ceiling. Wally shook his head and squinted hard. Although still indistinct, he could see that one of the men was down—shot—and another was sitting propped against a wall, holding some sort of large-bore personal cannon, its muzzle smoking.

Thank you, you gutless wonder, thought Wally.

Then he realized that two of the others had seen him. They struggled up off the floor, lifted their big, automatic rifles, and set themselves in firing positions. Another and then another rose to join them.

The four had leveled their weapons and were aiming for Wally when it finally occurred to his dazed mind that he might not be reacting as fast as he should. The world was still fuzzy and almost unreal, but he was in serious danger. He'd better get moving.

The first shot came and exploded into the cell beside him even as he leaped up and to his left.

Too close—moving too slow—wake up, Wally!

The second shot came hard on the heels of the first. Wally forced himself to extend and thrust and suddenly the oncoming shell was hanging in the air, midway between the gunner and the position Wally had just vacated. Twenty feet behind it, another projectile sat suspended, with yet another not far behind. Puffs of exhaust gas clung to the gun barrels beyond them.

Wally had made it to superspeed even as they had fired.

He had won the battle.

Wally loped over to examine the projectiles. His vision was still not one hundred percent, but he found if he squinted hard enough he could make out details. The shells were like nothing he'd seen before and he was more convinced than ever that they were prototypes from S.T.A.R. Labs' weapons division. That was something that needed investigation down the line.

Careful not to jar the explosive projectiles excessively, Wally slightly altered their courses down and toward the corner of the wall and floor. It would do no good to allow them to hurtle down the hall toward the unknown. As the three shells inched their way forward, Wally turned his attention to the six men who had stalked him. The man who had been shot—clean through the chest, leaving a gigantic, bloody aperture—was clearly dead. Smoke from the detonated charge still described a curve above the wound. Wally was sorry it had come to this but, if not for luck, that would have been him lying there.

The man with the cannon, seated on the floor, stared out into space with glassy, terrified eyes. Wally saw that one of the assault weapons lay smoking on the ground near him. Apparently, he had panicked when the rats crawled over him, fired blindly, and shot his companion. Then, in mindless desperation, he'd blown a hole in the wall with the cannon. Maybe just to relieve the claustrophobic tension because, when you thought about it, it made no sense.

Thank God they gave the panicky guy the cannon.

Wally gently eased the big gun out of Rat Fear's hands. At the speed he was moving, any careless jerk could easily rip off a finger or shatter bone. Although the man clutched his weapon with an iron grip, Wally could afford to work it loose patiently, knowing that, with his sight returning, he now had time on his side.

When he had freed the cannon, Wally collected all the other projectile weapons using the same persistence. He put them in a pile, did a quick analysis of their firing mechanisms, and methodically disarmed them all. The removed pins and springs were gently lobbed into the dark.

Checking back with the three in-flight shells, Wally determined that they were still on course for the corner of the floor and wall; he'd aimed well. He paused for a relative moment to watch as the lead shell slowly eased into the corner, its ceramic jacket gracefully peeling back against the resistance of shattering brick, until an internal detonator was touched and it ruptured into jagged fragments and a billow of white flame. The air surrounding the explosion rippled and expanded under the concussive pressure, but Wally was pleased to see that his decision to angle the shells into the joint was a good one; there was no ricochet and damage was minimized.

Now, before he pressed on, Wally gingerly removed the goggle apparatus from the head of one of his outmaneuvered foes. There was every reason to believe that there would be other traps set for him, and this device might help to even the advantage.

Slipping the thing over his head, Wally lowered the dark lenses over his still hazy eyes. Suddenly, the world focused into crystal clarity, with lights and darks modulated to allow detailed observation within either, as his eyes traveled back and forth between patches of shadow and sunlight. The goggles' lens mechanism apparently augmented the eye's ability to adjust to changes in brightness. The blinding glare of the strobes had been therefore cut by the lens, Wally reckoned, and what little light filtered into the dark cell block had been incredibly amplified.

A nifty gizmo, Wally decided. *I'm going to keep it.*

He left the apparatus in place over his eyes and ran down the hall in the direction from which the stalkers had come. He figured that probably eight to ten seconds had elapsed since Rat Fear had shot his wad. That meant the rest of the penitentiary stronghold had time to react. More than likely, there would be other frightened men on their way to the scene.

Sure enough, upon exiting the cell block through the door the stalkers had forced on their way in, Wally nearly stumbled over three other heavily armed men rounding a corner. He carefully removed the firearms of these as he had the others, but now opted to simply smash the barrels into ruin against a metal post.

Time, even such as it was to him, was limited. Chyre and Morillo would have seen the flashes and heard the shots and explosion, and would now be assuming the worst. Wally had said that this would be a simple reconnaissance jaunt, but fate had played out differently, and now he held an advantage that he wasn't about to let go. Regardless, to avoid creating further hazard, he'd have to keep things moving before the detectives did anything well-meaning but foolish—like force an assault.

First things first, he had to canvas the entire facility and disarm all combatants. With the vision-augmenting headgear he'd commandeered, this proved easy. Like the rats who had just aided in turning the table, Wally quickly and methodically ferreted his way through every open corridor and office, cell and alcove, nook and cranny, disabusing human statues of their weaponry as he went. The dark interiors turned day under the goggles' lens, he scanned carefully to avoid booby trap triggers, and in under five seconds he was confident that the thirty-two men he'd located represented all he was going to find.

Except . . .

Wally had found no arrangements for rest, no food, no tactics nor command center. That meant these necessities had to lie somewhere else, maybe with more troops. Maybe with Upchurch.

He'd avoided entering the central courtyard, where he'd been initially blindsided, having simply scanned it from a window in passing to insure it was clear.

Now he regarded it more carefully and noticed that a sizable trail had been worn through the dust covering the paving stones, leading to what appeared to be nothing but an old wooden door, boarded shut. Lots of travel came and went to that boarded door.

Someone was waiting for him on the other side.

Wally considered his options. He didn't want to phase through without any idea what conditions were on the other side. Plus, the helpful headgear with goggles wouldn't make the molecular transition and that was his ace in the hole.

He decided on a direct approach. Truthfully, he saw little choice but to plow ahead or retreat to the police, and Wally liked to joke that the Flash did not run well in reverse.

First, he cautiously surveyed the courtyard and was surprised to catch, at about a foot above the surface, the faint glimmer of dozens of thread-thin laser beams crisscrossing the open space, all at different angles. These, he realized, were the triggers that set off the strobe barrage. He had felt a tiny pull as he had tripped the one; they carried that much intensity. With the goggles they were all very visible—green and smoky against the wash of sunlight—if you were looking for them. That was how the men inside avoided them.

Wally appreciated the lenses all over again.

The laser placements were fiendishly clever, but logical if you took a moment to follow them, and Wally easily found a clear path to the barred wooden door.

He examined the perimeter of the entrance and the prop boards barring it. Nothing about it suggested that it was particularly secure. The door was clearly an invitation to another death trap.

Moving against the wall to one side, Wally grabbed a protruding board with both hands and ripped the door off its hinges. He was no Superman, but the momentum lent by superspeed, leveraged against the support of the wall, was more than enough for the task. Wally, flattened against the wall, watched as a surge of light oozed up out of the opening behind the doorway, an unfurling of languid cannon fire. The wall was shaking—undulating—to Wally's accelerated mind. He'd wisely sidestepped another booby trap—this time blinding light *and* concussive force.

Just to add to the confusion and uncertainty that he hoped were reigning inside, he tossed the door into a laser's path, setting off another barrage of the strobes.

With the goggles on, Wally was unaffected by the riot of light, but the men within couldn't know that.

As soon as the blast from inside the doorway had spent its radiating, sledgehammer force, Wally accelerated into the shattered gap. The strobes continued to explode behind him, reflecting confusedly on the sluggish cloud of dust filling the dark passage. The tremendous damage surrounding the inside of the doorway suggested the bomb burst had been set right there; small chunks of brick and mortar sank toward the ground, slow as the setting sun.

The goggles continued to prove invaluable. A few dark yards inside the door and the bottom fell out. It was a staircase leading down; this must have been a service entrance into the prison maintenance areas.

Wally bulled down the steps, fighting hard to keep his balance all the way. Even at superspeed—he figured he was doing about half Mach—he feared he would prove an easy target for someone aiming up the staircase. But he reached the bottom without incident and before him lay a dank hallway lined with fat, corroded iron pipes snaking toward a rectangle of light at the far end.

Without hesitating, he shot down the corridor.

It opened into a sizable chamber, the prison mechanical room, filled with steam pipes and the remnants of an ancient coal furnace and boiler. It was dimly lit and framed in black shadow by a string of bare electrical bulbs suspended on frayed cords from the high ceiling.

Wally took all this in in a microsecond. An array of horizontal pipes, as well as the furnace, lay directly across from him, perfect areas of concealment. Most important, he saw the green, smoky thread of light lancing across his path through the doorway.

He did not hesitate and stepped right into it.

The strobes exploded again, set in a high-velocity pattern similar to that of the trap outside. The goggles modulated their searing intensity to a pleasant fluctuation.

Twin lightning bolts shot out of unseen generators set on either side of the room's entrance, nearly catching Wally by surprise. But he caught them out of the corner of his eye and accelerated past their electromagnetic collision, which came close enough to raise his hair with static charge.

Two booby traps wrapped in one. Light and electrical discharge—not much else fast enough to catch a speedster.

Wally had to give the perpetrator credit, now that he was through what seemed like a last wall of defense.

From behind the pipes and furnace seven men were slowly, slowly rising and shouldering what looked to be grenade launchers. Their normal-time minds had yet to comprehend that the double trap hadn't worked. It was almost comical, the fixed, ritual snarls on their faces. Wally knew they were probably sounding a very fierce group war cry, but the fierceness just looked silly when you broke it down into slow motion.

For heaven's sake. Grenades in here? They'll blow themselves to pieces. These guys are seriously desperate.

Before they could come close to firing, Wally had the launchers out of their hands. Since they could conceivably cause further problems, positioned as they were to block any potential retreat, he decided he couldn't afford to be gentle this time and gave them each a tap at the base of the skull, hurling them into unconsciousness. That was a neat little trick he'd learned from the Batman, on a rare occasion that had found the Darknight Detective in an expansive mood.

Wally thoroughly searched the mechanical room and the doors leading off it. Two hid small storage areas and Wally flinched when he saw the racks and racks of weapons stacked inside. *These fanatics were ready for total war.*

Behind a third door, Wally found the secret army's living quarters, spare and utilitarian and currently unoccupied. That left one door behind the boiler.

He kicked it in, stepping back rapidly and to the side to avoid another explosive surprise. Nothing happened. Tentatively, he moved through and into another moldering, damp basement chamber.

A laboratory. A biological laboratory. Several heavy wooden tables held rows of beakers, racks of tubes and centrifuges and incubators. Spherical glass balls

of various sizes connected to one another by
corkscrew tubing, stained from some ochre liquid
stagnating within, vied for space next to a huge array
of microsurgical equipment. A lone computer rig sat
on a low metal cart, powered, as it appeared all electrical needs were, by a large diesel generator. Piles of
research papers lay scattered throughout, mostly on
the damp floor, many tumbling over into useless jum-
bles. It was a crazed, chaotic parody of the genetics
department at S.T.A.R. Labs.

In a far corner lay a mattress, strewn with unkempt
bedding and surrounded by bundles of clothing and
half-eaten food.

As filthy as your average fraternity house, thought
Wally.

And there were newspapers scattered throughout.
Layers and layers of papers. Recent editions of Metropolis' *Daily Planet*, as well as the *Keystone City Clarion* and the *Central City Standard*. Today's *Clarion* lay
on top of the bed, the headline screaming: "Serial
Killer Strikes Eighteen."

But what held Wally's attention was the tall boxy
shape, extending from floor to ceiling, that sat domi-
nating the center of the makeshift lab. It was a metal
tank, welded and riveted, broken by a series of glass
portholes at eye level. Three conduits writhed out of
the top—or what was left of the top—and connected
to what looked to be an industrial air-conditioning
unit mounted to the wall behind.

The top, and a good part of the upper third of the
tank, was blown open, the heavy metal walls split and

curled as if some great internal pressure had torn them apart. Inside the tank, Wally could see the ruins of some tall, cylindrical apparatus, the top of which bloomed into a Medusa's nest of shiny silver piping.

It reminded him of the tall thing with a crown of conduits he had partially seen through the haze of frozen vapor in the chamber at the end of the corridor at the S.T.A.R. Labs.

The labs. He remembered the note pad with *Allen* scribbled across its last page.

Allen.

Wally lost focus for one instant and that nearly cost him his life.

He decelerated. Temporarily lost in his troubling thoughts, confident that he had secured the room, he slowed down, almost to normal time.

There was a burst of light and a sharp report from a dark corner beyond the tall tank. Almost immediately, Wally felt a stinging something push his shoulder back.

He jumped back up the acceleration ladder, cursing his ineptitude. The firing of the shot and the impact of the bullet had registered in his mind at almost the same time. He had slowed down that far without realizing it.

You damn well deserve to die, making a fool mistake like that!

Back up to far above bullet speed, Wally rushed the source of the shot on an elliptical course, in case there was another shell on the way. But there was none, and the face of the man in the dark corner registered a blind terror that suggested he was lucky to have steadied himself for the one shot.

Wally removed the semi-automatic pistol from the man's limp hand and, taking no chances now, made another, closer inspection of the room.

He found nothing more. This was the end of the road.

The frightened man was well past middle age, bald and pudgy and dressed in an unbuttoned oxford and slacks that had probably been neat and professorial once, but should have been discarded long ago. His most outstanding physical features were a pair of enormous sideburns that crawled like caterpillars from the bird's nest of fringe hair that still grew above his ears and around the back of his skull. His eyes bulged in fear behind a pair of broken, taped bifocals.

He was moist and pale.

Wally decelerated, cautiously this time. As he did, the man sprang to quivering, dripping life.

Whatever it was that terrified him, it wasn't Wally.

As the speedster resolved into clarity, removing the goggled headgear as he slowed, the man almost did a double take.

"F-Flash? You . . . you're the Flash . . ."

But he continued shaking, and as his surprise dropped away, the look of panic melted into one of total despair.

"It . . . it doesn't matter. It's over. It's all over. For me. For us all."

Wally, his shoulder beginning to ache, smiled agreeably.

"Dr. Upchurch, I presume?"

CHAPTER 7

Cryptobiogenesis

Linda peeled back a corner of the thick bandage taped over Wally's shoulder and made a disapproving face.

"You had this looked at by professionals? I could do a better job."

Wally shrugged without thinking, and was rewarded with a painful twinge in his wound. It was early evening and he had just managed to slip his worn, battered body into a comfortable T-shirt and jeans when Linda had arrived home, all wired by the news of the Flash's actions at the old Quaker Penitentiary and the subsequent series of explosions that had blown the facility to smithereens.

"Ouch." Wally exaggerated his grimace, playing a bit for sympathy. "Morillo and Chyre made me go with them to emergency at Sacred Heart. They know as well as you do that we metahumans heal real fast and clean, but I went into the pen with their knowl-

edge, and then everything blew up in there, and I
didn't want them getting into trouble. So I played by
the books."

"And I'd say good for you, except this is the most
candy-ass job of wrapping a gunshot wound I've ever
seen. I could do better . . . I fact, I *will*. Stay put—I'm
going to redo this."

"Jeez, Linda." Wally rolled his eyes. "It's just a scrape.
It cut clean through muscle, and not deep. I'm *fine*."

Linda did not respond and began removing the
bandage with all the delicate precision of a first-year
medical student. Wally would have enjoyed the attention more were it not for the embarrassing circumstance that led to it.

"A gunshot wound. God, Wally, when I imagine all
the terrible things you might run into, all the awful
things that could happen to you—I never think—a
gunshot . . ."

"Yeah. I'm officially embarrassed. It shouldn't have
happened."

That was an understatement.

"But, you know, the strange thing is, I keep thinking about the fact that only, like, half an hour before I
let this happen, I'm on the Moon playing Steal the
Bacon with Superman. I mean, does it get any weirder
than that? One minute I'm competing with—well, he's
practically a god—and the next . . . the next, I can
barely hold it together against an old, loony egghead
in a filthy basement. What the hell is wrong with me?"

Wally hadn't told her any more than was necessary.
He hadn't told her about the booby traps, the high-

caliber explosive shells raining down all around him, his blindness, the rats, and he certainly hadn't told her about his experience at the mercy of the *presence*.

Why frighten her with information about things that couldn't be controlled? She knew very well he was in a dangerous business. Why torture her with useless details? Why let her know that a handgun was the least of the dangers he faced?

Actually, Linda did know that guns rated pretty far down the list of things that might kill Wally. But, unlike all the unnamed, speculative dangers she understood might befall her husband, Linda knew very well what a gun could do.

"A damn gunshot . . ."

Wally felt her hand shaking as she began re-dressing the wound.

She was crying.

The iron doors clanged shut behind Wally with their usual note of finality. For as often as he had entered the KCPD's high-security holding tank, he didn't think he'd ever become accustomed to the awful dread that sound inspired in him.

Morillo, loaded with investigation notes and files, escorted him in. Chyre was waiting for them in the dimly lit hallway outside the secure area's interrogation room, casually examining the goggled headgear Wally had turned over after capturing Upchurch. A couple of FBI suits, accompanied by a Detective Jenkins from Homicide, stood nearby, glum and disapproving.

Wally had thought he might actually have a few

hours to recuperate, some time to reassure Linda, when the call had come and Morillo was once again requesting his presence.

So he'd whipped the scarlet back on, too fast to be anything but a blur to Linda, but awkwardly slow to him, what with the sore shoulder. Then she'd gamely replaced the bandage, strapped tight with adhesive tape, over the stitched skin on his deltoid.

She wasn't happy to see him go again so soon, but she was a super hero's wife.

She was a gamer.

Gulping a handful of painkillers, and promising Linda that this would be nothing, Wally was at police headquarters before she could finish smiling her acceptance.

One of the feds spoke up, with ill-diguised contempt: "We'll be watching."

He meant they'd be behind the one-way mirror, keeping suspicious eyes on Morillo, Chyre, and the Flash's interrogation session.

"Whatever, just mind your own business," Chyre spit back. "You screwed your chance, now let us get to the bottom of this." The big man looked at Wally and shook his head in disgust. "What you gonna do? These mopes can't make sense of Upchurch, but they sure as hell don't want to be shown up, either."

"I take it Upchurch isn't rolling over on the eighteen murders?"

"Twenty-two, Wally," Morillo spoke gravely. "Twenty-two murders. Four more have turned up through the day."

"The times . . . ?" Wally's heart was sinking.

"They look like they all occurred within that midnight block. I didn't mean to scare you—there's no evidence of any more recent attacks."

Wally was somewhat relieved to hear that.

"To answer your question," Morillo continued, "Upchurch isn't saying he and his mercenaries didn't commit the murders. But he's not specifically saying they did, either. All that's clear is that he feels guilty as hell about something. He's scared half to death of something else and keeps referring to his army as *guards*."

Wally felt a touch of concern for the men in the penitentiary he had outplayed. "The mercenaries— you got them all out before it blew?"

Chyre waved a hand in exasperation. "All that we could find. We hope we did. They apparently began rigging the place to go up as soon as we'd stumbled in on them and they'd taken out Martinez and Albers. They were not going to let it fall into our hands. The negotiations were apparently all about them buying time to sneak out through an underground tunnel. We don't know just how many made it."

Morillo continued: "The boys are running ID checks on all we've apprehended. One we got—a Jorge Patadillo—apparently he's the straw who's been stirring the drink. We're thinking Upchurch met him through Weapons at S.T.A.R. Labs. It's not clear just who exactly this joker works for, but what little we can assess places him as a real player on the international weapons dealing scene. And, I guess, a true be-

liever in whatever it is Upchurch's research was leading to. The brain trust here seems to think he's the
guy who recruited and organized the army around
Upchurch. They were protecting him while he *built*
something."

Wally considered Morillo's report. "That much
sounds about right, but I'm still telling you, they
didn't commit the murders."

Morillo nodded. "And Chyre and I are inclined to
agree with you, now."

"Listen," Chyre spoke, "he wants to talk with you.
I don't know, he seems to admire you—like maybe
you're everything he wishes he had in a test tube. So
maybe he trusts you. Let's get to the bottom of this,
okay?"

"Absolutely. Let's. Take me in."

In contrast to the gloomy hall, the interrogation
room was overlit with hissing fluorescent bulbs that
washed everything to a ghastly monochromatic pal-
lor. Wally didn't think there was a shadow left in the
room and wished for a second that he was still wearing those light-modulating goggles.

One of the bulbs was flickering slightly, lending an
unreal, staccato effect to the scene, like a very old motion picture. *If this was meant to unnerve the guilty mind,*
thought Wally, *then I must be guilty.*

Actually, his slightly accelerated mind was probably
more distracted by the hypnotic pattern than were those
of the others. In this light, Upchurch's grotesquely
bushy sideburns seemed to quiver with life.

The scientist sat bolt upright in a chair on the far

side of a heavy metal table, square in the middle of
the room. Next to the door, reading a newspaper, was
a uniformed officer on guard duty. He glanced up as
Chyre led the way in and the big detective motioned
him out. Wally noted the rectangular mirrored surface
covering the whole of one wall to the side and imagined many pairs of intensely interested eyes glaring
through.

There was a thermal canister of hot coffee placed in
the center of the table and a set of mugs. Upchurch
had not availed himself, so Morillo poured a cup and
offered it. The scientist ignored the gesture, his wet,
glittery eyes fixed on Wally. He was still shaking.

"It's the Flash I want to talk with. I'm sorry if I
seem uncooperative, but only he will understand."

"And that's why we asked him here, Dr. Upchurch.
But it's important that you feel comfortable with Detective Chyre and me, too."

The scientist didn't seem to be listening. He shifted
his gaze to the bandage over Wally's left shoulder.
"I'm sorry I shot you."

Wally decided that Upchurch was going to take
some careful handling. He turned to Chyre and gestured for the goggles device. Chyre tossed it to him
and he held it out toward Upchurch.

"This is a clever little device. I don't think I would
have got through your warren alive without it."

Upchurch nodded receptively, as if accepting a
compliment from a peer. "Of course. The lenses were
designed to augment the vision of a speedster, as well
as a normal. Tell me . . . in your accelerated state, were

your perceptions of rate shift slowed as viewed through the goggles?"

"I'm not sure what you . . ."

"Oh, of course not. What was I thinking? You wouldn't be watching yourself."

Seeing Wally's questioning look, Upchurch continued. "One of the properties specifically designed into the lenses was an augmentation of the eye's ability to process and analyze high-speed visuals. To slow the perception of speed."

Wally got the drift. "All the better to catch a speedster."

"Why, yes!" exclaimed Upchurch brightly, warming to the conversation. Then he hesitated. "But . . . but not *you*. We didn't expect *you*."

Chyre, Morillo, and Wally all exchanged quick looks. Wally did something he normally wouldn't have done with a civilian. He slid into a chair across from Upchurch.

"Well, Doc, I've got to tell you, I am impressed. I'd like to order one of these things for myself. In fact, you had lots of impressive gear in your prison—very clever booby traps, weapons—"

"Wait . . . *wait*. I created the strobe traps and the electrical surge crossguard, of course. They came out of my superspeed research. Only I'd know how to effectively set them. But the guns and such—I can't take credit for them. Oh, I paid for them, but Paul was responsible for obtaining the weapons.

"Paul?"

"George Paul. The man who approached me about continuing my work after I'd parted ways with the Labs."

Morillo pulled a sheaf of photos out of the pile of files he'd brought. He thumbed through several before selecting one, and scooted it across the table to Upchurch. "Is this George Paul?"

"Why, yes . . . but I never saw him without a mustache."

"Jorge Patadillo," Morillo informed Wally.

"So . . . um," Wally continued carefully, "all this equipment, all those men—you were afraid of something. You needed protection."

"Of course. Why else . . ."

"You needed protection from . . . the people who were going to steal your work?"

Upchurch shot an exasperated look. Wally was afraid he'd played it too cute, had lost Upchurch's trust, but the scientist answered. "Of course not. No one outside my circle even knows my work. I needed protection from the Superluminoid."

That pulled Wally up short. It was an unfamiliar term, but he understood the meaning perfectly, and the hairs on the back of his neck rose.

"The Superluminoid?"

Upchurch nodded. "Yes. The being who moves faster than the speed of light."

Wally licked his lips. "The Superluminoid was trying to . . . kill you?"

"Well, I didn't know. I mean, I wasn't sure what it was thinking. But I knew it *was* thinking, and I knew that didn't bode well for me, no matter what its plans." Upchurch spoke as if it was all very obvious.

Chyre broke in. "So, Doc—that's why you hired an army? To stop this Super . . . lunamoid?"

Upchurch sat stubbornly silent.

"Please. I'd like to know, too," Wally coaxed.

The scientist continued, eyes focused on the Scarlet Speedster. "Hiring all those men, I don't know why we did that. It was Paul's idea. He said he needed to protect me until I could come up with a solution—a way of containing it. He wanted it to be controlled or destroyed. And so did I. But, I think, for different reasons."

Upchurch seemed to loosen up again. "At first, when the Superluminoid hovered around, I thought there was a chance. I thought I had done something wonderful. Then, when things had gone bad and it had disappeared, that's when we started worrying and Paul convinced me to give him the money to build our defenses. And to try to find a solution."

Morillo and Chyre leaned across the table, fascinated, as the scientist rambled on. "I went along with Paul's plan, I tried my best, but I never really believed it would work, you see. I never really believed there was a solution. It's unstoppable. I'm doomed. We're all doomed. It can get me—can get anyone—whenever it likes. The biggest army with the best detection and the strongest antispeed weapons couldn't stop it. You convinced me of that, Flash. Even you beat our defenses, and the Superluminoid is much more powerful than you."

Well, thought Wally, *I barely beat your defenses*. "I know, Dr. Upchurch. I fought your Superluminoid. It nearly killed me."

Upchurch's jaw went slack. He sputtered, trying to frame his thoughts, as Wally continued. "I found it lurking at a murder scene. The top of a man's head had been removed . . ."

The scientist nearly burst with morbid curiosity. "One of the series of people killed yesterday? It has to be! And . . . and the manner of death . . . the top of the head removed? It was the same in all the cases? Please, the papers don't say . . ."

He was so excited he even pleaded with the detectives now. Wally let Morillo take the ball.

"All right, Dr. Upchurch—you've been forthcoming with us. We'll share. Yes, all victims had the crown of their skulls displaced with surgical precision. Furthermore, the brains were all removed and the cavities cauterized as if with intense, concentrated heat. All this apparently happened instantaneously; the victims certainly didn't have time to realize what hit them. Oh, and I'm guessing it'll come as no surprise to you that they all were metagene carriers."

Upchurch groaned. "Fascinating . . . I—I mean, it's terrible, of course . . ."

Morillo pressed. "So just so I'm certain, you're telling me you were unaware?"

Upchurch snorted impatiently. "You think I could be responsible for wounds such as those? You show me a tool, a technique, that could do the kind of work you describe."

"Sorry, Dr. Upchurch, but we have to be clear—this is all procedure."

Chyre interjected. "We didn't get a chance to see what tools you might've had at your disposal in the pen. All we got from the deal is this goggle thing . . ."

"That wasn't my fault. That was Paul's doing. I had no idea he had fixed the entire facility to explode."

"That's okay, Dr. Upchurch. We're just trying to understand something that, from our perspective, is very difficult to understand." Morillo's tone was mollifying, but Wally could see Upchurch again growing defensive.

"Doc, the detectives are just doing what needs to be done. People are dead. They need to know if the killing is at an end or not."

The scientist slowly, firmly shook his head. "No, it's not over."

"Why?"

"Because, its trying to reproduce. It doesn't know how yet, but it will keep trying until it learns."

"Dr. Metz, at the labs, thought that, too. Why?"

"Metz? You know Samuel Metz?" Upchurch practically snarled. "Let me tell you, Metz is not so insightful. Any creature's first priority is to perpetuate itself. But I stood face-to-face with the thing. After it exploded out of the incubator, it lingered. I could see it growing, absorbing experiential data at an incredible rate. Even its growth was accelerated, something I hadn't anticipated."

Upchurch was rolling now. "It got into my mind and took what it could. It has great plans for itself, for its offspring. It has every intention of reproducing and that is not good for us. It has no respect for humans. No use. It has a great hatred within it. It will destroy us, and its progeny will inherit the planet. Surely, Flash, you saw that, too."

Wally sat silent for a moment, taken aback by the perverse excitement that flushed Upchurch's face and momentarily seemed to overcome his fear.

"I saw that it was stronger than me," the Scarlet Speedster replied. "Faster, too. And curious. About *me*. It could have killed me at any time, but it wanted—maybe it's like you said: It got in my mind and took what it could."

Upchurch looked at Wally with even more interest shining in his eyes. Like he had just realized something very intriguing. "Of course. You may be of interest to it. It may see the *relation*."

"Sure, it could see I'm another speedster . . ."

"No, no. Something else entirely. Well, not entirely," Upchurch seemed to consider his next words very carefully. "All right. Listen. I *will* tell you. I don't think you'll understand, but I will tell you."

The scientist sat still for a moment, his gaze turned downward, collecting his thoughts.

"If you talked with Samuel Metz, you must know that the S.T.A.R. Labs and I parted ways last year after more than five years of collaboration. The reason, I'm sure, he gave you was that the labs had ethical problems with my speedster-generation program. Well, that's hogwash. The directors of the labs were very happy with my research. My research was very promising. They were getting exactly what they wanted. *But* . . . there are many who do have moral questions concerning gene engineering and, for whatever corporate group-think reason, the directors decided they did not want the company name directly associated with my program. Maybe they think the public's unease with metahumans in general does not bode well for an acceptance of the purposeful creation of new ones, I don't know."

Upchurch began emphatically jabbing his finger in the air. "Regardless, they cut me loose. They canceled the speedster program and my contract. And that was that, I thought. But a week later George Paul, who I'd seen on occasion at the labs—mostly with the Weapons R and D director—approaches me with a scheme to keep the program going. Independently.

"Well, of course, I tell him I don't have the kind of money necessary to fund my research." The scientist grew even more animated. "But he says, 'Oh, I bet you've got more royalty money coming to you than you think,' and then, sure enough, out of the blue, here they come—huge royalty checks. More money than you'd ever believe, into a bank account Paul set up for me, all very secretively. Now, I'm not a sophisticated man when it comes to corporate intrigue, but I'm not stupid, either. It was pretty clear to me that the Labs wanted the project to continue. They just wanted a wall between it and their name."

Upchurch sighed. "I know I should have, but I didn't question Paul. I just wanted the chance to continue the program. I was so close, God help me. So I tell Paul what I need and he takes care it. All of it. The facility, the apparatus, independent electrical power . . . whatever I needed. I'd just make a withdrawal and he'd take care of it from there. The most important factor, however, was one that couldn't be bought. When the Labs had told me that the program was over, that I was out, I'd had the foresight to collect and spirit out the single most valuable element associated with my research."

He glanced at Wally. *Nervously,* the speedster thought.

"A DNA sample. The DNA of a metagene donor that held particular promise."

Allen. The name on the list in the Genetics department at the labs. The name without a matching vial. Allen.

Now the agitated zeal appeared to be draining from Upchurch. "It delivered on that promise, I'm sorry to say. With the facility set up to my specifications, with Paul taking care of all physical requirements, I was able to submerge myself completely in the program again. The quest to bio-engineer a new speedster."

"Why?" Wally couldn't help himself.

Upchurch looked at him absently, abstractly, as if the answer he was about to give was so self-evident that it didn't bear careful consideration.

"Because I want to understand. Because I couldn't very well go asking you, or any of your fellows, to submit to—*dissection*, could I? You're extraordinary beings. You shouldn't be able to do what you physically and mentally do. We need to know why. We need to understand, but none of you have ever been particularly cooperative."

With good reason, apparently. Wally did his best to suppress a shudder of disgust, but Upchurch seemed to notice a change in Wally's attitude.

"I'd hoped you would understand. There's so much we could learn from you . . ."

Wally regrouped. "Doc, I'm trying to understand. Believe me, I don't know what I'd do without my speed. But I need to hear the rest of your story."

All of the zealot's fire had gone out of Upchurch's eyes. "I suppose it doesn't make much difference at this point. There's not much more to tell. Nothing that anyone who wasn't a genetic engineer would care to sit through."

"The short version, then." Wally tried to sound agreeable.

The scientist shrugged. "I went back to work. I picked up where my research at S.T.A.R. had stopped. For six months, nonstop. Paul saw to everything I needed, I don't think I left that basement more than a dozen times. It's mostly guesswork, and process of elimination, of course. Matching the right metagene sequence with an effective primordial bath and the appropriate irradiation and voltage levels. It's not the sort of thing where you crawl closer and closer to success. No, at that point you know all the billions and billions of pieces. You just have to make them come together correctly—all at once."

A note of fear crept back into Upchurch's voice, as if in reaction to his hubris. "Well, I did it—I'm very

good, you know. I *did* it. Three months ago I finally
had a DNA sequence incorporating an aggressive,
dominant metagene, replicating in the Oparin-
Haldane apparatus. I transferred the seed to the incu-
bation tower, and for two days observed limited
growth.

"On the third day," the scientist paused to run a
damp hand over his now shiny face, "on the third
day, I was resting on the bed—I'd been monitoring
the situation for over twenty-four hours straight—and
I hear this *hissing*. The hissing woke me—it was very
odd. I see the incubator monitors are fluctuating
wildly—impossible readings—and this hissing, and
the heat, and the coolant tank is *swelling*. I swear it,
the top half of the steel coolant tank is swelling like a
balloon. Then . . . rivets start popping. The heat is incredible, it's like a *sun*. The air is all sticky. I can
hardly breathe—I can't *move*. I'm forced down into
the mattress like a great atmospheric pressure is
crushing me. My head is about to explode and all the
hissing has turned into a wash of—of *static* filling my
head. And then the incubator expands and twists and
the tower explodes in this great surge of *life*. You saw
the damage, Flash."

Wally noted that Upchurch was now trembling
fiercely and his eyes were bulging with terror, but the
scientist kept on with his tale. "And then it was before
me, observing me, so intelligent—already analytical
and curious and capable of absorbing all it could use
from my mind. I had not anticipated the rapidly accelerating development. I'd failed to predict that. It

sprang into being with the speed and fury of a new universe exploding from collapsing dimensions. It's birth was a little Big Bang. It was so—*inhuman.*"

The quivering scientist shook his head in wonder. "Who could have foreseen this? I was using human DNA, I expected a human result. An embryonic, human development. But not this, not a *monster.* I can't even begin to theorize why. The metagene is much more complex than we'd supposed."

Upchurch paused again and Wally, seething with a thousand questions, couldn't resist interrupting. "Why do you call it the 'Superluminoid'? How did you determine it was faster than light?"

A perplexed surprise twisted Upchurch's face. "I— I'm not sure. I guess . . . I just knew. I just saw enough of its mind to understand. I had no opportunity to conduct tests. I have no data to show you. But there were—*distortions* while it lingered with me. Time and space were no longer the constants as we perceive them. Even though my senses told me that the Superluminoid was there before me, in an undisrupted continuity of time, what I saw in its mind, as it searched through mine, was an endless series of countless *other* spacial reference points. It was jumping throughout our universe, exploring its new world with reckless abandon, effortlessly throwing itself across vast stretches of space, and returning so quickly my senses registered no absence. It was like it never left, but it was coming and going all the time. I don't believe it moves like you, or like any other speedster. He jumps—his moves are based on a pattern of jumps.

Patterns, you know, are the only things we know that can move faster than light."

Wally nodded. Upchurch's words put solidity to the chaotic impressions he'd received in his encounter with the thing. He believed the scientist's intuitive leap was accurate.

"I felt the same, Doc. But tell me, if it wants to reproduce—if it wants more like itself—why murder metagene carriers? Why lop off the top of their skulls and burn out their brains?"

Wally thought he could actually see Upchurch curling up, shrinking, as the scientist was forced to confront the enormity of the horror he'd unleashed. But he responded.

"I think it's the pineal it wants. And that—that information he got from me. Oh, God, that he got from *me*." Uphurch almost wailed. "He looked into my mind for his origin. He saw the procedures. He saw my impression of the DNA from which he was created. Now he's looking for that."

"But why the pineal, Doc?" Wally vaguely realized that his head had begun to ache. His shoulder, too. And his joints.

"Because that was what *I* always wanted! The pineal controls the growth of the metagene! It is the deciding factor in whether or not the metagene is activated. And it controls in which direction metapowers will develop! The pineal of a living metahuman would have meant so much to my work—it would have allowed me so much more understanding and control over the growth of my speedster! But . . . you can't just take a pineal body from someone. It's buried deep in the brain. You can't even biopsy one. Human life, however, means nothing to the Superluminoid. To it, we are simply sources of the raw material of life. It looked in my mind and saw that the pineal represented the greatest possibility of success. It saw my imagined collection of pineals and now it has begun harvesting the pineals of metagene carriers in the most efficient manner at its disposal, using it's unique powers."

The Doctor of Metagenics had now collapsed into an abject, quaking wreck. "Oh, God, when I saw the papers this morning . . . I suspected, I feared it had begun! After its birth, after it had lingered and searched my brain, it disappeared. For three months, nothing. I could sometimes feel its presence, almost as an afterthought. I suspect it was there and gone long before my conscious mind could sense it. It was keeping an eye on me, but it offered no contact. Three months must be an eternity to the Superluminoid. What did it learn, where did it travel, what did it decide in those three months? I had hoped it had lost interest in us. Paul feared otherwise, and now I know he was correct."

Wally felt sick, and it wasn't due entirely to Upchurch's revelations. He felt like the air was being squeezed out of the room at the same time that a low-pressure system was closing down the atmosphere. Inside his now throbbing head he felt a distant buzzing, but he stoically continued the interrogation. "How many more pineals does it need to collect before it's got enough?"

"No, no! It isn't *stockpiling* pineals! It's looking for the *one* pineal! The pineal carrying the metagene from which it developed! Its parent!"

Why, thought Wally, *why do I feel like my chest is going to cave in? Why is Upchurch screeching?*

"It will keep looking, and killing, until it finds the donor who provided the DNA that was its root stock!"

Morillo, who had been silently fitting Upchurch's words to what Wally had told him of his encounter with the Superluminoid, finally spoke. "Since the Flash had his encounter with your thing, we've seen no new attacks. No killing sprees since then. Is that a coincidence?"

Upchurch, teetering on the edge of panic, still managed to turn an appraising eye on Wally. "I don't think so. Earlier I mentioned that I thought the Superluminoid might have seen a relationship between itself and the Flash. I think it may see the Flash as a *connection*—as someone who will lead him to the donor. Up until it met him, it was harvesting at random. In the Flash, it saw something that was much closer to what it's after. Not exactly what it wants, but a trail it can follow. I think it is waiting for the Flash to lead it to its parent."

Through the cloud of bewildering static that was rapidly growing in his brain, Wally felt a strange combination of both anxiety and relief. What Upchurch said made sense, he thought, recalling *Allen*, and the missing vial at the labs.

"Then I guess the thing will be following me forever. Barry's long dead and gone."

Why do I feel so lousy?

"Barry? I'm sorry, I don't . . ." Upchurch was plainly confused by the reference.

Wally felt a twinge of doubt.

"The DNA sample you used to grow the Super-luminoid. Back at S.T.A.R. Labs I saw a listing for Allen. The vial was gone . . . but it was Barry Allen, right? Tell me the truth—the DNA you used to create this monster was Barry Allen's?"

The doctor looked aghast. "No, you're mistaken. The donor was an *Iris* Allen."

Wally's heart thudded into his stomach. Panic swept over him like a fever.

No, no. Please, not Iris . . .

Then the bottom of the world fell out and hell boiled over. Pain lanced into his skull like a lightning bolt and Wally instantly knew why. While Morillo and Chyre stared at the pale, anxious Upchurch blankly, insensible to the coming storm, Wally's mind, still running well above idle, finally understood his discomfort. He remembered the attack in Kevin Schull's house, he remembered the signs, the unease, the aura, the pain.

The Superluminoid was coming.

And there was very little he could do. Although he now might have a idea of where the thing came from, he still didn't know what it was. He still didn't know how to counter it. Wally plied his trade in a place where milliseconds were equal to hours and leaden seconds could be eternities. The Superluminoid came from somewhere beyond that.

It had been watching. From where, Wally did not know. But it had been watching and waiting and now it had decided it was time to move. It was coming in fast, and all Wally could do was accelerate as rapidly and as far as possible.

Why now? Why now?

Suddenly, it was in the room. Wally, aided by adrenaline and raw fear, had accomplished an incredible rush to Mach 500 by the time it appeared. Still, he could not see how it arrived, it moved so much faster. It simply blinked into a blurred, multiple exposure existence and regarded Wally balefully from across the petrified room.

As before, it appeared physically undefinable to Wally. It was a throbbing void of malignancy wrapped in a hulking, constantly distending caricature of human shape. It was here and it wasn't and it was here again, all chaos and indecipherable alien intent. The first time he had met the presence, Wally's fear had been cut by ignorance. His curiosity had not been tempered by knowledge of its incomparable power.

Now, Wally's mind was electrified by nothing but horror. He knew he was powerless and that the thing wanted Iris.

The thing has come for the source of its genetic structure. I am expected to lead it to Iris.

It was communicating its will.

With Wally.

It said nothing, but somehow Wally clearly understood: *I have been patient, but I am running out of patience.*

There was no bravado in that simple statement, no bullying, no taunting. It was a declaration of fact, cloaked in nothing more than the oppressive radiation of menace that was part and parcel of the Superluminoid.

Nonetheless, Wally completely understood that this was an ultimatum of sorts.

The Scarlet Speedster lunged, even though he knew it was a hopeless gesture. He did not have the space or time necessary to generate a speed that came even close to that of which he knew his nemesis was capable. The Superluminoid shifted and Wally missed, barely pulling up and cornering before he slammed through a wall.

If he could lure it outside, he might at least be able to maneuver, but he knew it didn't want to leave this room.

Wally wheeled, and there it was, hovering over the frozen form of Upchurch. Its message, however, was still directed at Wally.

He has served his purpose.

He no longer is an asset.

It then descended upon Upchurch, settling over the doomed scientist like a plague cloud. Wally watched in horror as the unaware man melted and blackened to an ember, then faded to a cinder. Wally knew instinctively that an incredible burst of heat had to have accompanied that surge of destructive power. Solar hot, but very localized, judging from the results he'd seen at the murder scenes. If not, Morillo and Chyre would have been fried, too.

Helpless rage choked Wally as he leapt forward again. To no avail; the monster neatly sidestepped him.

He threatens me, he kills my charges, and I'm too slow.

Then it was gone from the room but, judging by the continued psychic pain, Wally knew it was still nearby. Then the Scarlet Speedster had a terrible notion. He raced out of the room and down the hall of the secure area, to where the rows and rows of holding cells were crowded with the thirty-nine mercenaries waiting to be processed.

Again, too late. The cells were empty, save for the lumps of ash and cinder covering their floors. The guards, the homicide investigators, the feds—they all stood untouched and blissfully ignorant of the angel of death that had moved past them. But every man from the army formed by Upchurch and Patadillo was reduced to ash.

Desperate despair.

Sickening rage.

This was meant for me! Wally's mind screamed in its agony of futility.

He quickly searched the rest of police headquarters, but found no other casualties and no sign of the Superluminoid. It had made its point and left. It had targeted those that had accompanied Upchurch at its birth and, determining them to be more detriment than benefit, had made an example before Wally.

Show me to my genetic source, it had said. *Or else.*

It was gone. The atmospheric pressure, the stabbing pain, the nausea, and the infernal static had all disappeared with it, leaving Wally feeling nothing but hollow and defeated.

Worthless.

Or else I will reduce your people to charred ruins.

Back in the interrogation room, the one-way mirror, bulging inward, was just beginning to show a spider-web of cracks, the inevitable result of the power unleashed nanoseconds earlier. The fluorescent bulbs were stressing too, but they weren't so much a hazard as the shattering mirror would be to the men behind it.

Keep your head in the game, Wally. There are people here who still need you.

Resolving himself to damage control, Wally carefully moved the three feds and two homicide detectives out of the observation room and into the hallway. It was a more sensible action than trying to collect all those deadly pieces of fracturing glass. By the time he was done relocating the men, still holding their expressions of focused contempt, the mirror had indeed begun to fragment.

Chyre and Morillo, too, needed moving to be perfectly safe, and Wally was in no mood to witness any more misfortune, great or small. He slid their chairs away from the table, where they sat under the fluorescents.

As almost an afterthought, he moved the table to completely umbrella the pile of carbon that had been Upchurch.

He figured Homicide would be pleased if the remains were not contaminated by the falling glass.

Wally glanced around one more time to make sure he wasn't missing anything.

It was the goddamn least he could do.

Maybe the *only* thing.

Then he gulped two deep breaths and gave up the exclusivity of his accelerated world, sliding back down the ladder to normal time.

The stench of brimstone came in a rush.

The mirrored window blew into the observation room with a terrific crash. The fluorescent bulbs all exploded with dull, synchronized pops, spraying tiny bits of glass. Morillo and Chyre cranked back to life, like a couple of wind-up toys released. They both shot out of their chairs, jerking their heads about in stupefied confusion, unable to absorb the chaos that, for them, had exploded out of nowhere and in no time.

A recessed emergency light flickered on, casting the room in lurid red. Chyre reached for the automatic in his shoulder harness, then caught sight of Wally, now standing across the room, slumped and haunted looking. The detective let loose with a string of curses, and then, "What the *hell*? Where'd Upchurch go?"

Morillo had guessed by then. "Wally . . . don't tell me . . ."

Wally gave a jerky nod. He was trying very hard to calm his frenzied brain, to lower his reactions and thoughts to normal time.

Outside in the hall, there were more curses. The Homicide detectives and their guests were in a panicked rage.

But Wally wasn't listening, because suddenly, he

had a call, coming from that place inside his inner ear. *Wally—let me in, Wally . . .*

It was the Manhunter.

Wally realized—the other shoe was dropping.

As he'd been trained, he opened the little circuit in his brain that allowed for telepathic communication.

Go ahead, Manhunter.

The tone was urgent. *We've got big trouble, Wally. I suspect you are experiencing a related situation, but if there's any way you can respond . . .*

Wally didn't have to consider.

It's too late here. Give me a few minutes and I'll join you.

He turned to Morillo and Chyre, who had discovered the shrunken lump of charred carbon under the table.

"Listen up, guys, because this is going to have to be fast . . ."

CHAPTER 8

Cosmology

Superman materialized at a point in the atmosphere approximately five miles above latitude, seven degrees south, longitude, seventy-two degrees east. Through the thin, wispy layer of clouds below, he should have been able to see Diego Garcia, or at least some of the islands of the Chagos Archipelago, glistening like strings of pearls against the deep blue of the Indian Ocean. Instead, a filthy green-gray membrane of roiling opacity seethed ponderously from misty horizon to misty horizon, cloaking all beneath it.

The Watchtower's sensors and the panicked reports from the vast stretch of Indian Ocean affected had been accurate. This unheralded phenomenon, this global affliction that had manifested itself in the blink of an eye, covered literally hundreds of thousands of square miles of sea and island, wreaking who knew what havoc on the life now engulfed by it.

And it sure looked like it was alive—a living biomass the size of a moon, filling up the middle of the Indian Ocean and quite possibly extending deep into the Earth itself.

Superman shook his head in disbelief. He'd seen probably more sanity-challenging circumstances than any other inhabitant of the planet Earth. This was right there at the top of the list.

Tightening an alien muscle attached to his brain's frontal lobe, he refocused, and the lenses of his eyes magnified the shapeless behemoth one hundred times. Simultaneously, he jackknifed his body from the hovering position in which he'd arrived into a full power dive, pointed straight down. Arms fully extended for maximum streamlining, the Man of Steel plummeted, his eyes all the while fixed on the telescoped image rapidly growing before them. He figured he had one second before impact.

In that moment, he formed a clearer impression of the thing: Its base substance, on approach, was more translucent than he'd initially thought—layers and layers of depth were revealed within. It must tower at least two miles above sea level. And there were gigantic *shapes* floating and crawling and spasming within it.

Superman thought they might be organs, although some of them seemed weirdly geometric.

There were veins of fire—possibly energy impulses—writhing erratically between the variegated shapes. Growing closer, he realized that everything—the entirety—was quaking and heaving. Almost, it seemed, *sobbing*.

Closer still, and he placed the thing's substance at

denser than water, but less so than petroleum. It didn't exactly correlate with any material he'd ever encountered. In fact, the effort required to focus on it had started a sick pain curdling in his skull and that reminded him all too well of his experience with yesterday's fireballs, and the fragment.

Superman absorbed all this in the split second it took him to rocket down upon the monstrosity.

At the last instant, he decided to go straight in.

It was a considered risk, entering unknown matter, but one he was more than willing to take, considering the enormity of the catastrophe at hand. He didn't spend time convincing himself of the need, nor did he have to pump himself for battle.

There were lives at stake—both human and ecological welfare was threatened—and he was uniquely equipped to do something about it.

This was why Superman existed. This was his calling.

That was why all the others in the JLA looked to him.

I'm going in, he calmly broadcasted through the Manhunter's psychic link.

The Martian Manhunter, Wonder Woman, and the Green Lantern were nearby. Superman didn't know exactly where, but they had all been on hand when the alarms had sounded, when the unbelievable reports had tumbled over the outerband and into the Watchtower. They had all made teleportation jumps with the Man of Steel, falling down from the Moon to independent, various locations above the oceanic horror. They were all doing observations and analysis from their own perspectives. When any acted, when any had something to report, he or she would call out on the link.

But it was Superman who led the way. He sliced cleanly into the substance of the thing. There was hardly any resistance, the thin fluidity of what looked like milky jelly seemed to pull away from him, as if recoiling in terror.

Not unlike the fragment had behaved.

A prickly tingling, like a constant electric shock, ran the length of his nervous system, but other than that conditions were tolerable. He had filled his mighty lungs to their tops with air before entering the phenomenon's corpus; that would last him a good hour or so, pending any undue exertion or excessive atmospheric pressure. More than enough time to locate any humans here. Hopefully enough to get them out, if any still survived in this alien environment.

Superman sped through the blurry green twilight within the gargantuan organism, unimpeded by the viscous jelly that seemed to represent the vast majority of its bulk. The weirdly shaped bodies of denser matter he passed shook and jumped erratically, as if with seizures. He thought that if these were organs within the protoplasmic body of a vast amoeba, then something was terribly wrong with the thing. Although he couldn't have the slightest clue as to what passed for normal in such a beast, he couldn't believe that the palsied contortions indicated healthy functions.

Suddenly, a phalanx of bodies, all spherical and pale, all of a kind, swam out of the emerald murk. Unlike the other quaking organs, these moved with a definite, angry purpose. Their focus was Superman, and as they came, they spat glowing blobs of fiery energy at him.

Like antibodies, thought Superman. Organisms designed to destroy invaders compromising the cell.

Something like that.

The first of the barrage of energy packets broke against the Man of Steel with a weblike discharge of flickering lightning, and an impact that knocked him careening off course. His limbs went dead and numb for the briefest of moments, the defending body's weaponry apparently targeting his nervous system.

Superman fought to regain control and began a dodge as the second blob grazed him, exploding against a leg and spreading another wave of icy cold paralysis through his body. Jerking his head around, he summoned his own fire from its storage center suspended in his eyeballs' liquid cores. Concentrated and modified by his multifaceted lenses, the internally generated energy shot out of his squinting eyes in twin beams of intensely focused heat. Scything the beams across the field of battle, the Kryptonian cut through the closest attacking organs, rupturing their integrity, collapsing a dozen or so like torn balloons.

This did not sit well with him, the taking of life in any form, but the well-being of creatures he had sworn to protect was endangered and there was little time.

Hundreds more of the ivory spheres rushed in and hurled their bundles of numbing fire, but the defenders had missed their opportunity. They had lost the element of surprise without incapacitating Superman, whose agile mind and incomparable willpower had quickly recovered, forcing an evasive course of action upon his stunned nerves.

As fast as they were, he was faster.

Superman thought that the pale organs' attacks seemed uncoordinated, erratic—another sign that something was not well within the beast. If he was accurate in drawing a comparison to cellular antibodies then, he reasoned, there should be a hell of a lot more of these spheres responding to his intrusion. There should be millions swarming him under in a quick, lethal, and coordinated frenzy.

If they had kept their attacks coming relentlessly, he'd have had no choice but to retreat.

This effort, from a life-form so huge, seemed pathetic.

Now that he had their meter, now that he felt the rhythm of their attack, they were easy to avoid and outdistance, even though more and more continued to rush out of the gray-green nothingness and toward him as he corkscrewed and weaved deep into his host.

Suddenly he was wet, cutting through sea water. The protoplasmic material of the organism still surrounded him as well, its bulk extended below the surface of the ocean, mingling with the water. Superman quickly altered his course, angling up. He suspected the waters weren't deep here and he couldn't waste time burrowing through rock. He broke the surface without a sound or splash, as the all-pervasive alien substance seemed to deaden all energy.

Zigzagging low above the surface of the leaden waters, he suddenly caught sight of a ghostly configuration rising through the murk—stable, rigid forms. Redirecting his course toward them, he found himself above his destination: the American naval base on Diego Garcia.

The shapes had been the ships at anchor in the tiny island's harbor. Superman quickly counted a carrier, three cruisers, five frigates, and maybe ten to twelve supply and refueling vessels. Dry docks and cranes and the collection of simple concrete boxes that represented the base itself rose up beyond them.

Then, as he swooped into the midst of this technological oasis set weirdly against a protoplasmic universe, his eyes set on what he most feared.

Men and women, most of them in naval uniform, lay sprawled and unmoving on the decks and the docks and in the streets.

Activating his X-ray vision, he determined it was too late for them.

But maybe not for others. Without hesitation, he began searching the structures for survivors.

Wonder Woman appeared above the otherworldly biomass two hundred miles to the north and east of Superman's arrival point.

She, like Superman and the Manhunter, had been

in council at the Watchtower when this latest anomaly had popped into existence. She had the same scanty information as they, but whereas Superman had needed to make reasoned assumptions as to the nature of the phenomenon based on his observations, she intuited instantly that this was a living being.

This realization in itself made her queasy. The fact that her empathetic psyche detected absolutely no hostility radiating from the creature made things worse.

This was not an attack, she knew. She didn't think the thing chose to be here—in fact, Diana detected a note of fear. The situation was suddenly stickier than it first appeared.

Flattening her lithe, impossibly beautiful body into a glide, the Amazon angled down toward the green-gray mass, leveling off in an exploratory flight path about five thousand feet above the burbling, ever-changing surface. Part of it looked definitely akin to animal structure—much of what she saw reminded her of massive fungal growths from far on the distant shore of Styx. But she was sure it was not the product of myth and magic. Like the other undefinable phenomena, this was somehow part of the world governed by physics and logic.

This was not going to be easy. She knew there was a chance that humans caught within the creature might still be alive, but getting them out without further harming the thing presented a problem.

And the effort it took to focus on it made her head hurt.

She considered the probability that contact with the

alien matter might not be healthy for either the creature or herself.

I'm going in.

Superman. Over the Manhunter's link.

He didn't realize. How could he? He was no intuitive.

He was placing himself in terrible danger and Diana knew why. For Kal-El, the preservation of any human life was paramount. She knew that he was thinking that if there was anyone alive in there, their time was short.

"By Hera's golden stags!" she cursed, "if only he'd talk with me!"

Men would be the death of her.

Wonder Woman shook her head and dived. Whatever plan of action she would have decided on no longer mattered. Her course had been set by her headstrong teammate. She would not allow a fellow warrior to go into danger ignorant and alone.

Superman! she screamed her mind at him. *Your position?*

There was no reply.

Following Superman, she alerted the team in general.

Despite the revulsion she felt at the thought of violating the frightened creature, she plunged through the skin. The viscous plasm within recoiled, leaving her feeling like an unwelcome aggressor. Strange organs pulsed and spasmed in the the crepuscular green jelly that trembled before her. A line of pale, globular bodies seemed to attend to her presence, hesitate, and then fall away.

A persistent, annoying shock strummed on her nerves . . .

And her lasso—Hestia's Golden Lasso of Truth—suddenly burned against her right thigh.

She tried calling again for Superman.

No reply.

In fact, there was no response from any of the League. She began to suspect that the Manhunter's telepathic power could not penetrate the creature.

The fire in the lasso seemed to grow until its touch was an agony. Something was not right—there was something that needed to be addressed, the Lasso of Truth was alerting her.

Wonder Woman slowed her advance and unfastened the magic rope. Its fierce amber radiance grew brighter, casting a piercing light through the chloranemic depths. Once it was off her hip it no longer burned, and Diana, as skilled with the ways of the divine as she was with those of warfare, uncoiled it, allowing its luminous golden loops to extend and snake deep into protoplasmic oblivion.

The lasso did its job well. It *linked* Diana with the organism. She saw, or more accurately, intuited something of the truth.

She saw a different world. A different universe. A place outside the bubble of space, time, and multiplatformed dimensions humans and Olympians and Kryptonians and Apokoliptians and Oaans and the brain-stromatalites of Jityagkos Khel call "our universe." Someplace entirely outside our bubble.

She felt, she understood, that the biomass surrounding her was just a torn fragment of a greater living whole from that different place. There was no time and space in that other state, just one universe-filling, seething, growing, dying, feeding colony biomass that did not exactly think, but was content in its universe-filling sense of belonging and propriety.

Then, all that wonderful contentment and balance and perfect equanimity was gone in one terrible, cosmically violent instant as space/time imposed itself where it had never before existed. So violent was the act that the world ceased to exist, and some tiny portions of the universal life were torn and fragmented and dragged into—someplace else.

Someplace washed with terrible radiations and searing chemicals and so much pain and loneliness, and where was the rest of everything and where, and where, and *where, where, where?* So isolated, so empty, and so much cold nothing . . . *pain, pain, pain. . . .*

Through an enormous act of will, Diana shook herself loose from the emotional link with the tortured, dying creature. Almost beside herself with anger and sadness and pity for the fate of the strange and magnificent cosmos creature, of which this mass might represent the last, convulsing bit, she steeled herself to her duty and drove on again. Her lasso, having completed its task, was now cool and acquiescent in her grasp.

The last thing she had seen while under the lasso's spell was Superman, embattled and desperate.

As soon as he had materialized at his position along the northern fringes of the impossibly huge anomaly, the Martian Manhunter realized that he could establish a telepathic link of sorts with the thing. His scanning mind had immediately determined that it was a living creature and an overwhelmingly powerful broadcaster.

He wasn't so sure that the League link he effortlessly maintained between the team would stay clear in the midst of all its subpsychic noise. This, of course, worried him greatly. They were facing a total unknown and he didn't like the odds increased against them.

The Manhunter took quick stock of the situation. The Addu Atoll, the southernmost island group of the Maldives, should be swimming beneath him, just a scant degree south of the equator. But all he could see were coiling, whipping fronds of gray-green chaos, like a hurricane of tenuous, ghostly tissue. His eyes traveled to the horizon, and there to the north, obscured by oceanic haze, he could see the great uneven rim of the mass, with its gigantic tentacles and tubercles and cilia frantically waving at the sky.

To the south and west, it seemed to go on forever, its restless appearance altering every so often, as geographic features changed over the breadth of a continent.

J'onn J'onzz, a fascinated student of life in all its varieties and vagaries, placed this monster as, more correctly, a *them.* An aggregate of symbiotic organisms, each fulfilling a necessary function in the life of the whole.

A colony organism.

A super Portuguese man-of-war.

Or, maybe more accurately, an animal cell.

Or a fungal mass.

The Manhunter admitted he was stretching comparisons. The truth was, this represented something else altogether. Something for which there were no words, something on which it hurt to keep focus.

There is a certain similarity to the fragment, he mused.

I'm going in. It was Superman's measured, decisive tone. This didn't surprise the Manhunter. Superman generally did take point, that was his unwritten station. He was not going to spare even a second to analysis when lives were at stake.

But someone was going to have to figure the beast and the bigger picture. Things had gone too far.

Superman! Your position?

Of course: Diana.

Following Superman.

The League's strategic mastermind was maybe not always so tactically sound when she allowed herself to follow Superman's aggressive leads. Now half the team was committed.

He could abandon it all to fate and follow, blindly trusting that they'd learn what was needed to survive while on the hoof—

—He loved that allusion to earthly ungulates—

—Or he could hold back a moment and try to communicate with the biomass before committing.

Of course, he opted for the latter. The strength of the League lay in the diversity of their personalities as much as in their powers.

Telepathic contact and communication with such a powerful broadbander was not going to be easy. There was going to be a lot of mind-tearing noise to filter through in an attempt to locate and focus on the channel that could tell him something useful—and he knew he didn't have much time.

The Manhunter grit his teeth and steeled his mind against the psychic discomfort for which he knew he was headed and opened the receptors in his Martian brain.

The impact was immediate and overwhelming. He felt as if his mind as well as his skull were being whipped in circles by tornadoes of excruciatingly potent psychic power, none of which made any sense to him. None of which *communicated*.

Relentlessly, the Martian slogged through the various signals—some of which felt like the telepathic equivalent of his teeth being pulled down a blackboard—separating them out from one another, searching, searching for the one that spoke to him in impressions that crossed the gulf between alien consciousnesses.

With computerlike speed and precision, his telepathic centers filtered through the thousands of conflicting signals. Quickly, a path through the riot of conceptual static was determined, a sort of trail to the most likely of compatible signals. His mind raced against the pain, the awful, grinding babble, and then he had found it.

A clear signal.

One that made a kind of sense.

The Manhunter shut all else out as quickly as possible and gave complete attention to an interpretation of the confused, garbled impressions.

It was not intelligent, in any sense that the Martian recognized, but it did have a concept of self. It was very aware of *self*. It did not seem to have a concept for *other*.

It was everything, it was the universe. Unchanging, eternal.

Then something beyond comprehension had occurred. Something for which there were no impressions, no previous experiences. Everything that *was*, ended.

Except for this, whatever *this* was. Before, everything was right. Now, there was *this*.

The Manhunter understood that *this* meant Earth. Our reality. The biomass that lay before him was a living bit of an organic alternate universe that had somehow survived the annihilation of its *self* and been flung to Earth.

Picking through the pain and confusion, the Martian formed an image of its predicament. The majority of its mass was buried in the Earth, or rather was *interwoven* with the Earth in some primitive, protomaterial manner. Atoms and molecules did not seem to apply here. This event occurred on a far more primal level.

It was locked into the unbearable harshness of rock and the burning molten mantle beneath. The tiny fraction of the organism that the Manhunter could see suffered, as well, exposed to saltwater and atmosphere. It had no protection from the corroding forces of the chemical and radiant universe.

It was in excrutiating pain, and it was dying.

With all his powers of concentration centered on the deciphering of the telepathic mystery, the Manhunter unconsciously slipped lower and lower through the air, until he had descended close to the uppermost of the tendrils that swelled like growing thunderheads.

Suddenly, one, two, three of them elongated to whiplike flagelli that stretched and encircled him, enfolding him in a gray-green embrace.

The Green Lantern didn't know what to make of the burbling mass of repulsion stretching as far as his eyes could see. He wished he could have stuck closer to one of the senior team members. As capable as he'd proven under any number of challenging circumstances, there was still a big part of him that was all too ready to defer decision making to whoever else was ready to assume that responsibility.

He zoomed low for a closer view.

What to make of this monstrosity? It looked *alive*, for crying out loud.

Didn't appear aggressive. Actually, if anything, its flailing and pulsing seemed aimless.

Holy Ned, it *was* alive!

Kyle was in a quandary, a not unusual state for him. He was, potentially, the most powerful member of the League. He knew that because Superman, Wonder Woman, the Manhunter, and even the Batman, in his own obtuse, cryptic manner, had told him so. None of them were known for hyperbole. So he believed he must be what those stalwarts said he was, and that scared him more than the lantern's power itself.

He carried a great responsibility, but responsibility comes with wisdom, and he knew he had little of that.

He had no doubt the others had already sized up the situation.

I'm going in.

Of course—that was Superman's telepathic voice. There were lives at risk down there. Islands, ships, not to mention the whole of marine life. Aquaman's subjects.

What was the Man of Steel's plan?

Superman! Your location?

Diana.

Following Superman.

Kyle figured they knew what they were doing, but diving into an alien being? One that no one had a handle on? One that nauseated your brain anytime you concentrated on it for more than a second?

He wished he understood, wished he was that decisive. Wished they'd had time to strategize before heading out.

It was a living creature, for pity's sake.

He called in his mind for the Manhunter. He needed to corroborate his impressions with another's.

Strange that there was no reply. It was not like J'onn J'onzz. It was the Martian's nature to maintain easy telepathic access. Kyle did not like the dead air, the disturbing gap in communications.

He made his first decision. He was going to find the Manhunter.

Kyle knew the approximate location to where his teammate had teleported—only about one hundred miles north and northeast. Although he did not possess the raw speed of the Flash or Superman, the ring could carry him well into the supersonic realm. Flying a wide, zigzagging sweep, aided by a powerful emerald telescope apparatus, he knew that if the Manhunter was still maintaining altitude above the alien mass, he'd find him quickly.

Indeed, he sighted the suspicious bulge in the ethereal creature's contours from miles away. Magnifying the distant image, he was horrified to see a rigid Manhunter engulfed by coiling tendrils, slowly, relentlessly being pulled down, down. Kyle couldn't know this was a manifestation of the intense telepathic link shared by two extremely powerful broadcasters. All he knew was that two team members had disappeared into the beast, the third was going under, and their mind link had been severed.

That was more than enough for him. He was done equivocating. When there were no alternatives, when he feared for his fellows and stood at the edge of panic, then Kyle became very decisive.

This had to end, and quickly.

Kyle forced himself to look at the sickening, unnerving mass. To his mind it was disease and cancer and rot and plague. Which was good, because that gave him the mental image he needed. He called on his ring, the symbol and locus of his Green Lantern power, all the while envisioning a hypodermic syringe. He was very specific in his mental picture: This was the biggest, most serious needle ever, and it carried as its payload the most perfect, most potent disease-fighting agent imaginable. It was the ultimate serum designed to counter the worst plague.

Even as he thought it, the ring responded. It glowed as if in agreement, and an emerald ray shot out, expanding to a cone of light that flashed and dazzled and resolved itself into the perfect image of Kyle's imagined syringe, green and gigantic. It hung, for an instant, poised at the end of its emerald tether, and then Kyle spat another mental command and it launched itself like a living rocket into the mass. Kyle imagined it forcing its way down, down, down, straight to wherever the heart of the disease lay, and once there releasing its powerful antidote.

It didn't really matter that the weapon Kyle had created came in the shape of a syringe. The ring wasn't really delivering a medicine to a disease—Kyle knew that. But the mental image that Kyle formed was all important; it was the focus that allowed the ring to understand what its Green Lantern expected as a result. The image that Kyle asked the ring to make manifest was a communication of intent—the ring's pure, abstract power, focused and clear as to what its duty was, would do the job.

The syringe image had disappeared. Kyle hovered, holding his breath—one second, two seconds . . .

A massive convulsion heaved through the creature, pulled up from its depths like a pocket of gas bubbling out of a sewer. The entire organism shuddered and spasmed as a whole, all aspects finally coordinated in a death seizure. The tendrils and tentacles and tubercles stiffened. The convulsion passed through the thing and into the atmosphere, a mammoth shock wave radiating out into space.

Kyle saw the disturbance coming and rushed to the Manhunter, who hovered released and stunned, and encompassed them both in a simple ring-generated force sphere. The wave passed them without damage, but even a native nontelepath like Kyle could detect the nerve-wrenching subpsychic scream that accompanied it.

The last chunk of a living universe was dead.

It simply dematerialized, fading into nothingness. Like the fragment.

The Manhunter was shaking himself out of the deep telepathic trance in which he'd been locked, looking a bit surprised to see Kyle hovering next to him. The Green Lantern released the force field and reenvisioned his telescope, scanning the now clear sky and sea to the south.

Hundreds of miles away he found his missing teammates and shook his head in amazement.

Superman and Wonder Woman strained under the hull of an aircraft carrier. They had been flying it to safety when the organism had heaved and died.

"Wally." The Manhunter's voice brought Kyle back home. He turned to see that the Flash had just teleported in.

Wally West's legs were a scarlet blur, which always looked strange connected with his still upper body. A torso hanging over a red haze. But that, Kyle knew, was the only way the Flash could maintain altitude. He looked tired and kind of wild-eyed.

Kyle thought an emerald platform and the ring shot it out under Wally.

"Take it easy, Fleet Foot. It's over. You're too late."

CHAPTER 9

The Road to Heaven

Before Wally had teleported to his teammates above the Indian Ocean, he'd tried his best to quickly make a clear and concise report to Chyre and Morillo, but his words tumbled over one another as his mind darted uncontrolled between too many disasters. The Superluminoid wanted Iris. The Superluminoid wanted him to lead it to Iris. The Superluminoid had just executed forty human beings right under his nose. He was too slow. More were going to die, unless he led the Superluminoid to Iris. The League needed him. He was too slow.

Apparently, however, enough of what he said made sense to the detectives, because Chyre had said, "We can put her in a safe house, we can assign twenty-four-hour protection."

Wally gestured helplessly to the charred remains of Upchurch. "Doesn't matter. Didn't matter here. It can go anywhere. There's no defense."

Chyre had no response.

Then the room had erupted in panic and rage as the Homicide detectives and the feds had burst in, demanding to know what the hell had happened here in their own goddamn house, and no one whacks forty prisoners in the blink of an eye except a freakin' speedster, and how the hell could this happen? They glared at Wally, jabbed fingers at him, frustrated and fearful. Morillo and Chyre tried to hold them back, tried to reason with him, but nerves were frayed and fear ran hot and Wally was an obvious target.

This was no good. It was important that Morillo and Chyre have an idea of what had transpired, as he understood it, but now things had spun out of control and explaining to everyone's satisfaction was going to take a long time. Normal time. Time that Wally didn't have.

He touched his two friends on their shoulders. "Sorry. Got to go," he hoped they heard. Then he'd accelerated out of the room, out of the building, to where he could breathe and think.

Actually, there was not much to think about. It was time to shift to League mode. He opened his mind link to the Watchtower transport center and arranged with Plastic Man for an immediate relocation to the situation for which J'onn J'onzz had requested his aid. O'Brian's humor was forced and minimal, he'd noted, and that did not bode well.

Then he was over a sunwashed ocean with no danger in sight. O'Brian had brought him in near Kyle and the Manhunter. It was all over, his teammates were very relieved, but he was too late, and he didn't need Kyle telling him that.

In the great conference hall in the Watchtower, the League gathered and tried to assemble the pieces.

Wally dully noted the Green Lantern and Wonder Woman seated facing each other in an isolated corner. Kyle sat forward, his elbows on his knees, his hands clasped, his head bent low, looking anything but the hero. Wally knew he was in anguish. When the poor guy had heard the reports from the Manhunter and Diana detailing their contacts with the biomass, when he'd learned that he'd killed a terrified victim of inconceivable violence, he'd crashed into guilt. It didn't matter that they assured him it was dying anyway, and suffering greatly. Or that he had probably saved it from a great deal of continued pain. In Kyle's mind, he had made an ill-informed decision. He had been too quick to believe that his teammates were menaced. Diana had her hand on his shoulder, doing her best to convince him that he had done the right thing. It was odd, thought Wally, that Diana, the warrior, the League member with the least moral proscription against killing, was the one who was also the hands-down best crisis counselor after a death.

Wally himself felt sick and defeated.

Too slow, too slow.

The Martian Manhunter had assembled some early casualty statistics based on what they'd been able to gather in a series of quick observational runs before departing the Indian Ocean. Because the area compromised was so sparsely populated, the loss of human life was relatively low for a catastrophe of such range. The greatest hit had been taken in Diego Garcia, as Superman had feared, with over two thousand presumed dead. Those lucky enough to have been shipboard below steel decks had amazingly found sanctuary. The organism's substance, for some unknown, fortuitous reason, did not seem to penetrate steel.

Beyond that island, and including the Addu Atoll, probable fishing fleets from distant ports, and other ships at sea, he estimated maybe fifteen hundred more lost.

The cost to marine life was inestimable. The ecology of the Indian Ocean, and quite possibly the entire planet, would be damaged for decades. Aquaman, the Lord of the Seven Seas and erstwhile League member, had his minions scrambling even now, doing all that was possible to limit the extent of the submarine disaster.

In addition, several much smaller anomalies had been recorded as appearing at the same time as the monster on the Indian Ocean. One, materializing in Antarctica, had been attended by the Teen Titans, but disappeared before more than a cursory observation could be performed. Five others had been spotted in near-Earth space. They had since vanished.

All things considered, the Manhunter remarked softly, the world had gotten off a lot easier than it might have.

But it was still unacceptable.

It had to stop.

Wally nodded to himself, exhaled, and looked the Manhunter in the eye.

"I'm ready for that mind scan now."

He had already told his fellow League members about the Superluminoid's latest attack. About its origin and Upchurch. About what it wanted, what it needed. About Iris. About his role. About not being able to protect Iris.

The Manhunter and he had compared times, just to be sure. The attack and massacre at the Keystone City Police Headquarters had occurred precisely at the same moment the cosmic organism had appeared in the Indian Ocean.

"Why," asked Wally, "do you think it throws this alien crap at us while it's on a murder spree? Is it some sort of a misdirection?"

Superman had considered a moment before answering. "I don't think it's purposeful. I don't think it necessarily means to inflict the residue of other universes on us."

The Manhunter agreed. "*Residue* is the right word. When I was linked with the Indian Ocean organism, I think what I saw was an entire universe destroyed in an instant. I'm guessing as a result of your Superluminoid passing through. I think it may attain its faster-than-light speeds by jumping through connecting universes, using them as an infinite source of platforms to get from one point to another. Like the Ardavan-Ryan model has theorized."

Patterns, thought Wally. *Upchurch had spoken of the Superluminoid moving in patterns.*

"Unfortunately, it doesn't seem to jump cleanly, and maybe the residue of universes adjacent to ours gets pulled through," J'onn finished.

Wally remained thoughtful. "Another thing I don't understand—why do you suppose that with its superspeed it doesn't just tear through every metagene carrier in the whole damn world until it finds Iris? You'd think it could do that pretty quickly. Why is it waiting for me to show it to her?"

Wonder Woman fielded that one. "I've been trying to figure that out myself, Wally. My first guess would be that it exhausts its power relatively quickly. You may have seen as many surgical harvests as it can do at a given time, before its energy is expended. Let's face it, if it's hopping universes, it's expending incredible amounts of energy. So our one advantage may be that it is limited in the scope of damage it can inflict at one time."

Wally caught on. "Yeah, that might be true, but there were less than six hours between the first and second strikes, so I'm not sure how great an advantage that is."

Diana countered. "Strange to hear that coming from a speedster. I'd think that would seem like an infinity of waiting for you."

"Touché." Wally gave the Amazon a wan smile. "And I did get the impression that its patience with me is wearing thin. If it is limited in its actions before it recharges, it's going to take it a long time to single-handedly conquer the world. The sooner it can replicate itself, the more of itself it creates, the faster it'll get to its ultimate goal."

There had been a pause in the discussion, and then Wally remembered. "Diana, did you say you saw another possibility?"

The Amazon Princess shrugged and leaned back. "Well, realize that I can't help but be influenced by the myths and fables I was raised on, but what if it can't kill its own mother? What if it expects *you* to do that for it?"

Wally still shivered when he considered Diana's almost offhand remark.

"I'm ready for that mind scan now."

The Manhunter looked dubiously at the haggard speedster. "Are you sure? You've been through the wringer today. Two days in a row, actually. I may not be at my best, either. If you want to wait a bit . . ."

"No, now. This can't continue. You were right, this is bigger than what I thought and if I've got anything locked in my noggin to offer . . . I should have agreed to this yesterday. Before this round of disasters went down. I'm ready to do it."

Superman stood up. "He's right. Time is everything now. Let's get going and hope that Diana is right about it needing time to recharge."

Wally realized that he had been absently fingering his bandage. He'd forgotten that it still ached. It reminded him of home. "Linda. I should call Linda first. I told her I wouldn't be adventuring tonight. Ha."

The Manhunter chose a small darkened room for the scan. He could have performed it anywhere, but with all the confusion and distractions running through Wally's mind, as well as his own, the quieter and darker the better.

Wally took his seat in the middle of the room, with the Manhunter sitting directly across from him. The speedster knew the others were watching unseen in the dark. He was very nervous. He knew it had to be done. He knew this thing was bigger than him or his secret fears, but there was still that chunk of ego that desperately needed to stay in control.

"Now, on your honor," he said, gathering the remains of his sense of humor, "I want you all to promise that if I do anything to embarrass myself, you will leave and never speak of this again."

"If those were your everyday terms, we'd never have anything to talk about," the Manhunter deadpanned, revealing the dry wit he seldom displayed.

Wally mustered a sickly grin.

"Relax, Wally. Trust me. You'll feel nothing, you'll see nothing. All impressions will come to *me*. I'll be doing all the work while you take five. I am not going to be ransacking your mind in general. We don't have the time to look for scandal or childhood trauma or horrible social embarrassments, as much fun as it might be to do so. Nor will I be examining your self-image. If I stumble across something somewhere that indicates, say, a crushing insecurity"—Wally winced involuntarily, and hoped the Manhunter hadn't noticed—"I will back away from that place, and take any impressions I may have gained of that sort to my deathbed. Such is the moral code of a Martian telepath. You know me. You can trust me."

To Wally, it seemed that the Manhunter's voice was slipping into a soothing chant.

"I am only looking for the information buried in your subconscious that pertains to these victims and visitors from other states of being. I am only searching for messages and impressions of outside universes that may be harbored within you. I am only looking for clues that might save our world. Such is the code of a Martian telepath. You know me. You can trust me."

What the Manhunter had started in a relaxed, even jovial manner had gradually turned solemn and ritualistic. The Martian's face was lowered, his eyes were half-closed, unfocused. Wally wondered if the scan had begun. He didn't think he felt anything different in his head, but then, he vaguely realized, he wasn't thinking of much at all and he didn't think he could move had he wanted to, and . . .

Wally slipped off to another place.

He vaguely remembered the Manhunter telling him that he'd be aware of nothing, yet here he was. Words didn't seen very important anymore. In fact, they held no weight at all. Nor did anything else outside this place.

There was nothing but here.

Here was not really a here, either. There was no sense of space, of points and lines and planes and time to reference. No light, no dark, no color, no texture.

Here was a state of being.

"*Wally*." A state of being with a voice.

"Wally." A voice behind him.

He turned. He turned his self to another—another point of view. He turned to look behind.

There it was. Right behind him—the dark figure from his journey into the extracosmic fragment, so tall and spindly, with its plates of chitonous armor and its large, flattened head with huge, luminous eyes.

"Wally." It seemed to be swimming toward him. Struggling through gulfs of nothingness that swept against the figure like a surging current. Impossibly strong and graceful, yet unable to break through and join Wally.

Most of him regarded this with detached disinterest, but a small part of him somewhere deep inside was very concerned.

Then Wally blinked, or maybe the dark figure blinked, or maybe a mind shuddered. Suddenly the figure was much closer, standing right before Wally, gently sweeping its long, thin arms and oversize hands in a sculling motion, as if it were treading water.

He could see its sideways, football-shaped head with startling clarity now, the intricate overlapping of crustaceous plates, rich and black and filigreed with even darker alien inscriptions, shimmering with strange life. And the eyes—twin portals into yet another place.

The fierce, glowing eyes were so close, were burning right into Wally's, and there was something so familiar there.

"Wally." The voice was not really a voice. It was a reassurance.

"Wally, meet me at the great constant."

It did not come out as words. It was a concept and Wally understood perfectly.

Another blink and it was distant again, swimming against that invisible, irresistible current. It started to break apart, slowly at first. Little pieces of black chipped off the edges of its silhouette, carried away into the void. Then more and more of it melted away until it had dissolved like a sand castle overrun by the tide.

Or a structure vaporized by an atomic blast.

The eyes were the last to go.

Wally seldom felt calm, but he did now. It wasn't often his racing mind stayed low and patient of its own accord.

But it did now.

He contentedly drifted into the nothing.

The Manhunter was shaking his green head, talking very low to Superman and Wonder Woman. Wally blinked and remembered. The lights were dim, but turned up brighter than when the scan had started. Apparently it was over.

Superman noticed that Wally's eyes had reopened and nodded his way. The others turned their attention to him.

"Wally, you're amazing. I don't think I've ever had anyone fall asleep under a scan before." Despite the rib, the Martian's expression was grave.

"I didn't expect a nap. How long was I out?" Wally stood up and stretched. The truth was, he hadn't felt this rested in a long time.

"Only about ten minutes."

Wally felt good. Relieved. "So what did you dredge out of me?"

Then, slowly, he began to notice details. The expressions on his teammates' faces began to register and all the calm and relief seeped out of him.

Everyone looked grim.

The Manhunter was not happy. "Nothing, Wally. It didn't work. I failed."

"I don't understand—*nothing?*" *That couldn't be right.*

"Nothing I could access. There's something in there, but damned if I could get to it."

Now Wally was amazed. He didn't often see the Manhunter show such frustration.

"There is a discreet bit of memory planted deep in your core that I could not enter," the Martian explained. "I have never run into a mind I couldn't fully access unless it was protected by very powerful psychic blocks. This, however, was not protected by blocks, or by any defenses that I could discern. Regardless, I couldn't get in, no matter what angle I came at it. I don't know why. It is literally beyond me."

"So you didn't find the dark figure?"

"What dark figure?"

"The armored . . . alien . . . *thing.*" Wally struggled for words. He was starting to lose the pleasant state of serenity he'd so recently achieved. "Don't tell me *you* didn't see *that* swimming inside my brain."

The Manhunter slowly shook his head. "I didn't

see it, Wally. I assume it's locked inside that place I can't open. And *you* shouldn't have experienced anything unusual while under a mind scan."

"Well, sorry to put a wrinkle in your routine, but I remember seeing the dark figure. It came to me and . . . and it told me to . . . to . . ." —Wally fought to regain the elusive memory—"to meet it at . . . 'the great constant' . . ."

Wally's eyes lit up. "The great constant! The speed of light! The Speed Force! I need to go to the Speed Force!"

The others did not seem impressed. This was a riddle and they'd been looking for an answer.

"I thought the Speed Force was a sort of cul de sac—a dead end," Superman said skeptically.

"Well, it is, in a way. But it's more. The speedster mystics think it's heaven. Max Mercury preaches that it's where all speed power comes from and where it returns when we die," Wally explained, referring to the patriarchal speedster who had practically created a religion based on his beliefs.

"I've been there myself and don't know if I exactly agree with old Max. I do know that it's the end result of hitting the speed of light. Another plane of existence. It wasn't easy to leave, and I nearly didn't make it. Truth is, I'm not exactly sure how I returned. And I don't know if I could get out again. But it's a gateway and a meeting place for things beyond our world. It's possible to experience things there that are not possible here. It's very clear to me—this is what I have to do."

The others still looked doubtful.

"There's some kind of answer waiting for me there. I'm connected to this somehow. Look—what else do we have to go on? It's our only move."

The Manhunter did seem a bit relieved. "Damnedest thing. I never conducted a mind scan with this as a result. I couldn't get through, but something in the process apparently kicked back to you. It had to be a deliberate plant." He regarded Wally thoughtfully. "I don't think the Flash is . . . *um* . . . hallucinating."

Wally shot the Martian what he hoped was a withering stare. "Thanks for the overwhelming vote of confidence, J'onn. But it doesn't matter—I'm going. There's nothing else for me to do. I'm beaten—frankly, I think we're all beaten—unless this dark figure provides a key."

"And, what," Superman said, "makes you think this isn't a deception? What if your dark figure is a manifestation of the Superluminoid?"

Wally thought for a moment, but couldn't come up with a way of framing the answer that would make sense. "I don't know how or why, but the dark figure isn't malicious. I've never been so sure of anything in my life. I feel it in my genes." He wasn't sure why he put it that way. He wasn't trying to be funny.

Superman finally nodded his agreement. "I suppose you're right. There's nowhere else to go."

Wonder Woman smiled. "We're all in your capable hands, Wally."

It was the only thing to do, but he was glad to have their support.

Now, before he departed, there was one last matter needing attention. He faced them all.

"Just one thing. While I'm there—if I'm wrong—please do your best for Iris and Linda."

The road was long and dusty.

And straight.

Most important, it was straight.

Wally stood at a crossroads in what might have been the loneliest corner of North America. As much as his eyes were limited by the night, he could feel, more than see, the endless, undisturbed flatness of the high plains stretched in all directions. An infinity in two dimensions. The roads that intersected here cut arrow sharp through the low wheatfields that clothed the otherwise unprotected land and disappeared into imagined points on the line of the ghostly horizon.

Everything was defined by planes and edges. The cold black of the enormous sky held no clouds or moon, only the fine points of the stars, revealed now that the promised warm front had moved in from the south, sweeping the rain from the Midwest.

This was the land of simple geometry.

This was the best place in the world for building up a head of steam.

The light barrier was not easy to break. He had only done it once before and it had nearly killed him. He wouldn't even have attempted it if he hadn't been locked in a life-or-death struggle with the evil speedster Savitar.

But Wally had made it and he could do it again. It

would take road, lots of road, and a relatively long period of time building up to that final barrier.

The road to heaven cannot be easy. So said Max Mercury.

Savitar had got there, too, and he chose to stay. It was tempting, very tempting. It was speed paradise, and it had been very hard for Wally to leave. But staying entailed giving up your humanity and Wally wasn't quite prepared to do that.

Actually, ninety-nine percent of the approach would be relatively easy. It was that last push that required monumental effort, exacting reflexes, and unswerving, pinpoint willpower. It was that final acceleration past logic and physics that was the killer. Only he had ever gone past that barrier and lived to tell of it.

These high, flat plains were the best launching pad he could hope for. Hundreds and hundreds of miles of uniformly even land with few obstacles. He had carefully plotted his course: a giant figure eight, a Möbius strip across five states. The long, straight stretches and gentle curves would provide him with the ideal course for building tremendous momentum.

Wally stood at the crossroads at the center of his course. He would pass this point many, many times tonight. He tried to recall that sense of calm he had somehow taken from the mind scan, but it had slipped away.

He knew he should be feeling more urgency, but it all seemed too unlikely, too preposterous. The enormous notion that *everything* seemed to hinge on this run, it was just too big a notion to fathom.

Wally dug the toe of his right boot into the layer of loose dirt blowing across the macadam surface of the road.

This is, he told himself, *the most important run of your life.*

One strong, muscular contraction and he was on his way, leaving a smoking pocket of molten asphalt where he'd pushed off. He did not accelerate particularly quickly; a long, slow buildup was the key to this run.

Miles and miles of flat land. Plenty of room to gradually build controlled momentum. Wally's mind wandered to thoughts of all the speedsters born to this level country formed perfect for running. Was it a coincidence that the Midwest was the world's foremost breeding ground for speedsters? Or had the ancestors of speedsters been drawn to the open spaces for the sheer love of running unrestrained and had therefore created a metagene bank here? An invisible empire of speedsters tied to this land—their perfect, horizontal domain of speed?

Wally could not conceive of ever leaving this land, his home, and the infinite horizon surrounding him.

He patiently accelerated at an even, conservative rate, leaving a series of low, polite thunderclaps in his wake as he proceeded up through the Machs. Dust and road waste exploded out behind him, like waters cut by a hydroplaning speedboat. Then he climbed to a velocity where he no longer created resistance against the air, and all physical reactions to his passing stopped.

The miles sped by and he completed the second circuit of his infinity loop. All systems were working perfectly. His heart, his lungs, his sense of speed—all meshed efficiently.

Max Mercury, the patriarch, had roamed these plains long before they had been squared into fields and dotted with settlements and later cities. He was an immortal of sorts, a powerful spirit figure to the Native Americans of the plains, a super hero before anyone had ever invented the concept. Why he survived was anyone's guess, and he wasn't about to give the science boys a chance to pick him apart when all he needed was his personal church of the transcendent speedster to provide him with answers. He swore that there were others like him back in those days, other speedsters that predated him, that raced here past the seas of buffalo and rivers of elk before Europeans arrived.

This had always been speedster land. Sacred, holy land to Max Mercury, who believed to his core that he gained his powers from the Indian spirit world, a realm that somehow in his mystic belief system was closely allied with the Speed Force toward which Wally now pushed himself nearer.

Max had converted a lot of other speedsters to his quasireligion. Johnny Quick, the hardcore materialist, before he died. Quick's daughter and successor, Jesse, had turned to it in her grief. Wally thought that maybe even Jay Garrick, who wore the mantle of the Flash in the years before Barry assumed it, had toyed with the comforting system of belief it provided. Savitar, of course, had been an early disciple—but one who'd gone mad and created his own warped cult with himself placed squarely in the center.

There were many others. All the cryptospeedsters who chose to stay beneath the scrutiny of the public eye, living lives of apparent normality—sometimes in fear, sometimes in resignation. Not every speedster wanted to or could be a hero, or a villain, or even a public spectacle, and thank whatever for that.

Many, however, found something in Max's beliefs that grounded their strange lives, something that gave them a sense of belonging. Everyone needs to know for what reason they exist. Speedsters needed to know what their power was all about. Max offered answers.

But Max had never seen the promised land and Wally had. While he wished Max and his believers all the peace they had coming to them when their ends arrived, he wasn't so sure they'd spend eternity communing with God in the Speed Force.

Wally's course sped by faster and faster with every circuit. He'd lost track of the number of times he had passed the crossroads. For a change, his mind was in tune with the speed of the world his body inhabited; it was now matched and even challenged by his physical state.

His speed-altered vision resolved the nighttime into diamond-sharp clarity. The stars seemed to multiply and grow into great burning clusters of coal fire. They reflected their glory on the fields of wheat and the lights of distant towns grew in intensity, too, till Wally's night seemed bathed in phosphorescence.

His heart and lungs began to labor. An unaccustomed fatigue began to drag at his legs. He was reaching speeds that were not comfortable to maintain.

Barry Allen had never felt any attraction to Max's proselytizing. He was a scientist to the core and needed something to test if he were to even consider believing it. He spent much of his life trying to understand the why and wherefore of his speed power and, although he never found the answers, his honest, rigorous search had given him a form of peace.

Iris, too. Wally was so lucky that Barry and Iris had become the two great influences in his life. Both loved the truth and were not afraid to discard their beliefs if they didn't hold up to scrutiny.

And now, Linda. Linda was uncompromising. She had given him the strength to leave the Speed Force once before and he knew he could count on her again.

These were the people whom Wally clung to, who gave him his strength. That was why his mind rested on them, even as his body strained.

The stars and fields and city lights had blended into a whole, while somehow still remaining distinct. The night was no longer dark and lonely, it was crowned in radiance. Form and mass seemed composed of light, radiant light, and Wally understood that he was close to the barrier.

Now was the time to shut down his mind to all extraneous thoughts, to end the musings that up till now he'd allowed to keep him company. From here on in, there must be nothing but furious and laser-sharp concentration. To get so close and glance off the barrier because of a loss of focus, a failure of the will, would be unacceptable. This impossibly difficult transformation was not an option, it was of ultimate importance.

Failure is not possible, failure is not an option. Wally created a mantra for himself. A string of words to force his mind to the track, to keep the bit between his teeth.

His legs, which generally loped along with ease and spring, now seemed weighted with lead. There was an agony of fatigue throughout his body that was something more than muscular, something baser than chemical. It was the warning from the physical world that he was attempting something that broke a fundamental law. A perverse action that should not be easily committed.

His body pleaded that every step be his last. His mind forced his legs to pump faster, every step *faster.* There was no time to maintain, no place to backslide, no alternative but to run *faster.*

Failure is not possible, failure is not an option.

His lungs, shriveled and useless.

His heart, no longer the engine.

It was sheer willpower against the laws of physics. Speed power in defiance of the universal constant.

The atoms in Wally's boot treads had long ago ceased to bounce off the atoms of the road over which he virtually flew. Now his mind began to divorce itself from any remaining attachment to the physical universe. The definitions that were the road, the fields, the sky, and stars all faded until all that was left was the radiance.

The domain of light.

Failure is not possible, failure is not an option.

The radiance grew in intensity, then exploded into shafts and cataracts racing out to meet him, as he threw himself forward into one last surge, the last he had to give.

So beautiful.

He was lifted up.

High above, Superman scanned his telescopic night vision over the vacant plains one last time. He had lost sight of Wally long ago; not even his powers of speed and vision could follow the Scarlet Speedster's run beyond a certain point. When the Flash's accelerating progress had become too much to track, the Man of Steel had stabilized his attention at the crossroads and depended on his ability to sense infrared to mark Wally's passage as he completed each circuit. That tactic failed soon, too, as Wally's velocity outran any heat dispersal.

When five minutes passed with no sign of Wally, Superman decided the Flash must have made it to his Speed Force. Or evaporated in the attempt.

"You don't think he could kill himself trying to get there?" he asked Wonder Woman, hovering at his side and likewise searching the distant surface for clues.

The pragmatic Amazon scowled. "Clark, you're going to have to start trusting him someday, and this one's out of our hands, so it might as well be now. The fact that we still exist leads me to believe he made it."

Superman gnashed his teeth, a seldom-displayed nervous tic that created a grinding noise Diana found extremely annoying. He noticed her disapproving look.

"Sorry. You know I don't enjoy admitting I'm not in control."

"Well, there's a news flash." Diana allowed a smile—she knew him very well. "Given the circumstances, I think it's all right to admit we're all a little afraid."

Superman grunted. "I didn't say I was afraid. Wally'll do fine. And if he doesn't—we'll figure out something."

He didn't suggest *what*, but Wonder Woman decided to let it ride and began to hover up toward the stars.

"Let's get back. J'onn should have her by now."

CHAPTER 10

The Seventh Singularity

There was no doubt that the Flash had made it, because everything had changed. Where a nanosecond and an eternity before he had been in agony, now there was no pain, no gravity, no atmospheric drag. Just indescribably free and easy motion.

Wally was bathed in light. He was a part of the light. He had entered the Speed Force, which, of course, was light itself.

He had done it, he had broken the barrier.

To describe it properly wasn't possible, he realized. He'd never be able to explain what it was like.

Light was a dimension unto itself, with no real relation to our four familiar dimensions, and he was inside light.

Sometimes Wally saw it all rolling with him in waves, then he'd blink and it was shooting past in discrete packages—photons, he realized. But it was all the same: one luminescence, eternal and brilliant and powerful.

It shot through him like a current and he was riding that current, still and lightspeed all the same. Shooting up in lasers to the stars and motionless in the Cathedral of Lucifer, all the same, now and forever.

"*Wally.*"

Again, like during the mind scan.

"*Wally.*"

Behind him. He turned and there it was.

This time with no struggle. Towering over him, backlit with a corona, like an obsidian sun. Composed of black light.

A negative image, thought Wally.

The dark figure; this time still and commanding and in control.

"*Would you like less distracting surroundings in which to talk?*"

Wally nodded dumbly, or at least radiated a positive response.

The burning eyes blinked and the riot of scintillating luminescence surrounding them receded and disappeared.

He was now standing on an outcropping of rocks protruding from an otherwise unbroken landscape. To one side of his vantage, a vast plain stretched to an infinitely distant horizon. To the other, a calm sea did likewise, broken only slightly by low waves slapping on the littoral. The only sound was that of the gentle lapping. There was no smell of salt air or dusty earth. Nothing.

Wally knew it was an illusion. He was still traveling with the speed of light.

Even as he thought it, the voice came again: *"Of course. The world within the great constant, what you call the Speed Force, is confusing at first. It can take some time to master. But anything can be formed from light; and I thought this projection might suit you."*

Wally looked and the dark figure was standing across from him, at the pinnacle of another rock on the outcropping. *"I thought this setting might help you to focus."*

"I was here once before." Wally felt compelled to divulge the truth. "In the Speed Force, I mean. It was very seductive. I almost couldn't leave, but then I knew I wasn't meant to stay."

With a ringing like that of a golden carillon, the figure laughed, somewhat shocking Wally. *"Do not ascribe too much purpose to the Speed Force. It is a quantum state of being and can be a narcotic, but it does not determine fate. For us right now, it is most importantly a means of communication."*

The figure seemed to have decided that the situation was going well, because it suddenly relaxed, folded its spindly, strangely jointed limbs in on themselves, and sat down. Wally joined it, crossing his legs and stationing himself facing it. His rock did not seem uncomfortable.

The figure stared at Wally and Wally stared right back. There was something so familiar . . .

"You are curious as to who I am?" The figure spoke in English—or so it seemed to Wally—conveyed through the air in bell-like, sexless tones. This was not telepathy this time. It was using breath and sound. Yet

Wally could see no movement to indicate a muscular source.

"Our voices are illusions, too. Sound does not exist here."

"Oh. Right." Stupid to have considered otherwise.

"Please, take off your mask. I would like to see you face."

Wally didn't see the harm and peeled the fabric back. He thought the figure almost gasped.

"It is a wonderful face."

Wally suddenly had the notion that the figure's odd, oblong head, with all its plating and intricately woven detailing, was a mask, too. Or a helmet.

"How about yours? Let's see your face."

The figure shook its head slowly, almost sadly. *"I am sorry. That is not possible."*

Then, after a pause: *"Do you know who I am?"*

Wally wasn't sure how to handle that one, coming as it was from out of the blue. "Should I?"

The figure shook its head again. *"It is best you do not know. In the world I come from, I serve a purpose somewhat similar to yours. A role involving a dual identity."*

Wally corrected the figure. "I keep no dual identity. I'm Wally West, the Flash—one and the same."

The figure was silent, and then, *"Even so, it is better this way. You will have to be satisfied to know me in the same manner the world of a distant future on an Earth of another universe knows me. I am the Seventh Singularity, who was thrown into the gravity pit of a dead, shrunken star seven times and each time emerged stronger. I am a quantum warrior, reaching out across infinite universes and endless time, to teach you how to stop the evil that has grown from your universe, stalking out to annihilate us all."*

Wally scratched his head. "You're a super hero."

"That would be the closest analogy."

"I had hoped . . . I had a feeling . . . I first saw your image in that fragment of a fireball, yesterday . . ."

"There are many ways I have tried to contact you, Wally. Imprinting the remains of a dying universe was one, but it is very difficult to sustain a connection long enough to communicate coherent information, one universe to another. Too much interference, too many unresolvable physical discrepancies. I needed to convince you that you must come here, to the great constant that holds true in all universes. This is a physical reality that transcends and connects all. The speed of light is a conduit for exceptional telepaths of all places and times."

"Why me?"

"You are the speedster. The ultimate speed potential in your world."

"But it's more than just *that*," Wally argued. "I saw the name Iris West—my aunt—in the fragment! And my own *face* . . ."

"Iris West and you are intimately connected with this catastrophe. Genetically. The being you call the Superluminoid was born from your aunt. Its genetics are her genetics—and, to a large extent, yours. You and it are cousins, on many levels."

Wally felt the hollow, sick feeling return. He hadn't allowed himself to think of it in those terms. It was the offspring of Iris, his father's sister. It carried his genes, too.

"*Believe it or not, you both have a similar potential. No one and nothing else has any hope of catching and countering the Superluminoid—but you alone.*"

It's all in the genes, thought Wally.

"*Iris West, you know, carries an incredibly powerful package of metagenes. Potentially, the most powerful. She, herself, of course never manifested in your universe. If she ever had a child, however, that child might have surpassed you.*"

The figure—the Singularity—had said *she never manifested in your universe.* What did that mean? Wally chose to let it slide for the time being.

"*As it is, however, by the nature of your blood relationship, you have a very close second to her package. You do not find this surprising, do you? You and she have always shared a unique bond.*"

"Sure—but that's *personality*. We just always got along."

The carillon sounded again. "*Excuse me. I'm laughing at myself. Your response reminds me to remember your culture's level of scientific understanding. Trust me, your aunt's and your personality mesh was not coincidental. Your metagene packages are very closely related and that speaks to your bond.*"

Although he was wandering from the urgency of their meeting, Wally decided to take advantage of the chance to address a point that had been bothering him. "Why didn't she ever manifest?"

The Singularity paused thoughtfully, all the while staring at Wally. "*That is a very complex question. Having the metagene is one thing, manifesting is quite another,*" *requiring a host of synchronistic influences. As you know, the influences seldom all occur in the necessary concordance. No matter how powerful the potential, probability dictates many beings will never manifest."*

"But you said she never manifested—in *my* universe."

Another pause. *"I did?"*

Wally did not reply and instead waited expectantly.

The Singularity finally continued, and for the first time, a note that was a shade less than totally relaxed crept into its voice. *"I suppose I did—and so what? What is the harm, really, if you are shown some of the bigger picture,"* his dark companion seemed to argue with itself.

Then: *"Do you understand this concept of alternate universes, Wally? Do you understand that there are an infinite number of variations on Wally West existing on an infinite number of Earth variants in universes without number? Coming into existence and disappearing from existence with every split second? That is not theory, that is truth. For every action we take, for every minuscule event that occurs in any universe, defining the forward progress of time, there is an alternative action taken. And that other action forms a new universe.*

"Everything is built on probability, Wally. Every action has a probable set of alternatives that serve as springboards to form minutely variant universes. It is happening all the time. We, here, right now, have created immeasurable legions of variants. All our conscious and unconscious moves that have served to further this continuum have, at the same time, sparked another universe in which we acted differently."

"That's a lot of universes. And wasteful." Wally was not one to allow his imagination to overwhelm his practicality.

"Yes, Wally, it is a lot of universes. More than you or I can ever conceive. Splitting off from each other, rejoining each other, splitting off again—everything in a constant state of flux. That is the nature of the system. That is the way everything works. It is not wasteful. And—this is important, Wally—all are essentially independent of one another. Information and event do not generally flow between universes. What you know is the result of what you have learned from your senses interacting with your universe alone.

"However, sometimes there is a flow of information between universes. Most of the time it is completely ambivalent—harmless. At your point in time, in your universe, I know that scientists have at least seen some evidence of divergent universe interaction. This is where they learned of the underpinning state of physics—quantum phenomena. They see the results in subatomic particles and their ability to exist in two separate places at once. They may not realize it yet, but what they are briefly seeing is a particle as it exists in both your and another universe, adjacent and for one nanosecond, interactive. Quantum phenomena are the result of interaction between neighboring universes."

Wally felt he'd gotten the point, although, in truth, abstracts left less than a memorable impact on him. "Okay—but you seem to have a lot of knowledge of my world, and here we are, sharing a crapload of information."

"Because my world is scientifically far in advance of

yours. Through millennia of painstaking experimentation we have learned to interface with other worlds through the application of probability mathematics. Your world will get there eventually, led by the works of Deutsch and, later, Kesperti."

Another pause. *"You'd probably better forget I mentioned Kesperti."*

Interesting, thought Wally, *but I doubt you have to worry about that.* What was it about the Singularity that seemed so damned familiar?

"I—and my associates—monitor the universes and the spaces in between. We sweep and scan for abnormalities that could prove disruptive. Oh, there is nothing in the system itself that could fail, but sentience—that is another ball of wax.

"There are intelligences *that occur from time to time, from world to world, that, sometimes consciously, sometimes unconsciously, wield the power to undo worlds. To annihilate entire webs of probability. We meet these disruptive, malignant beings and do what is necessary to counter them."*

"Supervillains." Wally felt he needed to cut to the chase. "And you and your associates—the Justice League."

"Roughly correct."

"So why me? Why do you need me? Why don't you just take care of the Superluminoid yourself? You can't tell me you don't have the power . . ." Wally had hoped that it might bristle at his pointed insinuation, but the dark figure still seemed totally lost in its mission to make Wally understand.

"We have all the power necessary—but our actions must stay confined to our own universe. If we unleashed our forces in any other world, the results might well be the same as that of this menace we now seek to end.

"As you may have deduced from your encounters with the bits of other universes blown into yours, the arrangement and nature of matter varies—sometimes considerably—from world to world. Physical interaction never bodes well for either of the universes involved.

"What my associates and I can do in such extreme cases as that which we now face is telepathically contact agents from a concerned world. Reach them in spaces of quantum interface such as this. Give them what they need to counter the malignancies.

"You, Wally West, in this case are the appropriate agent."

"Because I'm connected—genetically connected . . ."

"Yes."

Wally scowled. He wasn't by nature violent, but in this case he just wanted everything reduced to something he could hit. Just something simple and straightforward, something he could put his back into. *Just let me hit something.*

But it didn't seem like that was about to happen.

"So. Give me what I need."

"*It is not that easy,*" said the Singularity, with an apologetic tilt of the head.

The speedster's scowl deepened. "I didn't think so."

That bit of sarcasm didn't seem to sit well with the Singularity. Its voice suddenly turned brittle, slightly tinged with anger. *"When did you stop growing, Wally? When did you stop learning?"*

This sudden, paternalistic attitude angered Wally further—the thing was assuming too much familiarity. He chose to ignore the needling questions. "What else do I need to know?"

The Singularity, too, moved past the outburst. *"You need to understand our enemy."*

Wally nodded, submitting unhappily to the inevitable.

The Singularity paused, perhaps for dramatic effect, and then unfolded its sticklike limbs, standing tall and magnificent against the colorless backdrop of nothing above the sea and sand.

"We spoke earlier of the host of influences that must occur in lockstep if a metagene carrier is to manifest. It happens seldom enough, and the odds are increased only slightly by conscious manipulation, but the laws of probability require the extraordinary to occur eventually.

"Jonas Upchurch, aided by random factors of which he will never guess, let alone employ, midwifed an extraordinary event. His sole act of genius was identifying the metagene package of Iris West as one of superior potential. His actual attempt to incubate new life in the form of a speedster would never had succeeded if it were not for the chance synchronicity of a series of unsuspected environmental and quantum factors.

"Such is the mystery and the science of probability. May we never forget that. May we never deny that."

Wally was suddenly aware of a ritualistic bent that

the Singularity's speech had taken on. The figure's words now flowed in rhythmic cadence.

"Jonas Upchurch created a new life. He released the potential in a powerful gene package, and it was tangled and augmented by factors from not one, not two, but three other worlds. That was statistically unlikely, but distinctly possible.

"Such is the mystery and the science of probability. May we never forget that. May we never deny that.

"Upchurch worked no evil himself, and the being he created has no intent other than self-preservation, but it is still a malignancy, a destroyer of probabilities.

"Upchurch succeeded in creating a speedster, though by no great skill of his own, but by chance and probability alone.

"The thing is a stalker, a speedster whose power has manifested in the most terrible of manners. It moves past light speed by a series of jumps. It possesses the power to jump from one universe to another—a series of quantum reflex actions sprung one after the other in a pattern so rapid it exceeds the great constant. It is a true, native quantum being whose every move carries it through and past an infinity of unique and separate universes.

"In truth, it cannot be still. It must always move to continue its existence. It must always stay in a state of motion, or it ceases.

"And this is the horror. This is the evil: Every world it passes through, every universe it uses as a stepping-stone in its course, is destroyed in its wake. Totally and eternally erased by the incompatible, alien energy released in that world's discrete physical structure.

"This is why we of the Tel'kulyp must act. Not in denial of possibilities, not in interference with probability. But because the stalker annihilates untold billions with its every move. Because the weave of the fabric is coming undone as it jumps, ignorant of the catastrophes it leaves in its awful wake. Because its trail of ruin is so great that it threatens the system and the continuum of any and all.

"Such is the mystery and the science of probability. May we never forget that. May we never deny that."

The Singularity swayed, as if weakened by the intensity of its incantations. Then it collapsed its limbs again and returned to its seat, its head lowered.

This time Wally was impressed. The alien ceremony, the ritualistic fervor, had communicated more than words, it had done its job. Wally had seen something of the empty gulf of nothingness that confronted the Many Worlds that no longer existed after the Superluminoid's passage. What had seemed impossibly distant and unrelated a moment ago now seemed all too terribly immediate and urgent. All the horror and pain of his encounters with the Superluminoid, his helplessness in its cold, calculating scheme, the dank, depressed basement in which it was born, the weird sickness in his chest that came with the extracosmic anomalies, the bullet to his shoulder, the brainless bowls and charred cinders that had been human, all those memories returned at once and came crashing down on him, and were placed in their larger context.

"It's that powerful?" Wally asked, somewhat rhetorically.

The Singularity raised its patient eyes to Wally. It seemed weary. *"Yes. It is the end of us all. Of everything. And we can do nothing but recruit you and hope."*

All the giddy euphoria and lightness of being that had come with his entrance into the Speed Force was dissipated.

"So if it does succeed in reproducing itself—"

The Singularity interrupted: *"It will. It has the knowledge."*

"Then, I assume, we'll have multiple Superluminoids annihilating everything that much faster than one alone. Doesn't it realize it'll destroy itself eventually?"

The Singularity shrugged. *"It is only doing what is in its nature to do. Predators do not stop killing when they are hungry, even if the prey is scarce.*

"The Superluminoid is the loneliest thing that has ever lived. It can relate to nothing else. It feels for nothing else— nothing except you, Wally. It found you and saw that you and it are related. It saw that you can lead it to Iris West."

"It was pretty clear that it hates me."

"Because it sees itself in you—except that it has nothing but itself. You have everything it wants. You have community. You have Iris West."

"But it would eventually find her for itself?"

"You have that figured right. But at a tremendous expenditure of energy and, from its accelerated perspective, over an enormous period of time. It badly wants to be quickly lead to Iris West. That is the most important card you hold.

"You see, once it had physically encountered you, once it actually touched you, the Superluminoid was able to con-

nect and determine your genetic construction. It sensed you are closely linked to its mother. You can call it out by simply going to Iris and touching her. The connection will be made and it will know."

Wally felt a wave of panic well up inside as he considered what might have been. He remembered searching Iris out at her work, checking on her from outside the building. How might have things played out if he'd decided to move any closer?

"And every time it moves . . . ?"

"Uncountably, infinitely huge numbers of universes are annihilated, and he never stops moving. They are dying even as we speak."

And here we are, wasting time? I should be out there doing something now! Wally fought for patience.

"What can you give me? What can you give me to stop *that* before it's too late?"

"I can give you knowledge. I can show you your potential."

Silence. The dark figure was not going to be rushed.

Then: *"You know little of your own power, Wally. Maybe not entirely through willful ignorance—the science of your day has a long way to go. My associates and I have decided that, the dangers of extracosmic interference aside, you must be made aware of the true nature of your speed abilities.*

"Do you ever wonder, Wally, at the mechanics of what you do? At the factors and forces that allow a creature of soft carbon and brittle calcium and mostly liquid to attain the speed of light?"

Put that way, he seemed so pathetic. *Why is it trying its best to piss me off?*

"Well, the science boys say I ought to wonder. They're certainly licking their chops, hoping for a chance to take me apart, screw by screw.

"Barry used to speculate. He thought we were protected by a kind of force field, one generated by our accelerated molecular frequency. Of course, Max Mercury says that the Speed Force protects us. I guess I never bothered to look for answers myself."

"Barry Allen's theories were well thought out, but wrong. He was barking up the wrong tree, and his knowledge of physics was limited by the times in which he lived. Barry cared, though. He wanted the truth—he wanted hard answers. That is something to be respected."

If that was supposed to make Wally feel insufficient in comparison, it had worked. He'd always been satisfied just knowing he was fast.

"Well, Wally, although it is always preferable that a superbeing learns, or does not learn, the nature of his power by his own volition, in this event it is necessary for you to be schooled."

Why the hell had he started to feel disappointed in himself? Did he care if he didn't have the approval of this weird figure from a distant world?

"The truth is this, Wally, and it is essential: Your speed ability is merely a byproduct of your true power.

"I spoke of your great potential. That is something that transcends how quickly you can move. It is something beyond physical skills and tricks. Your true gift lies in your ability to access and control quantum power. You speedsters of Earth—you are quantum beings and you do not even know it."

Wally must have looked especially uncomprehending, because the Singularity took a moment to let its words settle before continuing.

"How do you think you survive the violence of accelerations that should pulp you instantly once you have pushed off—if you are only flesh and bone? There is no magic force field, there is no mystic Speed Force, benevolent and beyond comprehension.

"How do you attain speeds that approach that of light when your equally increased mass should make such rates impossible to maintain? There is no physical course that would allow you to achieve this—if your power were merely physical.

"But, you must understand, your power is not physical. *Your power is your ability to harness the quantum state to your bidding. Involuntarily, it would seem. We see no evidence that you make any conscious decisions as to its use. The skill comes to you naturally, written right into your genetic code.*

"You do start your run with a muscular contraction, but once you are in motion, the forces that govern your relationship with your universe change from those of gravity and electromagnetism, to those that underpin reality—the quantum forces."

Wally stared blankly. The Singularity rephrased, patiently.

"Wally, when you run, you are no longer subject to the restraints of the physical world. You are wielding quantum power—you can do pretty much whatever you want. It is like your body's atomic structure has been transformed to what you call tachyons—*particles that can move faster than the speed of light."*

This made enough sense to Wally to realize it made no sense. "Then why can't I match the Superluminoid?"

"Because your genetic instructions didn't go that far. The Superluminoid's did. That is one difference in your genetic packages—the Superluminoid seems to access faster-than-light involuntarily."

Wally threw up his hands. "I—I just don't see . . . I mean, look, I can barely make it here—to the speed of light—and then I'm trapped. The pain I feel getting here sure seems physical—it feels like I'm going to *die.* If I was made up of tachyons or whatever, it should be as easy as falling down. It shouldn't be any effort at all."

The dark figure nodded. *"It won't be, if you let me teach you. Your genetic instructions have allowed you to go so far, but your outer limits are capped by your psychological attachment to physical reality. You can learn to move beyond that. There is so much potential in you that is unused. So much greatness.*

"If you are prepared to work with me, if you are ready to open your mind and learn, then you will find yourself able to do things you never dreamed possible, Wally. You can match the Superluminoid."

There was no choice, of course, and Wally guessed that the point the Singularity was making was that if he didn't shape up and pay attention, this would all come to naught.

He was feeling more and more like a dull child. A dull, resentful child. A disappointment. A failure.

"Wally, you can do this."

He looked out to the rolling sea and then to the infinite, unchanging flat land. *Is that my problem? Am I afraid I can't do it? Am I afraid I won't measure up?*

"You cannot afford to stay secure in your own little world anymore, Wally. We need you."

Hear what it's saying, Wally.

"All of us."

Get past the attitude. Get past the fear of failure. The whole world is waiting. Worlds. Plural. There's no one else but you.

"You can handle it. You are bright enough."

Too big. Too big for me. No one to blame, no limits, no excuses. I just want to be a hero, I just want it to be simple.

"Wally."

Step up and be the hero.

Wally looked back to the Singularity, with its disjointed alien proportions, its black, lustrous exoskeleton set with rich, writhing inscriptions, its unwavering, unblinking eyes. He saw that familiar *something* again . . .

. . . And this time he recognized it for what it was.

The Singularity believed in him. It trusted him. He could feel its confidence in him radiating out, no matter what its words were. He hadn't remembered feeling that in a long time. Not coming from a fellow professional. Maybe not since Barry.

It made all the difference.

Wally stood up. "I can do it. I'm ready to work with you."

The Singularity could feel the difference, too, he guessed, because this time there were no more caveats, no more questions. Wally knew it knew he was ready now.

"Then come and be initiated into the knowledge of the Kabkorthex, the PanCosmic Chomjee and the Tel'kulyp. Come and learn the secrets of the quantum warriors."

The Singularity again stood, unwrapping its long, spiny extremities. This time, however, it didn't stop growing. It continued to expand and transform, revealing new limbs and appendages and more mass until it blotted out the sky from the amazed Wally's eyes. Scales and joints folded out into shapes for which there were no names, and then there was more Singularity than anything else, and then still more, and then all was black, black, black and Wally was sinking into the everything that the Singularity had become.

Tiny, distant stars.

No, wait, thought Wally, *those are galaxies.* Tiny, distant galaxies. Winking in and out of existence with frightening speed.

Galaxies, or electrons, *yes*—and photons—popping in and out of the vacuum in unending multitudes. Space was thick with them, sticky with them. In truth, there was no space, just a sea of frothing, seething quantum particles.

"There is no space. The quantum world is everywhere. It is your friend, your lifeboat, your courage, and your good death."

Wally turned his head and the Seventh Singularity was floating beside him, on the virtual sea of sub-atomic particles. It looked at him and revealed itself, just a little:

"I was born on an Earth very similar to yours, at a time very close to yours. My Earth and yours were distanced by very little. Only a handful of minor alternate actions disassociated our worlds. One of those alternate actions, however, involved my abduction. I was torn from my Earth and the people I loved by the Loth'ku, whose true name is damned.

"The Loth'ku were genetic raiders, gray-skinned horrors from a distant future who for eons had sought to manipulate ancient breeding stocks to their own imperialistic ends. They sought to control probability—may they be seven times cursed.

"They saw the metapotential in the human-that-I-was and, drawing me back into their future, committed me to their gene pits. They altered my structure, they transformed me, and then they threw me into the black hole, the all-devouring neutron star cluster that rages at the heart of their galaxy. Seven times they threw me in, and the final time, I survived.

"I survived and transformed into something far more than even they had hoped or feared. Something over which their control failed. They had created the first quantum warrior.

"I destroyed them all. An entire race, in a single moment of insane fury."

The story, which Wally witnessed as much as heard, seemed to linger a second on that last bloodthirsty detail. The Loth'ku must have been—*are,* Wally corrected himself—terrible, indeed, to have earned such ferocious hatred.

The Singularity's story continued: "For ages following my act of blind, cataclysmic rage, I wandered my universe and did penance. I learned the extent of my powers, learned to control them. I formed a creed for myself and fought for justice and stability on the many worlds I visited.

"I traveled to the Rhuyk-i nebula and fought alongside the plasma beings of Quoud in their telepathic war with the marauding Huyroyu. I met the mollusks of Sellib, sank through the philosopher sands of Ji'Khiivu, and beat back an invading armada of living comets outside the Tranop cluster. And more, and more. I saw more of my universe than could be described in your lifetime.

"I settled on the black planet Denebru for centuries and there learned the science and ethics of probability from its Coleopteran inhabitants, the Deng. The gift of their insectoid armor protects me and gives me this form.

"Denebru also gave me peace and understanding, but it was not home. In time, I moved on and searched for ages more, until I had returned to the world of my birth.

"Until I had found Earth.

"Earth—but not the Earth I had known. The Loth'ku had taken me forty-seven centuries into the future. My time, my people, were long, long dead.

"But the Earth of the sixty-seventh century was no less in need of protection than mine of the twentieth. It still cried for heroes to ward off the forces and sentients who envied her riches and beauty and stability.

"I stayed, and was adopted, and eventually was made stronger still with the gathering of a host of fellow metahumans and quantum warriors. Together we form the Tel'ku-lyp and the PanCosmic Chomjee, our mission to guard the

*system-that-works against all that would disrupt and rend
the chain of probabilities that keep the Many Worlds intact.*

*"Such is our mission: to protect the mystery and the science of probability. May we never forget that. May we
never deny that."*

The story, like a song, lingered here again, skipping
a few beats, allowing Wally's mind to stretch and absorb some of the cosmic scope involved.

*"As I have already told you, as you now understand,
seldom have we seen such destructive potential so realized
as in this being you call the Superluminoid. It wades
through the quantum sea with immunity, barging through
universes without end, snuffing out each in turn, as if they
were burning matchsticks on which it treads.*

*"It holds the power to access the quantum state, with no
understanding of responsibility, no manner of control."*

Wally had a horrible thought. It jumped into his
mind, from where he didn't know, but it seemed very
relevant and immediate. He couldn't help interrupting the Singularity's narrative—his mind screamed
out involuntarily.

*But won't I do the same? If I access the quantum state
and cross universes—won't I destroy all those innocent,
unknowing worlds as well?*

The Singularity seemed pleased that Wally had
come to this realization himself.

*"Of course you would. That is why you cannot receive
the knowledge of how to release your power without also
learning to control it. That is why this is not so simple as
you would like.*

"The Superluminoid has no ethics, no control, no under-

standing of its power. It is a bludgeon, a simple hammer, smashing its way through the Many Worlds.

"You, Wally, will be a scalpel, slicing a path so fine that any disruption left in your wake will heal immediately."

There was time again to let this sink in. These rhythmic spaces felt right to Wally now, and although he still felt the urgency of the situation, his impatience had left him. Everything was happening in due course.

"Now it is good. Look at me, Wally. Do not focus on my eyes—be aware of all of me."

The Singularity, treading beside him in the depths of this sea of evanescent particles like a black crustacean in a galaxy of meteoric plankton, began to move its impossibly long arms in a pattern that etched invisible symbols across Wally's eyes. Faster and faster the arms weaved and swept, and the spiky fingers, too.

They wrote instructions and explanations and references and ethical guides and history and theory and strategy, all of which burned directly into Wally's brain. He understood every bit of it, although he had no idea how that could be.

He was changing.

Motion is just a means, and what lies outside the start and the stop points is just as important.

Sometimes it is good to stop motion.

When the Singularity was done teaching, and Wally was done learning, they dropped the illusion.

Wally's mind again registered the reality of him and the Singularity flowing through the great constant, what Max Mercury called the Speed Force.

The riot of photons and waves no longer overwhelmed Wally. He understood it. He understood that he really was a part of it, that he could come and then move beyond it whenever he pleased. It was a pleasant way station, but it was no end point.

His training was done, his time with the Seventh Singularity almost over, and his mission lay before him.

"You understand," the Singularity's undisguised telepathic voice still carried a bell-like quality, *"your new knowledge and control is only temporary. It is not good that you keep what you did not discover yourself. Someday you or your descendants will unlock the potential of your own accord, and then it will stick."*

Wally understood.

"And you understand that nothing is guaranteed. We did the best we could to put you on equal footing, but the Superluminoid is strong."

Wally attempted some humor: *Well, if I don't beat it in this universe, I guess there'll be another in which I will.*

The Singularity laughed softly. *"Not in this instance. Make sure you stop it in this universe."*

Wally got that, too.

There was one last question that gnawed at him. He wasn't exactly sure how he wanted to phrase it—the fact that the subject it raised had not been addressed by his quantum guide led him to believe that maybe it should be avoided.

Finally, though, Wally decided he had to lay it on

the table: *We've talked about connections. How Iris and the Superluminoid and I are all connected, and that's why I'm the man who's right for the job.*

But there's still more to it than that, right? I understand enough now to know that you couldn't have reached across universes and time and into the great constant to contact me—if there weren't some connection between you and me. You just can't do that. Not without a strong—connection. Between you and me.

The magnificent quantum warrior seemed to ignore Wally's question for a painfully long time, closing down its telepathic link completely.

But then: *"Yes, Wally."*

That was all it would say.

CHAPTER 11

The Eleventh Hour

The Martian Manhunter hesitated for the umpteenth time, and then went ahead and morphed his native green form into that of a human postal delivery man. Something seemed wrong with that choice, and it took the alien a second more to realize that, of course, residents of the United States did not expect their mail delivered to their doors at 10:30 P.M. An appearance by a postman at that hour might even be reason for alarm.

The night air was warm for April, but damp from earlier rains. He stood in a shrub-secluded corner of the front yard of a small, neat house on Early Street, fidgeting and indecisive. This was a very uncomfortable assignment, one for which he might have been well suited, but so fraught with social awkwardness that he wished it were any other Leaguer but he in the garden outside the little house.

It was a predicament, this not knowing what disguise to cloak himself in. He had convinced himself that a disguise was necessary because the woman must not be frightened by his sudden appearance after so many years. He couldn't alarm her.

A commonplace, respected human agent delivering—*something*. That would be reasonable, right? That wouldn't be so unexpected, showing up at a lady's door at 10:30 P.M.

That's what he told himself—he needed to ease her past the League's reentry into her life.

The truth was, he was embarrassed that he hadn't done better to stay in touch. He hadn't talked with her, the widow of a dear comrade, in probably years. He didn't *want* her to know who it was banging on the door, unannounced, after all that silence. Once he'd explained the situation, once that settled in, *then* he'd reveal himself.

Yes—then she'd be pleased to know she was in the safekeeping of the Martian Manhunter.

No.

That made no sense.

At 10:30 P.M., for pity's sake.

J'onn J'onnz was miserable. Sometimes his ignorance of human need and response drove him crazy. All he wanted was to save her as much anguish as possible.

And himself, embarrassment.

Unfortunately, time did not allow for the careful and protracted examination of every cowardly option.

In the end he gave himself up to the fact that he was guilty, and he'd have to deal with the embarrass-

ment and that was that. Returning to his massive,
green Martian form, he marched out of the shrubs
and up the porch steps.

He rang the doorbell twice and was considering
knocking loudly, when the curtains parted from the
inset French windows and there she was, staring out
at him with wide eyes.

The Manhunter shifted uncomfortably and attempted a grin. She didn't look like she hated him, so
he hoped she'd open the door soon. He really didn't
like the idea of being spotted by the neighbors loiter-
ing on a porch with his cape stuck between his legs.

Thankfully, she had the bolt thrown before he'd
finished the thought. He stepped back as she swept
open the door.

"Hello, Iris."

She looked confused, and then, suddenly, anxiety
rushed in to take its place.

"Wally . . ." she said, almost gasping.

This was exactly what he'd hoped to avoid. She
had jumped to conclusions. If only he could have figured an appropriate disguise.

He hurriedly reassured her: "No, Iris, it's all right.
Wally is—fine. He's all right . . ."

Not smooth at all, but the worry lines vanished immediately and Iris's face went slack with relief.

"Oh, God, I'm sorry. But just showing up like
this—I remember what it was like with Barry . . . I'm
sorry, J'onn, what am I thinking? Come in. Get off the
porch."

The Manhunter was very impressed that, despite

the distress he'd just put her through, she was still alert to his uncomfortable position standing outside and exposed.

After all this time, she still instinctively filled her support role.

Ducking his head, he squeezed through the small foyer. Iris motioned him into a comfortable, simple living room.

"Arts and Crafts," he noted, proud that he could identify the early twentieth-century decorative style Iris had chosen for the interior. "I never thought of you and Barry in terms of what interests might fill your day-to-day lives."

Iris gave him a quizzical, stiff grin, still obviously trying to wrap her mind around her visitor's unexpected appearance.

"Actually, we never had furniture like this. The money Barry and I made always seemed to need to go to something else. It's only been in the last couple of years that I've had the time and money to do some refinishing, do some interior decorating."

Then, before he could reply: "How have you been, J'onn? It's been a long time."

He wasn't any good at this. "Yes. It's been a long time and I haven't stayed in touch. I haven't been there for you. None of us have. I'm ashamed."

He felt better for having dropped the baggage, even though he knew he did it badly.

Iris motioned for him to sit in one of the oak-and-leather easy chairs. He did so slowly, very aware that his mass, if carelessly lowered, could easily snap the wood braces. She sat on a sofa across from him, graceful and, to all appearances, not unhappy with him.

"I hope you don't feel bad about that, J'onn. I mean, we're all busy. You and the League most of all—I still follow your careers through the news. We all owe you."

Iris was exceptional. She had changed little in the maybe four years since he'd last seen her. Her chestnut hair was still cut short, with just a few strands of gray above her left temple. Her blue-green eyes, accented by perfectly arched eyebrows, still pierced or laughed, depending on the moment. She was dressed in a simple house dress that fit her comfortably. And she was poised and balanced, in fighting trim—the Manhunter couldn't help but appraise her in light of his profession.

Barry had always said she would have made a great super hero. She had that disposition, that quality.

She was calm and collected. She could lead anyone through any crisis. Smart as a whip, too.

Barry used to brag how she'd helped him. Assisted in his crimebusting with nothing but brain power and guts. How many other heroes had life partners they could rely on like that?

"Well, we owe you, too, Iris. More than I suspect we know."

She laughed, clear and light. "That's so very dramatic!" Then she shook her head and refocused. Her expression turned serious. "Why the visit now, J'onn? Be honest—is Wally in trouble?"

The Manhunter spread his hands in a gesture of ignorance. "Honestly, Iris, Wally is in no more danger than any of us. What I came to talk about was *you*."

He paused before coming to the point. "Do you remember—did you ever knowingly give a DNA sample for metagenic research?"

Iris thought for a moment. "I guess I did donate a mouth swab for metagene-related disease research—yes. A couple of years ago. You knew that I was a carrier, J'onn?"

He shifted uneasily in the confining chair. He wished it could have been anyone else there but him. "That information became relevant just recently. Listen, I've got to tell you a story . . ."

And he did, softening some of the sharper angles and leaving out what she didn't need to know. He relayed Wally's discovery that her DNA had traveled to S.T.A.R. Labs and then to Upchurch's hands, and how it apparently was an important component in creating a new form of speedster that was causing Wally, and now the JLA, a good deal of trouble. Most important, he stressed, they had reason to believe that the artificial speedster may be targeting her.

Iris furrowed her brow and seemed not at all concerned with the threat.

"I don't suppose these serial murders that have got the city tied in knots are connected?" She arched an eyebrow and searched his face for the truth.

The Manhunter rolled his eyes in an exaggerated manner; he wasn't going to be able to gloss over the unpleasantness. She was too sharp.

"Ohhhh. No. That means—this speedster killer, it's got my metagenes?"

The Manhunter nodded, reluctantly.

"And Wally's?" She was putting together the pieces he'd wanted to keep from her.

"It's killing because it's looking for something—you say it's targeting me? It's looking for me? It's looking for its—*mother*?"

"It sort of looks that way, Iris. It wants Wally to lead it to you. That's why Wally hasn't been harmed, we think. It seems to need a genetic trail to follow to you."

Iris finally looked appropriately stunned.

"That's why Wally hasn't come. Wally knows he can't come anywhere near you. The reason I'm here, and not another Leaguer, is because I'm a telepath, Iris. If the speedster—the Superluminoid—tries to reach you, we're hoping I'll detect him in time to afford you some protection."

Iris shot him a knowing, rueful smile. "You think you'll have time to save me from a speedster who has Wally flummoxed? Don't kid a kidder, J'onn."

The Martian reluctantly conceded the point. "It's the best we can do, Iris. But the plan is—we want you to come to the Watchtower. We think we can devise something more effective there. We need to do whatever we can to protect you from this thing, and our stronghold is on the Moon."

Iris did not look impressed.

"Iris, the thing's going to keep killing until it finds you. With or without Wally leading it, it will eventually find you. This won't come out sounding right, but there's much more than just your life at stake. If it does find you . . ." The Manhunter faltered, unsure how much information he wanted to divulge.

Iris finished for him: "It'll have my DNA. It'll be able to reproduce itself. I'm not stupid, J'onn. And it also occurs to me that if the League is involved with this, then the stakes must be pretty damn high. The whole ball of wax, maybe?" She sighed. "Where does Wally stand on this?"

Great Deimos, thought the Manhunter, *she's taken control right out from under me.*

"Actually, Wally doesn't know anything about this. We—League Command—decided it would be best not to give the Superluminoid any more trails to follow. It seems to be psychically connected to Wally."

"Oh, dear. They *are* blood relations, I guess." The worry lines between her brows were deepening again. She could take personal threat and the implication of widespread catastrophe without batting an eyelash, but her front began to crumble when her nephew's well-being was in doubt. She still carried that devotion, the Manhunter acknowledged admiringly.

"Where is he now?"

There was no longer any point in half-truths.

"He's looking for an answer to the thing. He's in that state he calls the Speed Force."

Iris bit her lip and began twisting her fingers together.

"It's that bad, huh?

She stood up and straightened her dress.

"Then we better get going, because when he comes

out, things are going to happen fast. Fly me to the Moon, J'onn."

It was one thing to find the Martian Manhunter ringing your doorbell, it was quite another to be greeted on the Moon by Superman and Wonder Woman.

Iris had been around super heroes most of her adult life; marriage to a lifetime member of the League guaranteed a certain amount of social contact and had erased from her much of the almost superstitious awe in which the general civilian populace held their protectors.

The years of relative isolation since Barry's death, with only her occasional visits with Wally maintaining the link to her past, had not done much to lessen that easy regard.

Superman and Wonder Woman awaiting her arrival at the teleportation dock, however—*that* was impressive.

"Hello, Iris. Welcome to the Watchtower. We haven't had you up before, have we?" Superman's words were warm and simple—but he was, for Christ's sake, *Superman*.

No one ever grew completely comfortable with the Man of Steel.

Nor with Wonder Woman, an icon of equal mythological power transcended only by her incomparable beauty.

The Manhunter was just the messenger boy, Iris realized, not meaning to be uncharitable.

The appearance of these two, patiently waiting for her and her alone, sealed the sense of urgency she had taken from the Martian. Any feelings of unreality and distance that still lingered were dissipated like mist beneath twin blazing suns.

Wonder Woman took her hand in courtly fashion. Iris supposed that a Bronze-age Greek would have done the same.

"We don't see each other often enough, Iris Allen. We miss you—and Barry, as well."

If it had been anyone other than these two, Iris would have wanted to roll her eyes. She would have said, "Well, its not like we hung out together before."

But this being Wonder Woman, and that being Superman nodding his head in agreement, the urge to comment did not surface. There was a fierce sincerity that radiated from the royal couple that did not allow for cynicism.

There was also a very palpable urgency. Even as they exchanged introductory pleasantries, Iris was being hustled out of the teleportation chamber and down a mammoth corridor, vaulted like a cathedral. She recognized little of the science and engineering principles behind this fantastic haven of giants; this was the home of a class of beings who saved planets and defended galaxies. There was a hard-eged practicality to the place, but also a melding of cultures and talents that extended far beyond Earth's orbit. Iris was vaguely aware that she was gaping like a tourist.

"You've never been to the Watchtower before?"

Wonder Woman repeated Superman's question, as they politely but briskly herded her along.

Iris didn't believe for a moment that they weren't very aware of all who had seen their inner sanctum.

"The Watchtower hadn't been built when Barry died. There was never any reason for Wally to bring me up. Do you hold open houses?"

"No—no." Wonder Woman almost fumbled. "I'd forgotten that Barry had passed before we built . . ."

The Manhunter grinned as Iris easily stole the initiative from her guardians. "Has there been any word from Wally? Is he back from the Speed Force yet?"

Realizing the extent of Iris's comprehension, Superman and Diana shot the Manhunter sharp looks. The Martian shrugged his shoulders, indicating helpless resignation.

Then, apparently conceding that she would not unquestioningly submit to circumstances, Superman answered Iris with professional bluntness. "We don't have word from Wally yet. He warned us that there could be a time displacement factor involved in accessing the Speed Force, so we're not sure when to expect his return. We think the Superluminoid needs to rest and recharge for a period between assaults. Wally is aware of this. We're hoping to have him back before we estimate it can strike again."

"So what exactly is Wally looking for in the Force?"

Iris's direct question was followed by a moment of uncomfortable silence. Their measured but urgent walk, however, did not slow.

"We're not sure," Wonder Woman finally offered, "It's all very . . . ambiguous . . ."

The Manhunter picked up the thread. "Wally was contacted by an intelligence that offered a connection to the Superluminoid. That's really all we know."

Iris gulped, tried to hold down her rising fear. "He's not stupid. He wouldn't have gone if he didn't have good reason. He won't leave us defenseless."

Superman placed his hand on Iris's back and guided her toward a large door off the corridor. As they approached, it silently slid open. "Of course he wouldn't. We just don't know what to expect, and that's why we decided that it was best to be proactive and get you here—just in case. We can't take chances. We just don't do that. We need to protect you to our maximum capabilities."

Iris stopped in the doorway and turned to face the three super heroes. She bit her lower lip to keep it from trembling. "I'll do whatever you think is best. But don't bet against Wally. He won't fail."

Iris turned and entered the room beyond the doorway. It was huge and cylindrical and its metallic walls glistened in the light from an incandescent dome, high above. Packed onto the floor and crawling the walls was an assortment of gleaming apparatuses and contraptions, towering and terrifying and completely meaningless to Iris's untrained eye. She couldn't know, but much of it represented the fruit of alien science, presented to the Watchtower over the years by League members from other worlds. To her, it just looked disquieting and dangerous, this confusing array of jumbled technologies. Like an army of insects camouflaged as machines, lurking and waiting to pounce on unsuspecting prey.

Wonder Woman, who, like the others, was perfectly at ease in the metal jungle, explained. "This is our physics lab. We wanted to get you here as quickly as possible. There's someone here you need to meet."

There was a man gliding toward them—at least Iris thought it was a man—through the inky shadows cast by the grotesque equipment under the dome light. He almost seemed a part of the shadows, a black-and-gray wraith wrapped in a cloak that rippled with a life of its own. The man drew closer and more distinct, and Iris saw that his head was encased in a black cowl crowned on either side by pointed—*ears.*

As the astonishing truth sank in, Iris felt the hairs on the back of her neck rise. This, indeed, was a mystery revealed—something far darker and more unsuspected than a trip to the Watchtower.

He was no simple urban legend, then. He truly *did* exist.

The Batman stopped before Iris, slightly inclined his head in salute, and addressed her in a voice as darkly silky as the night. "Ms. Allen, I've been asked to see to your welfare."

Good Lord—*the Batman.* Not even her own husband would ever confirm the existence of this legendary denizen of the Gotham twilight.

As the Dark Knight did not seen inclined to speak further, Superman offered a partial explanation: "Batman is responsible for integrating all our technologies, Iris. He hard-wired much of the Watchtower."

"I'm sure the Batman's credentials are good." Iris did not feel nearly as self-possessed as she tried to sound.

Suddenly, without pretense, the Batman took her gently but firmly by the arm and steered her into the quagmire of glittering hardware. He obviously wasn't one for idle chitchat, and Iris was surprised when he suddenly spoke again.

"I'm sorry I never got the chance to offer my condolences, Ms. Allen." He didn't get any more specific, and then: "You should know that your nephew has become an excellent warrior."

"I know."

"Ms. Allen . . ."

"Iris."

"Iris—you know that you are part of an extraordinary circumstance. I've come to the Watchtower to engineer a system for protecting you against a possible attack founded on extreme speed—"

"She knows the situation, Batman," Superman interjected, "you can be straight."

The Batman, giving no indication that he'd heard the Kryptonian's interruption, continued. "What I have designed, based on the most complete data available, is a flexible environment fitted to counter ultrahigh-velocity maneuvers."

He offered no more information. Apparently, he felt that what he had given Iris was comfort enough.

They hurried around the corner of a monstrous,

blocky contraption that looked like it must be extra-terrestrial in origin. Behind it, Iris was confronted by a raised dais, and by the remainder of the League. On closer inspection Iris could see the disk-shaped plat-form actually hovered about five feet above a series of power cells embedded in the floor. *Antigravity*, she supposed. Standing stock-still on top of the disk was the new, very young Green Lantern, his right arm raised, his hand in a fist, and a beam of his famous ring's emerald power shooting straight up to flare out into a ghostly, conical shell that curved down and fit over the circular dais. Next to this bizarre apparatus, Plastic Man was attending a control console, his rub-bery arms and fingers extended into tendrils that worked keys and levers with rapid-fire efficiency, his head bobbing comically on an elongated stalk of a neck, his eyes darting back and forth between the Lantern and the controls.

Neither Plastic Man nor the Lantern gave the new-comers more than a glance. Iris thought they looked much too tense.

Without a word, Wonder Woman strode over to Plastic Man and took her place beside him, assisting at the controls. Like this had all been rehearsed.

The Batman glided to the disk platform and turned to Superman and Iris.

"We don't have the time needed to fully rig an au-tomated system, but I've been able to piece together Rannian, Kryptonian, and some of my own security technologies into something that should be effective.

"If the Superluminoid is moving faster than the

speed of light," the Batman continued, "and I'm accepting that Wally would have no problem recognizing that, then it's expending tremendous amounts of energy. That power drain must be somewhat telegraphed and we're going to catch that drain. Simply put, it's going to trip an alarm."

For some unknown reason, a shiver suddenly ran down Iris's spine.

The Gotham Guardian motioned to Superman. "Kal-El, please lift Iris onto the isolation disk next to the Lantern . . ."

Unexpectedly, her head started to throb.

"May I?" Superman asked. Iris nodded, and the next thing she knew he had smoothly swept her off her feet and hovered up onto the disk. He placed her down by the motionless Green Lantern, his fist still held high, the ring's energy field radiating about the edges of the platform. She might have better appreciated the fabulous absurdity of the situation if her head wasn't pounding so damn awfully now, and if she could stop thinking about what she'd seen just before she'd left her home and been teleported to this other world of worried, hurried titans.

All of a sudden, without apparent reason, she found she couldn't stop obsessing about the beetle—the big, powerful june bug that was at the screen in her bedroom window.

She'd opened her windows early this spring evening, a warm front having followed the rain. Then, before they'd departed for the Watchtower, Iris had left the Manhunter in the living room to go get a sweater—who knew what the temperature of a super-hero headquarters on the Moon would be?—and she'd heard it bumping against the screen attracted to the light inside. Inexplicably fascinated by something she hadn't thought about in years, and at this, the most inappropriate of times, she'd forced open the screen, and the big beetle had flown into the room, lighting with an audible clunk on her vanity. Strange, she had thought—it was very early in the season to see one of these large, black beauties. Iris could re-member spending many a summer's evening with Wally on her brother's screened porch in Blue Valley, watching the dull glisten of the beetles as they awk-wardly clattered their armored bodies against the screen and porch, the starry night sky framing them, mysterious and driven.

For some reason she took the beetle's arrival into her house as a sign. It reminded her of Wally.

Wally was going to be all right.

Now she couldn't get the black beetle out of her mind.

Her ears were buzzing with a strange, dry static, like the rustling of hidden insects.

From somewhere very distant, she could hear the Batman continuing to give directions—to explain. These people were always explaining.

". . . Powered and triggered by the Lantern's ring . . . no time for any other rig . . . will have to maintain security force field until we can get some-thing more permanent . . . strobe patterns to confuse . . . my configuration based on Wally's experi-

ence with Upchurch's traps . . . and tachyon disruption . . . fail-safe is zetabeam mechanism . . . instantaneous . . ."

It didn't seem to be of much importance.

Where's Wally? she wondered. Her joints ached
terribly.

Then she was vaguely aware that the Lantern was
staring at her. His mouth was moving very slowly
and she could see the words form on his lips. *Your—
nose—Ms.—Allen—your—nose—is—bleeding . . .*

But her head was going to split, her lungs were
crashing to her stomach, she couldn't breathe . . .

The world exploded into motion.

Everything occurred simultaneously, she later realized, and far too fast to recall accurately. But she had
distinct impressions.

Superman, alarmed and turning with lightning reflexes, but stopped short by an invisible blow that
sent him cartwheeling into the massive, blocky contraption near the platform.

The Lantern, staring at her in concern, flung off the
platform and smashed violently into a wall of sparking electrical equipment.

Beyond him, the Manhunter collapsed to the floor,
clutching his head, his face nerveless, his eyes in agony.

The Batman, spasming and falling as well.

Wonder Woman and Plastic Man, lost in a glare of
writhing energy and flying metal as the control console exploded in their faces.

A vibration overlaid with a violent quaking, as if
the Watchtower's foundation was shifting and failing.

A flutter of blackness and light as whatever energy source powered the Watchtower faltered and reset.

The feeling of her heart in her throat as the anti-gravity cells failed and the platform beneath her collapsed to the floor with a terrific jolt.

And then it was over. In a split second all those impressions—and then stark, shocking stillness and silence, save for the hiss and crackle of ruptured power conduits.

She was lying on the top of the fallen platform, slightly stunned by the sudden five-foot drop. The awful pain in her head and joints was gone.

But she was looking at something growing in front of her. It was a visible *ripple* spreading out of thin air that suddenly began resolving itself into some kind of dark matter and then into an anthropomorphic silhouette.

Something streaked with gray and black.

It began loping toward her.

CHAPTER 12

Superluminal

It was easy, leaving the Speed Force.

The only hold it had on him had been psychological, Wally could now plainly see. It was the thrill of pure and constant speed and the fear of never being fast enough that had made existing in a state of speed of light seem so spiritually attractive.

With the Seventh Singularity's telepathic presence departed, Wally dropped down to a subluminal state instantaneously, without struggle, eager to meet and resolve the catastrophic matter at hand. For the first time in his life, his mind was clear and set. His thoughts were all of a kind, there were no distractions. He knew his capabilities, he understood the Superluminoid's capabilities, and he knew how he was going to go about meeting the thing.

He did not dwell on failure.

The physical world, his home, sprang into focus and he was racing down long, dark highways toward

Keystone City. He could have traveled at the speed of thought, had he wished. He could have fully employed the quantum abilities he now recognized and understood, and have made the particle jump before he could finish thinking the thought. But he didn't need to do that—in this case, he was moving fast enough.

Fast enough.

In five seconds he was in Keystone City and racing toward his apartment.

Linda sat at the kitchen table staring blankly at her laptop's screen. Her report wasn't getting done. Her fingers had not touched the keyboard all night, and instead danced without rhythm on the edge of the table surface.

A hardened veteran of the late-night vigil, she seldom allowed herself to be rattled, but something about this case in which Wally was involved had her completely unnerved.

She could sense it in his attitude. He was back on his heels. He wasn't confident. That's what had led to his taking a bullet—a mistake unheard of for a speedster. There was something big, very big, happening, and she did not have the comfort of knowing this was something the Justice League could shoulder as a team. For some reason, this was coming down on Wally alone.

He had called shortly before 10:00 P.M., from the Watchtower, to apologize. Things had not gone as he'd assured her they would before he'd left, with her crying over his torn shoulder. Stupid, to give him something else to worry over. He didn't need to be distracted by her emotional state while he was out there *somewhere*, dealing with *whatever*.

She could tell he was distraught. Things were not going as he had hoped.

Things were spinning out of control.

That was two hours ago. And then Iris had called.

Linda knew her paper wasn't going to get done tonight.

The air above the seat next to hers began to ripple. Linda caught the odd effect out of the corner of her eye, and by the time she had turned her head, Wally was sitting next to her.

Smiling, relaxed, and confident. So different from the scattered, confused man she had bandaged hours earlier. His bandage was gone—the wound was healed. For a split second a superstitious dread fell over her and she feared she was seeing a ghost. The romantic notion of Wally as a guardian angel come back one last time . . .

But then he had her in his arms and he was warm and there was no doubt it was really him.

"Is it over, Wally?"

He pushed her gently back and, brushing her hair from her face, looked into her eyes.

"No, Linda. But soon—and for good. It's going to be okay. You don't have to worry about me now. I won't be taking any more bullets."

She could see that. He was changed. He radiated a calm, reassuring power. It was almost frightening—almost inhuman—but it was also totally Wally.

"Believe it or not, Iris is at the center of this. That's part of why I've been way off my game. But I've got answers now. I've got to get over to her, but first I needed to see you."

Linda looked at him quizzically. "You don't know?"

He stared blankly.

"Iris called me, less than an hour ago—she said the Manhunter was with her. He was taking her to the Watchtower. She wanted to make sure you'd know . . ."

Wally's face showed only mild surprise and then he smiled. "It makes sense. You know, a couple of hours ago this probably would have pissed the hell out of me, but I can see why they did it. They weren't about to put all their eggs in one basket, and why should they? They had good reason for keeping me out of the loop. They're thinking the less I know about her location, the less chance I might inadvertently tip off the Superluminoid."

Linda didn't understand, but she knew that now was not the time to ask for an explanation. "Well, no matter what the League thinks, Iris wanted you to know."

Wally stood up and began to glimmer and glisten. He smiled as he faded into sparks.

"Things are going to be different once I'm done with this."

Seconds later, Wally was carefully decelerating through police headquarters. Tonight the aging structure's interior was a diorama of tension and chaos.

Rigid figures filled the entrance and halls—teams of forensic experts, the commissioner and his brass, and what looked like every cop and detective in the city. Wally even recognized the mayor and his public relations team addressing a group of reporters and cameramen, herded to one side. The speedster glanced at the big wall clock over the duty sergeant's desk: 11:47—it had been less than four hours since the massacre in the holding cells. Wally hadn't been sure how much relative time he had spent in the Speed Force. Now he figured probably about an hour and a half.

He jogged up the main stair gallery, slowing just gradually enough to effect a neat stop in Metahuman Hostility's open office. As he'd expected, circumstances had chained his detectives to their posts.

Wally hadn't counted on finding two other plainclothes cops looming over his seated, miserable-looking friends. They were, no doubt, picking Chyre's and Morillo's brains for details concerning the massacre. *Of course*, Wally realized—it had happened under their noses.

The interrogators were no doubt jacking them up over the Flash's involvement, too. Hopefully—and Wally felt a touch of fear here—the Superluminoid had not struck again.

Wally decelerated his mind smoothly, in perfect coordination with his potential speed factor. Both mind and body bottomed out together and his concentration stayed true as Chyre and Morillo jumped up in relief, and the two interrogating detectives flinched backward.

"Jesus, Wally!" Morillo found his voice first. "Where've you been?"

The interrogators recovered quickly. "You goddamn better stay put! You're part of a police investigation!"

Wally ignored them. "Please tell me there haven't been any more attacks."

The voice was calm, but Chyre seemed to sense the urgency behind the words. "Not that we've heard, but then, we've been kept busy having our asses busted—"

Morillo broke in. "Nothing, Wally."

He felt grateful for that; it was what he'd hoped to hear. Wally knew there was no way this could have played out faster, but he was relieved another round didn't have to die.

He was going to be fast enough.

Wally glanced over at the two interrogators, just so they could feel included. "Listen—the next time you see me, either our problem is over or we're all wearing wings. I'll give you all the report you need then, but right now I've got to end this."

He looked back to Morillo and Chyre. "It's okay, guys. I've got a handle on things."

Then, before another word of protest could be voiced, he was down to the foundation and in the morgue. This time he had flexed his quantum powers fully, transforming his subatomic makeup to a particle blend similar to, but more versatile than, tachyons. The world of matter dissolved before him to one of particle instability, and he was past walls and doors and security blocks without ever encountering them.

Police medical personnel stood, caught in the act of prodding and probing the forty grim remains of Upchurch and his hired guns, spread on shiny metal trays before the meat lockers.

Wally floated down the line until he had found the lump of carbon marked "Upchurch." Staring into the colorless mass, he allowed himself to fall into it. And as with the fragment from the fireball, as when he had looked into the skulls of Alvin Hurst and Kevin Schull, he felt the malignant presence of the Superluminoid, lingering, marking what it had claimed as its own.

Altering his constitution just slightly, Wally reached for the remains and interacted with the matter on a physical level. He brushed his fingers lightly over the lump and collected loose ash, then pulled those fingers over his cheeks and nose leaving long, gray stripes behind.

War paint. Camouflage.

He wasn't exactly sure why he did this. It was primal, instinctual, and came directly from that state where consciousness interacts with the particle world, the state that tells birds and salmon where to migrate, bees how to navigate to their pollen, rats when to desert a ship, and all life in general how to recognize its own.

Then a blink, and he was on the roof of headquarters, searching the warm, clear night. To the east, rising between the shadows of two skyscrapers, he found the Moon, close to full and waiting for him as he gathered himself for his first unaided journey through space.

Not space, Wally reminded himself—a foaming sea of particles, winking in and out of existence far too rapidly to be recorded by any sense or telemetry working in normal time. But real, nonetheless, and affording a speedster fully in control of his power a medium for passage as far as the stars, should he wish.

He didn't need to think the process through—the Singularity's painstakingly precise lessons were imprinted on his genetic instructions as involuntary reflexes. Wally simply realized his goal and the means necessary to achieve it, and the world again revealed itself as constructed and driven by particle function, the law and force underlying the physical.

The Watchtower.

He ran straight toward Justice League Headquarters on a cushion of light.

Then Wally was in the Watchtower, on the Control Deck, now vacant, managed solely by Kryptonian-hybrid drones. Of course—all League members present would be attending to the emergency defenses, rushing against time to prepare a system for protecting Iris.

They, no doubt, still hoped there were a couple of hours before the Superluminoid could recharge and strike again. But Wally now understood this wasn't the case. The thing could strike right now, and continue to, growing stronger and stronger with time. Wally wasn't going to give it more time, though. He was going to give it what it wanted *now*. He was going to make it show its hand before it reached maximum power.

Wally transferred himself to the science deck and the physics laboratories. He immediately spotted the throbbing energy signature that identified the Green Lantern's deployed power and was only slightly surprised to recognize that its emerald "magic" was only another aspect of the particle state, where all probabilities are accessible.

Then he saw her—Iris, next to the isolation disk over which Kyle maintained a force shield. She was surrounded by Superman, the Manhunter—and the Batman. Ha! The Dark Knight himself had come up and organized the defense. Diana and O'Brian were to one side, coordinating systems control. Wally analyzed the arrangements and understood that the Lantern's ring power would serve as a kind of early warning system. There were no doubt all sorts of disorientation weapons attached to a speed-activated trigger, much like Upchurch's traps. And there—that was a zetaray transportation mechanism, aimed right at the hovering disk. That would be the fail-safe device—Iris would be transported to the far side of the galaxy as a last-ditch resort.

None of it would work. They had no conception of the speeds that warped matter and energy. The Superluminoid would be long gone before the trip could trigger the response.

Actually, Wally believed they probably did suspect it was futile—but what else could they do? He appreciated that they were fighting for Iris the best they could.

Satisfied that he understood the lay of the land, Wally focused on Iris. She looked very tiny and fragile surrounded by the towering members of the Justice League. And yet, he noted proudly, with fire in her eyes. But for the vagaries of probability, she could be standing here as an equal.

Wally was sure she was not happy being placed in the center of attention. That gleam in her eyes—and the narrow, sideways glance frozen on Superman—probably signified annoyance more than anything else.

Now, Wally realized, was the moment of truth. The one act that he still dreaded. There was no turning back, there was no choice. Everything was set.

He had to give up Iris. He had to bait the trap with his beloved aunt.

Wally strode up to her, slipping between the Martian and the Kryptonian, and decelerated to slightly below light speed, but still far too fast to be detected by Superman or any of the Batman's sensors. He would do the deed now, before they set her within the Lantern's trip wire.

It's been too long, Iris.

Please forgive me if this doesn't go well, but it has to end now.

Then he slowed the relative speed of one hand and lightly, carefully touched her. The subatomic particles that composed his hand just barely interfaced with Iris's shoulder.

That was all. That was the necessary physical connection, their quantum personas made temporarily one.

Here is Iris West! the action seemed to scream across the quantum sea. *Here is the source of your life, the mother of your existence!*

Here is the reason you have been watching me! Here is she for whom you wished!

Here is Iris West Allen!

Wally moved his hand from her shoulder and shot back up to light speed, again neatly avoiding the danger of becoming engulfed by that state.

Almost simultaneously, there was a vibration from very far away. It surged and receded somewhere on the very edge of his brain, a shock wave from some inestimable distance. From many worlds away.

The message had been received and the Superluminoid had not taken long to respond.

There was another surge, incrementally more forceful than the first. The Superluminoid was lunging ahead eagerly—greedily, Wally imagined. The bait had been taken, and he imagined it jumping and crashing through doomed universes, annihilating billions and billions of innocent lives, eager and impatient.

Wally had been wrong to feel relieved that the Superluminoid had not struck again in Keystone City. He had forgotten all that would be sacrificed beyond this universe in the final action.

He hoped it would not be too much.

There was no incomprehensible pain to herald the thing's approach, as he had experienced in the past. The Flash was above pain now and only felt the steadily advancing drumbeat. But the pattern of jumps came from so many worlds away that Wally knew there was more than enough time to set the trap. Even moving past the speed of light within a particle state, the Superluminoid would require whole seconds to manifest in this world.

There was time, but the thing was strong.

Forgive me, Iris, if I'm not good enough.

Wally again accessed the particle state, accelerating far past the speed of light. The physical world again fell into a dreamy half-life, subordinate to the quantum reality in which he now moved. He knew he had to chose carefully, and very wisely, as he put his strategy into effect.

Motion is just a means, and what lies outside the start and the stop points is just as important.

Sometimes it is good to stop motion.

The lessons from the Singularity were burned into his brain, had shown him his power in a different light. Although Wally had always looked at greater and greater speed as the solution to whatever problem presented itself, the truth was, he had another option.

He could lie motionless, waiting within the shadows of worlds.

The Superluminoid could not. The Singularity had revealed that if the thing did not keep moving, it would not exist.

That was the horror of its existence, and its weakness. It was the speedster reduced and elevated to nothing but pure speed and motion. It had no choice. It could never rest, it could never reflect, it could have no peace. It was all motion, with no humanity.

The Superluminoid probably didn't even know what it wanted. But it was a life-form with the instincts of self-preservation and self-perpetuation, and the power to ruthlessly act on those directives.

Wally determined he would have no pity on the brute.

The drumbeat, the ripple of quantum shock waves, was growing noticeably more insistent. He needed to make a choice.

The relative "direction" through which the Superluminoid was forging was easy for Wally to identify, and he oriented toward it.

Wally steeled himself, swallowed hard—and then dived ahead, knifing straight through the particle interface between universes, cutting precisely across probability, and entered an adjacent universe.

Astonishing—the jump had happened just as the Singularity had said it would. With his power disciplined and focused, Wally had slid into the new world with no disruption, no terrible destruction. He was not trampling universes, as did the Superluminoid, but *entering* them.

He was actually existing in an alternate universe. He had actually transferred outside everything he had ever known.

Well, not exactly, it seemed.

This universe looked awfully similar to his own. Through the swirling, sparking sea of virtual particles, Wally focused on the physical state beyond. What he saw appeared no different than what he had left—the tableau in the physics lab was incrementally progressing as he would have suspected. It looked like Superman was turning to address Iris.

Was Iris wincing slightly? *Did she feel the Superluminoid coming?*

Whatever it was that had caused this reality to bifurcate from his, it was not readily evident.

He decided to move farther on. Again orienting himself toward the approaching waves of ethereal disruption, Wally pushed himself on through the interference and into yet another cosmos.

This world was different. He was on the Moon, but there was no Watchtower here, there was no sign of human handiwork, only rolling plains of gray dust and a low line of soft hills on the horizon. He looked up into the airless void above and was reassured to see the Earth still there, full and streaked with blue and white. He looked closer, and thought he could distinguish the outline of North America peeking out from under swirls of cloud, but he couldn't be sure. It didn't look quite right.

He pushed on again and came to another universe. Here there was no Moon, no Earth, only distant stars and vast clouds of cosmic gas pinwheeling around an empty black nothingness that sucked everything toward it, even the microcosmic particle world that carried no mass. It was very lonely, and he began to distrust his ability to find his way back home. What was more disturbing was the fact that he could no longer see Iris or his teammates. They didn't exist here, at least not in the same way they did in his world.

Wally had to decide how much farther to go. He

had to estimate the strength of the Superluminoid and he had no yardstick for measuring that. Should he hold here and hope that he'd dug in deep enough, or go on to another universe and pray that he hadn't overextended?

The job was first and foremost to keep the Superluminoid away from Iris. He'd go one more. Once again he located the direction of the being's approach and sliced straight through and toward it.

This alternate world—the one he now found himself in—confounded his notions of *universe*. The concepts of matter and energy, self and other, were all lost in a cosmic scum of pink, radiating, homogenized plasma. It was a universe of one state, with no differentiation.

Now Wally was truly unnerved. Anyone would have been. No human mind, no matter how advanced, would have been prepared to receive and resolve such an alien state. Fortunately, his own corpus kept its integrity and he did not go immediately mad. Regardless, Wally could feel this reality tearing at his sanity.

Almost instinctively, he made one last move beyond that horrible universe, but pulled up short of the next one, lingering in the particle interface between realities.

This was his strategy—this was where he would lay his trap, in this boiling quantum ocean between universes far from his home. In this space he could sit perfectly still, waiting for the Superluminoid to bull past, unsuspecting. Unable to detect ambush until it was too late, Wally could drag it down from behind, countering its momentum until it was held motionless well before it reached Iris.

That was the plan.

Now Wally hunkered down in the shadowy nether between universes, more alone than any man had ever been.

Making himself still, he waited. He instinctively understood that he could maintain himself in this quantum state without true forward motion. It was another skill that had always lurked within him, but had not been written into his instructions. Motionless in the quantum unreality between universes, he would be as invisible to the Superluminoid as he could ever be.

The artificial thing had sunk a hook into Wally's mind when the speedster had first forced himself to look inside the fireball fragment. Something of its awful malignancy lingered like radiation in all the results of its handiwork, and provided a telepathic link to those things to which it was *connected*. Wally's persona had been sucked into the fragment by the message from the Singularity, but had been captured by the Superluminoid. All three of them, somehow, connected and related.

Ever since, Wally had come to realize, the Superluminoid had kept a distant eye on him. The initial contact had been reinforced when he looked into the pit inside Alvin Hurst's skull and then into the ruin of Kevin Schull's. That had been enough to call the monster out. It knew then that Wally was an important factor in its survival, and after that it watched him, waiting for him to lead it home.

Wally again thanked his lucky stars that his instincts had kept him from approaching Iris.

But the danger here was still great—the thing might still be able to detect Wally, hidden as cleverly as he was between worlds. The ash of Upchurch drawn on his face, rotten with the Superluminoid's own evil radiation, would help to disguise him, would confuse the being, he hoped.

That was the plan.

He knew that, Earth-normal relative, the time frame in which he waited only represented seconds, but in his accelerated state he felt his patience stretched over centuries. The distant surge and ebb had grown to a regular, booming disruption.

And it set his virtual teeth on edge.

It was coming.

How long? How long, his racing mind wondered? It was taking forever for it to jump its way from so far.

All those worlds ending, untold billions dead, all so one mistake could move and live.

His patience holding, Wally did not move.

He did not leap out to confront the destroyer as it annihilated universe after universe, even though his heart screamed that *something must be done!*

The martial cadence continued to grow and grow, filling his mind with world-ending explosions.

His patience stretched thin.

His self-control at its limit.

The shattering theme an anvil on his brain.

Wally forced himself to create an illusion, a visual mechanism on which he could focus and maintain.

He made himself see the system of universes as an endless series of rooms, all connected by closed doors, each one in a line. The Superluminoid was blowing open the doors, with a terrible, booming shock, and roaring, fiery and terrible, through each room, leaving charred ruins behind.

And each explosive shock brought it closer to the doorway in which Wally hid.

There!

The quantum shock and pressure had just grown enormously. Wally steeled himself because he knew that the time had come, it was very close by . . .

Maybe the next, maybe the next . . .

It was on him, and Wally, even with all his new knowledge and power, could hardly comprehend the force of nature that blotted out his transuniverse station.

It was, indeed, a monster. Its motion made it terrible, much more terrible than the presence Wally had perceived in the Schull home. Then, and at the KCPD, Wally's relative perceptual slowness had not allowed him to see the thing's constant state of agitation—the quality that Upchurch had described as its seeming to be there and not there at the same time.

Before it had simply been too fast to comprehend, but now Wally saw it in its true shape of faster-than-light motion, and it was terrible.

But, also, terribly beautiful in its purity.

Wally leapt and accelerated as the thing flashed through his vacuum. If he couldn't grab onto it, if he couldn't catch its momentum, he would be marooned in nothing, with no universes surrounding him.

He had to catch the Superluminoid and *hold*, or he was lost, and so was everything else.

Wally pushed himself again—he exploded into pure kinetic energy—and *reached* . . .

He had it.

His virtual fingers sank deep into the yielding, sticky, sparky substance he had pummeled during that first encounter.

The Superluminoid screamed. It wailed into his mind. It was afraid. Nothing had ever caught it unaware, had taken it by surprise.

It knew it was attacked.

Then Wally saw in a flash that the Superluminoid's momentum had carried them through to the horrible, plasma-state universe. Wally pulled back, dragging against its forward rush—and began sinking his own quantum being into the corpus of his cousin. He had to slow the monster, he had to stop it before it jumped to his universe and to Iris.

The Superluminoid thrashed and struggled and writhed like a monstrous centipede in its efforts to dislodge the Flash. It howled in fear and rage and turned a portion of its primitive consciousness back toward its tormentor.

It saw Wally there, his face covered in the remains of its creator. Wally got the distinct psychic impression that the thing was shocked.

Wally later remembered that impression, and thought that it seemed like the thing had never looked back before. Like it had never inspected its wake of past deeds.

Suddenly they were in the next world closer to home, the world of no Earth, no Moon.

Wally sank in deeper, continued to pull back, even though the sparking had grown to bolts of lightning shooting through his corpus, seeking to tear him into disassociated, random photons. He refocused and bore in, creating more and more drag.

It was working. The Superluminoid was slowed, although not nearly enough, not soon enough.

Wally couldn't believe how strong the damn thing was. He hadn't figured on such raw, brute energy. It *was* more a force of nature than an offshoot of the human race.

How could it have been born of man?

What strange agenda hidden in the metagene had led to this?

The thing was changing, though, as it slowed. To Wally's perception it was now becoming more solid, more anthropomorphic. Not unlike when Wally had sucker punched it down the velocity ladder back at Schull's house and it had seemed to nearly take on an almost human form.

As it slowed it lost its monstrous, terrible beauty and some of its raw power.

It needed speed. The Superluminoid gained power from the universes it ripped apart. The more annihilation, the more power.

When it lingered on Earth, when it slowed to perform its dreadful caricature of surgery, ripping out pineals, it lost power.

It hated that.

It hated that its cousin was on its back now, slowing it, weakening it.

Inarticulate expulsions of rage and red confusion burst in Wally's mind. *Why? Why are you doing this to me?*

Let me live!

At the same time the disintegrating force seeking to tear Wally apart grew more frantic, even as his cousin's power waned.

Wally hung on for dear life—there was no alternative.

The thing crashed them through to the next world over, and Wally was horrified to recognize the physics lab interior. They were in the universe adjacent to his! Despite Wally's efforts, the Superluminoid's course had stayed true—it continued bulling straight for Iris.

It was drawing too close!

It had to end here!

Wally couldn't believe that he hadn't moved far enough down the line of intersecting universes to effectively brake the thing's advance, but it was far stronger than he had ever imagined.

He had miscalculated. He had been sure he'd gone far enough, and he had been wrong.

He couldn't let it go any farther.

As a blur, in the midst of whip-saw thrashing and rending energies, Wally saw this alternate universe's players standing at their stations, waiting for their drama to unfold, looking identical to his own teammates and Iris. In another nanosecond the Superluminoid's completed passage would reduce them and their reality to nothingness, but Wally had no time to appreciate that particularly wrenching tragedy as he strained to pull back, *back* on the battling, bludgeoning behemoth.

The Superluminoid seemed to grab him by his throat. It was fighting him psychologically now, with its extraordinary telepathic power. This was the one angle of attack against which Wally's defenses were weak. He was not a strong telepath, and no instructions and guidance from far-and-future heroes could create something from nothing.

The thing had him by the throat, was throttling him, and turned around to look into his eyes, even as another part of it continued to fight toward that jump into the next universe. It turned and looked him full in the face in a form made clear by its forcibly retarded motion—and Wally saw his own features, made insane with rage and aloneness, desperate and hollow, glaring straight into his own eyes.

His own face.

Let me live!

Let me create more of my own kind!

I will annihilate you!

Wally's mind reeled. And for one infinitesimal moment, he relaxed his concentration. The thing seized its opportunity and, digging its virtual claws deep into his neck, flung Wally free of its corpus and into a universe that was collapsing under the strain of its passage.

God, no!

This was it. The end.

All was lost if he fell behind now, enveloped by the nothingness of a hollowed-out universe.

But his athletic training served him again, even here, in this state below the physical world. His mental reflexes responded with machine precision and, instead of engaging muscles, forced an acceleration to faster-than-light speed, in reverse of the direction he had been thrown.

It was a blind and reckless move, reversing momentum so abruptly, but it was all he had and it worked. His particle corpus kept its integrity despite the strain, and his sense of direction still stood him in good stead—there was the Superluminoid, right before him, jumping out of this dissolving world. Wally leaped and stretched himself to his maximum and caught his cousin's trailing heel, just as it disappeared.

He was carried through with the Superluminoid, back into the universe of their origin. Back to Iris.

The Superluminoid was caught off-balance by Wally's grasp, and faltered as they crashed into the familiar setting of the laboratory. It rotated toward Wally, now more solid than ever. Still and void and unknowable in substance, but increasingly human in shape, it snarled a wordless, telepathic obscenity at him from lips too much like his own, and swung a ferocious backhand.

The telepathic attacks were failing. It was resorting to the purely physical now, as Wally succeeded in dragging it down past light speed.

Wally ducked the scything swing of its clawlike

hands and returned a cross, straight into its chest. The thing buckled—it could feel pain, or at least some sort of disruptive distress.

Solid, Wally thought. *It grows more solid as it slows relative to my speed!*

Wally lunged for his artificial cousin, hoping to pin it helplessly, but he underestimated its feral ability to recover and respond. It twisted and, clever as a martial arts master, used Wally's forward momentum against him, hurling him over its body and straight at the seemingly frozen figure of Superman. Wally, accelerated against his will too close to the speed of light, had no time to react, and caught the Man of Steel square in the chest, sending the frozen giant slowly spinning toward the massive bulk of the alien machine the Manhunter had named the Promethium Interocetor. The impact with Superman would have blown apart a weaker being, but the Man of Steel's great mass kept Wally from exploding straight through him and plunging into the machine himself.

Still, it hurt like hell.

Wally scrambled, fighting to recover his wits—his ill-advised tactic had left nothing remaining between the Superluminoid and Iris.

Sure enough—Wally's blood went instantly and absolutely cold—there it was, on the antigravity platform, hovering before her.

The Green Lantern was hurtling through the air, flattened against a wall of equipment.

The defense system's control console, shattered by the wily being, was glacially erupting in a spew of shrapnel and fire before the uncomprehending eyes of Diana and O'Brian.

The Manhunter and Batman were crumpling to the floor, overcome by the powerful, undisciplined, telepathic outrage.

It had her.

It had Iris.

It had found the source of its life.

The genetic wellspring of its new race of world-ending superbeings.

The Superluminoid held the fate of the Many Worlds in its grasp, frozen and helpless . . .

And it hesitated.

It had hesitated. Wally screamed and launched himself with animal ferocity straight at its heart. He caught it full-on, tearing it away from Iris and driving it off the platform and out of the lab and straight up to the speed of light in a blinding instant.

The searing, luminescent splendor of the Speed Force burst into diamond clarity as he jockeyed in his stunned foe. He *chose* to take his dark cousin into this place beyond and between all worlds.

It had hesitated.

It had hesitated before its mother and Wally had not. He had seized the initiative, had taken momentum, and gained the higher ground.

Most of all, he had been *patient*.

Now, here in this state of constants, in this dimension of universal stability, he was going to smother the life out of a weakened enemy who could not free itself, no matter how it struggled.

It had lost too much speed—and power. It needed movement and time to regain its strength. That was its downfall.

Wally held it still, held it locked in this one state. Held it motionless relative to the speed of light.

The Superluminoid writhed and flexed and screamed and tried to dart, but Wally's grip did not fail, and it grew weaker and weaker.

From out of nowhere, the Seventh Singularity suddenly appeared before them.

It looked down on Wally, observing him patiently as he crouched, smothering his cousin. Wally could vaguely discern the shapes of several other anthropomorphic forms floating in the brilliance behind it.

"*Wally, let me have it,*" the Singularity spoke.

Wally was incredulous. "I don't—*are you crazy?* You know what this thing will do. You know what it's *done.* I can't let it up!"

"*It did not do it.*"

"It what?"

"*It did not kill Iris West. It could have, but it did not.*"

"But it's destroyed billions of universes! You told me! I *saw* . . . !" Wally choked on his outrage.

The Singularity held still and silent for a long moment, and Wally, continuing to strangle the artificial speedster, got the feeling that the quantum warrior was struggling with itself.

Finally it spoke again, very deliberately. "*Look at me, Wally.*"

Something opened in the strange, black, sideways head of the Singularity. Something not material was opened and, for the briefest of instants, something was revealed.

Wally looked past the surface, gazed into the darkness, and stared shell-shocked at the truth. His mind reeled, but he finally understood. He understood the connection, the familiarity. He *understood*.

The Singularity had chosen to share something very privileged with him.

Everything was changed, and so much that had intrigued him now made sense.

"Do you trust me, Wally?"

The Superluminoid's struggles were very feeble now, almost imperceptible. It was so close to death.

Wally could have ended it then.

So easily.

Instead, he handed his cousin to the Singularity. Curiously, it had shrunken in form to something like a blobby, unformed child.

The Singularity almost sighed in relief. *"Thank you, Wally. You have made it safe for me to take this lost creature to my world, where some good can come of all this.*

"As you tumbled with it through all those doomed worlds, locking your mind with its mind, your will battling its will, part of you crept inside it and it was changed. You have given it the beginning of a conscience—and that makes all the difference in the Worlds.

"Such is the mystery and the science of probability. May we never forget that. May we never deny that."

Wally, still struggling to comprehend, couldn't help but offer one last protest. "It's so powerful. How can we risk the chance that . . . that . . ."

Words failed the speedster, and the Singularity did not waver.

"Someday you will know that you did the right thing."

The Singularity cradled the embryonic Superluminoid and, accompanied by its fellow phantoms, began a slow and graceful fade, no doubt returning to whatever mysterious future lay in store for them in their alternative universe.

At the last moment, Wally couldn't help blurting out: "Why?"

"You tell me," the answer came back, floating out of nothing.

Then they were gone.

Wally dropped out of the Speed Force and back to the Watchtower and the physics lab.

The knowledge that he had gained from the Singularity, the instinctual understanding of his unlimited powers that the majestic creature had written into his genetic code, was already fading, as promised. It was only right—the knowledge had freed his abilities for an emergency situation, but it made perfect sense that the prescience leave him, and he relearn it on his own, in his own manner and time.

But the knowledge of that of which he was capable—that would never leave him.

Wally's vision onto the particle world of quantum power disappeared and the lines and planes and solid textures of the lab sprang into sharp focus. He decelerated neatly into normal time, and his mind did, too. It didn't linger in high gear, he was pleased to note; it slipped easily and evenly down with his physical state.

He felt no impatience.

And there—there before him was Iris. The platform had collapsed—the Superluminoid's jump had no doubt triggered a power outage—and she was lying on top of it. She looked dazed and her nose was bleeding, but she was otherwise unhurt.

Unhurt. Iris was okay.

Wally saw her look up toward him as he materialized into normal time. At first her eyes registered disbelief and then horror. Wally imagined that his deceleration from the quantum world, coupled with the grimy remains of Upchurch smeared over his head, probably *did* look terrifying.

He strode forward and fixed his aunt with a big grin. Only then did he see recognition sweep across her features, as Iris started laughing in relief.

Laughing her familiar laugh, clear and bright as a bell.

In a split second his fellow Leaguers would be bouncing off the carpet—spoiling for a fight, mad as hornets—and Wally would have the happy task of telling them that it was all over.

Everything was okay.

But right now, in this split second of stillness, he could marvel at the incredible web interlacing all the universes.

The Singularity, in that final moment, had revealed their connection.

The reason why it alone could reach across time and universe to teach him.

A connection so similar to the one who had taught him so much as a child.

A connection that would continue to guide him, if he was smart enough to allow it.

The Seventh Singularity had been born to an Earth very similar to Wally's own—only the slightest degree separated the two.

But on that other Earth a young woman had been taken from her home and her time and had manifested metapowers that she would otherwise have not.

The Singularity had for a moment lifted the veil and shown him their connection—as strong as blood.

It was a *she*.

Iris.

The Seventh Singularity was Iris West.

And Wally West was the Flash. The Fastest Man Alive. The man who had just saved the Many Worlds.

He was good enough. He was *fast* enough.

Iris and Barry had always known that, and now so did he.

About the Author

MARK SCHULTZ has been in the cartooning and illustration business for sixteen years. His most well-known creation, the award-winning comic book *Xenozoic Tales*, has been adapted to television as the animated series *Cadillacs and Dinosaurs*. In addition to his own works, Mark has scripted or illustrated many popular twentieth-century icons, including Superman, Batman, *Aliens, Star Wars*, Flash Gordon, and Tarzan. He has just completed illustrating volume one of *Robert E. Howard's Complete Conan of Cimmeria* (Wandering Star, 2003). He believes in diversity. This is his first novel.